PAST CONTINUOUS

PAST CONTINUOUS

Denise Goff

Hodder & Stoughton

First published in 1995 by Hodder and Stoughton
A division of Hodder Headline PLC

10 9 8 7 6 5 4 3 2 1

British Library Cataloguing in Publication Data

Goff, Denise
Past Continuous
I. Title
823 [F]

ISBN 0 340 62880 4

Typeset by Phoenix Typesetting, Ilkley, West Yorkshire.

Printed and bound in Great Britain by
Mackays of Chatham PLC

Hodder and Stoughton
A division of Hodder Headline PLC
338 Euston Road
London NW1 3BH

Contents

I

The Class
1960

Emily, Alice and May.

I chant the names in my head. My aunts will all be at 'the class', my mother says. Even Aunt Emily, whom I don't remember.

Emily, Alice and May—

Great-aunts, my mother says they are, not ordinary ones, because they're Gran's little sisters. This makes me laugh because they aren't little at all. They're big, and old. Well, old like my mother, but not as old as Gran.

'Your gran was born before the first war,' my mother explains when I ask why this should be. 'Your aunts were born a good while after.'

I don't understand, but it makes me think that they were once babies, that once they must have been five years old like me.

Emily, Alice and May—

To the tune of 'Popeye the Sailor Man'.

The car begins to go faster. I jump up to look out of the back window and catch a glimpse of sea, a triangle of deep blue wedged between the amusement arcade and the ice-cream parlour.

On to the new road, past the cigarette factory, Wills' Whiffs and Wills' Wild Woodbines. I like travelling in the car, spying places and faces, and no one spying me.

But by the time we reach Newcastle I've had to begin counting. It's taking too long. Along the quayside, down a cobbled street, the old castle hunched black and sooty on the hill, past the station, all fidgeting and squirming and counting some more. *It's taking too long.*

If I can count to ten without seeing a red car, then I'll be all right.

One—
Two—
We're through the commons, and there's the library! Turning into Gran's road, the red pillar-box marking her house in the distance, rows and rows of joined up houses, the monkey puzzle tree, a chimney smoking— and finally we're there. Outside the blue door. I press my nose to the window and grab the door handle. I wasn't car sick once! I clamber out.

'Why on earth didn't you say?'

My mother stares at the wet patch on the car seat.

'For heaven's sakes, Megan—'

The cross voice. The one with a bit of a slap in it.

Quick hands push me through the gate and up the short path. There's no time to count lilac candles, but I steal a look at the patch of grass; great sprinklings of daisies, there'll be daisy chains. But I keep looking down, had better look sorry.

The rap at the door echoes round the terraces, setting off dogs, barking from further and further away like ripples on the park pond. Lots of dogs on Gran's estate, not like at home where they're all on a leash, blowing along the beach or pier dragging windswept owners behind them. Here they go for walks on their own. But there's often a sack covering a bump in the middle of the road and I know what's under it. *Squished dog.*

I wait, moving from foot to foot, the tops of my legs damp and cold, trying to count how many dogs I can hear. But they're going quiet again, and someone's unbolting the door.

'Sorry, Mam,' my mother says. 'Our Megan had a bit of an accident in the car— Not like her at all.'

And the voice is soft again, the slap gone, but still I stare at my feet. A hand lifts my chin. I look up. Green eyes smiling down at me. I grin back.

'Now you be good, mind, with Gran's ladies.'

I tuck my hair behind my ears and nod vigorously.

'And nice and quiet when you have to be, eh?'

My mother's arms enclose me and I hold on tight, but I don't really mind her going. Not this time.

Over my mother's shoulder, Gran winks at me.

'Well, I expect it was just because you were excited, eh Megan? This being your first "class" and all?'

I try to wink back, but it takes both eyes.

'And we can fix you up in no time at all, can't we?'

I take the offered hand, too excited to remember to wave goodbye until it's too late. But today that doesn't matter either. Up the dark stairs into the bathroom, damp and shivery, even in summer, bitter smells from the orangey soap, coal tar, which should be black, but isn't. Waiting while underclothes are quickly found, followed by the rough and tumble of taking off and putting on.

'I bet it even happened to the Queen Mother sometimes,' Gran mutters, lifting me high in the air by the waistband of my new tights and shaking me down into them.

A kiss on my cheek.

'There you are. Clean and dry. Now you run along. I've not finished the baking yet and they'll be here any minute.'

I watch her clump downstairs, then hug my arms. Where should I start? I'll have to be quick to see all the things.

I pull back the corner curtain in the smaller of the two bedrooms. Scraps and rolls of material lie all in a heap, rough heathery tweeds, ivory slippery silks. I tug at a piece of stiff yellow stuff – Aunt Alice has a dress of this – and look through a square of dark-blue lace. There was a party frock for May out of that. I hold it closer to my face and the world changes.

Next Gran's room, the curtains closed against the sunshine, on the dressing-table the three silver brushes, Grandad's stretchy armbands— and the old photograph of Gran with her three sisters.

They don't look alike, at all, my aunts. Aunt Alice is tiny and dark, a bit like Gran but much younger, Aunt Emily is tall and fair (what does she look like now?) and May fatter, somewhere in between. May's hair is red. Bright red the last time I saw her. I put the photo back, had better be quick—

By the bed, the big-faced alarm clock. I pick it up with both hands and look at it hard. Sometimes I can tell the time, but the hands aren't in the places I know. What if it's time now!

Down the steep stairs, into the tiny living-room, the table already pulled to the centre of the swirly carpet, two packs of playing cards ready on the best white cloth. Had better be quick—

Up on the chair, over the window-sill, stretch, careful fingers— the Green Dragon Vase! I take a breath and turn its face towards me. It glares back angrily, eyes redder than rubies, blackened nostrils

3

flaring. Green and shiny and mean as mean. Carnations growing out of its back today.

The sideboard cupboard. I jump off the seat, open the door and sniff deeply, my head right inside. Raisins and glacé cherries and spicy marmalade and woody smells.

On top, the diamond fruit bowl. Moving it back and forth, scanning the ceiling, quicker and quicker—

At last.

A rainbow.

Now they can come. Now I'm ready.

The kitchen is warm with the smells of baking. I stand on tiptoe at the bench. There's a chocolate cake on a doily with icing still dripping down the sides, buns with cherries on top, scones and jam.

'Who's coming?' I ask. I know about my three aunts, Emily, Alice and May, but there'll be other ladies too. 'The girls', as Gran calls them, even though some of them are *really* old, older than Gran herself.

I stretch further to see quick fingers roll up scraps of pastry, kneading and pushing, and a round appears, as smooth and white as a snowball. Maybe for me.

'Well—' Gran puts the dough to one side and begins adding spoonfuls of jam to pastry cases. 'That one's for your little Aunt Alice – *if* she comes. As for this big fat one, well, that must be May's,' said with a wink. 'Aunt Emily's—'

'Tell me about Aunt Emily,' I say.

'Again?'

I nod. Aunt Emily doesn't live in Fenham, which is what you call this part of Newcastle.

'All right. What do you want to hear?'

'How she looks like a princess, how she lived on a desert island, how she lives with the Queen in London, how—'

Gran laughs. 'Not quite, our Megan. You're a bigger story-teller than me. Here—'

And she gives me the spoon to lick.

'I'll get the photo and show you. We've just got time.'

She's back in a moment, wiping one hand on her apron.

'Here we are. The cutting should be in the back.'

4

I take the silver frame in both hands as Gran smooths out a piece of newspaper. It shows the same picture as I'm holding.

'It's the girls again!'

'I'll read you a bit.'

I move closer.

'*Knitting class twenty years old today!*' she reads in a funny loud voice. '*When we started, they said "the class" wouldn't last, that it would just be a gossip shop, said Mrs Rose MacIntyre of Fenham –* That's me,' she nods – '*But the original twelve grand dames of the class –* the reporter was a cheeky young bugger – *still meet every other Tuesday. Except instead of knitting woollens for soldiers, it's to play whist for sixpences—*'

She folds up the newspaper. 'Ee, the rubbish they write nowadays. I've never bet a sixpence in me life.'

But I can see that she's smiling. I put the photograph on the bench and move my finger along the line of 'girls'. There are twelve of them, all standing in a row with arms linked behind their backs, all with one leg lifted in the air, like the Tiller Girls on TV.

Gran is at one end, smiling a bit, but not with her usual smile.

Then Alice— looking funny. Her dark hair is blowing about her face, but you can see she's wearing a big smile, and you can also see that she's blinked, because her eyes are tight shut. Alice is my favourite because she's often funny, even when she doesn't mean to be. She says it's her happy pills.

Then May, next to Alice. You could make two Alices out of one May—

I move on to the next 'girl'. I don't like to think too much about May at the moment.

I know most of the girls. I see them with Gran in the coffee shop of the big store in town. Ladies in fur coats with huge handbags, all talking loudly over the scream of the silver machines that make the steam. They all look a bit the same. Short, curly perms, tight skirts with round stomachs, jumpers with bosoms like bolsters.

But Aunt Emily doesn't look like that.

'Is that her?' But I already know it is. My finger stops.

She's tall and slim, with long golden hair swept up at the back of her head and she's wearing lovely floaty clothes. In the photo she looks a bit like a doll, because her eyes are wide open and she's not smiling. But I imagine her really looking like a princess. Everyone

5

says she's a 'beauty'. I'm not sure about this, but I know she isn't an 'auntie' because Gran told me so. She likes to be called 'aunt'.

I suddenly remember the month before, having tea at Gran's one afternoon, when May said I wasn't to call *her* aunt any more, because she didn't like it.

'In that case why not just call me Alice too,' Alice said with a cross look to May. 'Because then it sounds like I'm your friend, as well as your aunt.' Which made me feel a little better, but I still don't like to think about May at the moment.

'Yes, that's Emily,' says Gran. 'Remember her now?'

There's a rap at the door, followed by a distant crescendo of barking. She takes off her apron.

'You go in the garden and see if there are any caterpillars.'

But that's for ordinary days, and today it's 'the class', so I follow behind her like a shadow.

'It's May,' calls Gran. Then she tuts. 'And she's on her own.'

I walk quickly back to the kitchen and stand ready by the back door.

'Bloody hell, Rose! I've spent the last forty-five minutes getting here!'

May's voice is loud. It fills the whole house and spills out to where I'm standing. I take a step further into the garden.

'I went for Alice. You know what she's like at the moment. So many pills in her she rattles. On another planet half the time, the daft bugger. Well, she'll bloody well have to make her own way here now.'

I hear Gran muttering. They're coming closer. I glance around and see the door to the coal shed is open. May's voice won't be so big in there.

But it is.

'I put myself out, I did. Knowing her, she might not have realised it was Tuesday, let alone the class, or even whose bloody class.'

Gran replies in a low voice I can't hear.

'Aye, well, and maybe I should,' the big voice protests. 'I did try. But she was in one of them belligerent moods. You know how she is at the moment. I don't know what the hell's got into her! I keep thinking I must have done something wrong, but I'm damned if I know what.' She sighs. 'Anyway, if I'd waited, neither of us would have got here this side of tomorrow.'

They're at the back door. I can just see May through the window, her bright halo of red hair, the startlingly blue eyes in her pale, powdery face.

'I know, I know it's not her fault, but she's so bloody *dopey*!'

I like this word. It would make a good name for the cat.

'Can you believe she'd dropped off and burned a bleeding great hole in her jumper with her cigarette? She only woke up when I knocked. Honestly, she could have burned the house down and not noticed. One too many Valium. Or else paralytic—'

I like this word too. I try to repeat it, but it has too many bits.

There's a silence, then Gran murmuring again, then:

'Why? What's *she* doing here? Cramps the style having a kid at the class doesn't it?'

Gran is outside now.

'Alice's young Jane was at *her* class last time,' she says. 'And I've been promising Megan she could come after her birthday. You'll just have to put up with it, May.'

Footsteps across the concrete.

'She's probably in the cabbages looking for caterpillars. Megan!'

Footsteps up the garden path. Then May's voice, low, 'Bloody kid's tea party next—'

I stand as still as I can. I can't come out now. They think I'm at the bottom of the garden.

Silence. More seconds pass, and then gradually my heart begins to thud more slowly.

Suddenly May's face appears at the cracked window.

'She's in here, Rose!'

I step back, stumbling into a pile of wooden boxes.

'What the hell are you doing in there?' the face shouts at me.

'Out, our Megan.' Gran sounds cross. She takes my hand and yanks. 'Now look. You're all mucky again.' But she doesn't mention the torn tights. 'Upstairs and get clean.'

I run indoors.

'The girl's just a bit shy. You know what they're like at this age.'

'Thank Christ I don't,' I hear May say with a laugh as I climb the stairs.

Most of the girls have arrived, Gran comes in to tell me, but I'm still busy. I'm standing on a stool at the kitchen bench, with a tea towel pinned around my middle, rolling out pastry. You have to concentrate or it sticks itself to the rolling pin. I sprinkle more flour on to the greying dough. I've decided to make three. A boy, a girl and a 'something', currants for eyes and buttons.

'Mmm, they're good, Megan.' I know it's May standing behind me watching, but I don't want to talk to her, so I don't turn round. I can hear her breathing. She 'humphs', then is gone.

'And how's my girl?'

I'm suddenly lifted off my stool, clasped into a fur coat and swung in a circle. But cautiously, the scullery, as Gran calls it, is only narrow. I laugh. I know who *this* is. *I* knew she would come.

'Alice!' Gran sounds surprised. 'Are you all right? I thought you weren't coming. May said—'

Alice's pale face looks more tiny than usual above her big, shiny black coat. She raises her eyebrows.

'Oh aye? May exaggerates. She just couldn't be bothered to wait for me, that's all. Of course I'm fine. Look at me.'

And she twirls me around again, singing:

> *'She's a big lass an' a bonny lass,*
> *An' she likes her beer,*
> *An' they call her Cushy Butterfield*
> *An' I wish she wor here.'*

'Alice!'

My feet bang against the wall.

'And look at your coat,' Gran tuts. 'The child's got flour from one end of the place to the other.'

But Alice just plants a kiss on my forehead and goes off laughing.

Back on my stool, I look at my reflection in the glass. Cushy Butterfield— with lipstick lips right in the middle of her forehead. I giggle.

I start on the buttons, listening for the front door. *She's* not arrived yet. *Aunt Emily.* The voices soar up and down in the next room. Gran's girls are always loud. Suddenly there's a pause. Then the kitchen door opens.

'Megan?' someone says quietly. 'Do you remember me?'

I turn round. She doesn't look like the photograph at all, because she's smiling and there are crinkles at the sides of her eyes. And she doesn't look anything like a princess either. She's just wearing a plain white dress, no velvet, no jewels, nothing. Her pale-gold hair is tied in a simple knot at her neck, there's not even a curl! I look away, disappointed.

'A bit shy?' she asks, smiling. She sounds different from the others, she doesn't sound Geordie.

I go back to my pastry, mumbling that I'm busy. She watches me in silence for a few minutes, so that my cheeks grow hot. Then she pats my head and is gone, leaving spicy perfume in the air.

She might be pretty, but she's nothing like a princess at all. I bet she never even lived on a desert island either. It was just one of Gran's stories. I chop and hack, suddenly bored with my pastry creations.

It grows quieter in the room next door. There's not so much laughter and chat, until finally, silence.

Then:

'Hearts is *trumps*!'

'You daft bat. You should have hung on to that one. It went!'

A raised voice. 'Hey, that's mine!'

Silence again.

'I'll have that—'

'Off!' Loud and pleased.

Lots of groans.

'Twenty-seven for me, Rose.'

'Five. I was off meself then!'

Another moan. 'A right handful. Forty-three— and I'd just picked up the ace!'

Gran's girls can be funny.

Suddenly, 'What the hell are you doing with those in your hand. They went!'

'They did not!'

Angry voices. I stop what I'm doing and listen.

'They bloody well did! She played the eight, Emily the six and then—'

'*You* should mind your own business!'

The other voice grows louder.

'*You're* a one to talk. Never could keep your nose out, or your hands off what belonged to others!'

'And what do you mean by that, Alice?'

Alice. It's Alice and May—

There's a clang of something metal. I imagine the big silver and brown ash tray being crashed down on the table.

May and Alice—

'Stop it, you two!' Gran sounds cross.

Someone 'humphs'. Who? May makes noises like that. I climb off the stool and stand closer to the door.

'If you two don't make more of an effort, I'm going to stop you both coming,' Gran says.

'What's this all about anyway?' Aunt Emily sounds surprised. 'You always used to be as thick as thieves. I leave the country for a while and come back to find you enemies?'

'They've been carrying on like this for months,' Gran grumbles. 'Like a couple of kids. Don't you think it's time to sort out whatever your problem is and give us all a little peace?'

'There's a man involved, I'll be bound,' comes a voice I recognise as Gran's neighbour, followed by a cackle. 'Someone been playing away from home, eh?'

'You're not kidding,' says someone sounding like a nasty version of Aunt Alice.

'Alice, Alice, what the hell's got into you?' May says, and her voice is suddenly soft, and she sounds more like she used to, because May *used* to be nice. 'I've got problems of my own without this—'

'Really,' says Alice drily. 'And what problems do you think *you* have?'

But there's no answer.

Everyone suddenly starts talking at once.

'Tea-time!' Gran shouts over the noise. 'Alice, you clear the cards. May, the cups and plates are on the sideboard.'

There are sounds of scraping of chairs. I climb back on my stool to my pastry men.

'They're nice, pet.'

Gran carefully transfers the grey shapes to a baking sheet. One of the legs drops off in the process, but I don't mind. It was the something's leg, and 'somethings' don't have to have two legs.

I like having tea with the girls. I sit next to Aunt Emily, who I suppose can't help not being a princess. She keeps giving me things and I don't have to have any sandwiches at all. I think I'm going to like Aunt Emily.

'She'll be sick,' Gran mutters.

'Rubbish—'

Another jam tart appears on my plate.

The room seems to have grown smaller, suddenly full to bursting with ladies— and hats! Lots of hats, brown hats and grey hats and hats with pins in. Only Gran and my three aunts without a hat. Faces eating, red lips on teacups, chat, chat, chat, lacy hankies out of bags for wiping crumbs. Except for Alice. Alice doesn't eat at all. And she doesn't drink tea either. She fills her cup from a little silver bottle she keeps in her bag. But May eats. May has a big bit of chocolate cake stuck to her chin. I try not to stare.

Gran polishes off the last jam tart and sighs.

'We're one short,' she says and puts down her cup. 'The numbers are all wrong. Someone will have to sit out or we'll have to play rummy again.'

Tuts and mutters.

I go to the sofa and pull the old books into my lap. Inside each one is my mother's name, but not my mother's name. Elizabeth, instead of Betty. MacIntyre, instead of Thompson. I've been told, but I can't remember why. The room gradually grows quiet until there's just the flick of the cards being dealt, the flare of a match, a murmur, chuckles, and then the clock ticking loudly in the silence. In the shafts of afternoon sunlight the dust motes twinkle and dance—

I open my eyes to the sound of my name. For a second or two I don't know where I am. The air is thick and blue with cigarette smoke. Sunshine is streaming in through the lace-curtained window, making dappled patterns on the worn carpet.

'Yes, let's play something the bairn can play. She's been sitting there, good as gold, all afternoon.'

'What about blind horse? She might manage that.'

'Eh, our Megan? Can you play blind horse?'

Alice is talking to me. I rub my eyes and climb down. Someone gives me a pile of halfpennies.

'Then you would put the four on the five,' says Aunt Emily.

'Or the six on the five,' says Alice.

'And then the seven would go on the six.'

I yawn and nod. I'm going to play cards.

I make a careful column with the halfpennies as they talk.

'And so it's one for the kitty and one for his nob. Right? All right, pet?' Alice repeats.

I smile. *I'm* going to play cards.

Someone spreads the cards in my hand into a fan shape. Reds and blacks, curly shapes and diamonds. I know the hearts. The Queen of Hearts is beautiful. Her dress is red, with jewels, and she wears a crown in her black hair.

Hands occasionally reach over and pull one of the cards from my fan. It's getting smaller. I don't want the Queen to go.

I yawn, then look up to see if anyone has noticed. May opposite is puffing on a cigarette. Suddenly two fat pillars of smoke pour from her nose. Right out of her nose! I look over at the Green Dragon Vase, then back at May. The smoke is still coming out! And now she's talking, and it's coming out of her mouth with every word!

'Come on! Who's got the Queen? We've all bleeding knocked and I'm damned if I'm going to pay again!'

I gaze entranced at the smoky words leaping off her tongue.

'Here! What's this!'

Rough hands stretch across and tug at my fan. The cards fall to the table, the Queen uppermost.

'Would you look at that,' May says. 'The bloody kid's had it all the time!'

May pushes her face half-way across the table and glares at me.

'*This* is the Queen and it goes *there*! We've all been waiting for you!'

'May,' Gran tuts. 'She's only a girl. Where's the harm?'

I take my hands off the table and hold them tightly in my lap, nails digging into my palms. I've done something wrong.

'She's ruined the bloody game! That's where's the harm! I had to pay twice because of her. Sitting with the King I was. I would have been off!'

Gran speaks sharply. 'For God's sake, May, that's enough. Never mind about Alice, what the hell's got into you these days?'

May humphs. 'Needs a good clip round the ear to wake this one up, if you ask me.'

'But we're not, May,' says Alice drily, stroking my head.

'And that's no way to speak to a child,' says Aunt Emily quietly, but I hear.

May rubs her eyes. 'I know, I know,' she says after a while, sounding suddenly very tired.

I look at the table-cloth, my eyes blurring, trying to keep them open as long as possible so that the tears won't fall. I've done something wrong. They won't let me come to the class again.

'I think I should go,' says Aunt Emily. 'I'm due back in London tomorrow.'

'We're off as well,' chime two of the others.

They're all going. Because of me. *I did something wrong.*

Through tears I watch Gran's neighbour put on a bright-orange scarf, hat slipped a bit to one side, red lipstick outside her lips pretending to be a bigger mouth, cigarette waggling up and down in the corner as she talks.

'Good to see you, Emily. London's not so far away as that island, Greece, wasn't it? Or Cyprus? So don't be a stranger—'

Aunt Emily's smile doesn't quite reach her eyes.

I slide down under the table, up the other side, and close the door quietly behind me.

It's darker and cool in the bedroom. I feel hot and my eyes hurt. Alice follows me up.

'Your Aunt May just isn't used to children,' she says after a while, stroking my hair from my face. 'So pay no attention. She's not a bad old soul.'

The door closes and it goes quiet. I lie down on the coats, my face in a fur smelling of lily of the valley, like Alice, and play with a scarf that feels cool against my cheek, spicy, not flowery, like Christmas cake— and Aunt Emily.

'Megan?'

I turn my head. I didn't hear the door open.

'Megan— It's me.'

Quickly I sit up. In the half-light, May's big, powdery face looks very white. She sits close beside me, on the edge of the bed.

I hold my breath. May doesn't like me. May doesn't like children. After a while, she sighs.

13

'You're not to mind me, pet,' she says. 'I'm just not nice sometimes.'

I sit, hardly breathing as she takes hold of my hand, puts something cold on to the palm, and closes my fingers around it.

'In fact,' she says, standing and briskly buttoning her coat. 'You're not allowed to mind much in this world, Megan.'

She sounds sad, but I still don't say anything.

I wait as she walks heavily down the stairs and the front door bangs, and then I open my hand. In the dusk the new sixpence gleams like a white light.

2

May
1943

'Are you sure you don't want me to stay?' Emily asked again, her face anxious. 'You don't look too well, May. Maybe we should have asked the doctor to come out to us again.'

May shook her head. 'You go. I'm fine. Really. And you're already late for your night class.'

Frowning, Emily bent and kissed her cheek.

'Well, if you're sure—'

'Quite.'

May watched her elder sister weave her way gracefully out of the crowded surgery, aware that the eyes of all the men in the room would be doing the same. Not that Emily would ever notice. She was always oblivious of the attention her looks prompted. Emily seemed to live in a world of her own for much of the time.

May waved reassuringly as her sister turned and hesitated by the door.

'Off you go,' she mouthed.

She sat back, pressing herself against the waiting-room wall, trying to keep as much distance as possible between her and the overblown crowd before her. It was the first time she'd been out in a month and the world seemed to have grown brighter, louder, more vivid. Or her nerves more raw.

A young boy playing with a truck looked up and grinned gap-toothed as it ran over her foot. One of his eyes was infected, crustily closed. A woman stood and clipped his ear, her legs stick-thin beneath a huge stomach, like a caricature of pregnancy. The girl

15

opposite moaned and began to rock herself softly. In an effort not to look, May fixed her eyes on the too-bright posters.

'Come into the factories' one invited. A woman, arms outstretched, planes overhead, warships and tanks at her side.

'Eat more greens' another exhorted. While the third was curt: 'No spitting'.

The surgery door opened. A woman shuffled out on swollen ankles. May knew her. She turned away.

'May Charlton? May—'

The doctor stood smiling in her direction. He held the door and patted her shoulder as she walked through. He'd known her since she was a child.

'Well, you're looking better than when I last saw you, anyway,' he said.

With an effort she smiled back. She waited as he wrote in his notes. A fire burned in the grate, the glass in the bookcase behind him reflecting back its flickering flames. A clock on the mantelpiece ticked in the silence, loudly marking each second.

Finally he put down his pen and looked up at her.

'So, May—'

He asked a few questions. She gave short, quiet replies.

'Much pain?'

She shook her head. Some, not much.

'Well, we'll just have a look then, shall we—'

The examining table was cold and hard.

'Draw your knees up— Now relax— That's right.'

She closed her eyes. But it wasn't so bad. Not like the last time. Then there had been such pain.

There was a clang of metal in a dish.

'Finished, all done.'

She let out her breath.

'Good girl, good girl—'

She stared up at the ceiling. She was almost eighteen. He still thought she was ten. Which was oddly comforting.

'You weren't well enough last time, May, but now I think we need to have a talk,' he said, as he washed his hands.

He didn't sit behind the desk, but in the chair next to hers. His voice was stern. Her cheeks blazed at his words as she sat, head bent, unable to look at his face. But after a while his tone softened.

16

'You're all right now, lass, and that's the main thing,' he said, patting her hand.

Then his instructions were brisk and to the point. After all, his kindness had to be spread thinly. A whole mass of humanity waited at the other side of the door, and they too expected their share.

Outside, the evening air was cold. May checked her watch, realising she could have a long wait. The night before the Germans had mistaken a rain-washed road for the Tyne and they'd bombed the goods yard, thinking it was a shipyard. The sugar and butter were still blazing, the trams disrupted. She could be here for ages. For a moment she wished she'd allowed Emily to wait with her. But then there would have been questions— and what could she have said. She needed the time to think.

She stood shuffling from foot to foot, watching a barrage balloon that had broken free of its ropes. It hung suspended above the city, a whale in a dark sea, occasionally dislodging a roof tile as it drifted with its anchorless chain. Alice had told her about it earlier that day. She'd said it had floated over her college and there had been chaos amongst the girls. Together they had laughed. But now May watched without interest as a gust of wind moved it on to new waters.

The pain low in her abdomen had begun again. She shivered. She was going to be late. And it was their night for the knitting class.

The tram hissed like a gander as it stopped. She took a seat at the back and winced as it jolted into action, but as it moved smoothly the pain faded. Dry-eyed, empty as fallen leaves, she looked through her reflection into the darkening city.

Oh God, she whispered.

Oh *Joe*.

Joseph Graham. What have you done now?

Another lie—

'Joseph! Joseph Graham,' the teacher snapped that first time. 'What have you done now?'

They had been seven years old, sitting next to each other at Wellbeck Primary School.

17

'You told me that you needed pencils, because you had none yourself.'

Joe had nodded, wide-eyed with innocence, as usual.

'So what's this?'

The teacher lifted the desk lid, exposing a treacherous array of coloured sticks. 'A lie, that's what it is!'

And the reluctant hand was flattened, followed by the swish of the cane, and Joe's face had crumpled.

That was the first lie she'd seen him tell. And the first of many punishments. Not that the punishments ever stopped him. But it was always the crumpled look, never taken lightly. Joe was too sensitive really, to be a rogue.

All through Wellbeck Primary, Walkergate Junior, Welling Secondary— And Joe was so clever. He had no need to lie.

He ought to be going to university, the headmaster told Joe's mother, who laughed like a drain at his words. But it was true. Joe was a reader – novels, history, poetry even! *He had no need to lie—*

'It's just my pathological compulsion to bend the truth in the face of authority,' he used to grin, making her laugh.

But he'd never lied to her. Only this once—

This time he *had* lied.

They'd been the best of friends for years, even when he reached the age when other boys teased him for walking to school with a girl. He'd taken black eyes for her. And given as good as he'd got.

May leaned against the window of the tram, the glass cool against her forehead. Joe, Joseph Graham. In and out of each other's pockets, each other's houses, each other's lives, for how many years?

The ghost of the crumpled look had been there when she'd told him about Will, and that she was getting married.

A few seconds' confusion. Then, 'Good. Champion, May. I'm really pleased for you both.'

Another lie.

'Will's a good bloke. He'll take care of you.'

Then the strained smile and the suddenly remembered appointment.

May closed her eyes. But perhaps she'd known how he felt about her, even before that. Perhaps she'd always known.

The tram clattered through the darkening city. The pain was getting worse. But not much longer now. If she breathed evenly it would pass. Outside, the rain was mixed with sleet. Winter was on its way, the summer just a memory—

Well, more than just a memory, now. Now she would never be able to forget.

He'd called for her early that morning—

'May! May? Are you up?'

She'd heard the first time. It was too early. Groaning, she turned over and put the pillow over her head. If she didn't respond, maybe her mother would call for Alice instead.

'May! Can you hear me, our May? Joe's here to see you!'

She sighed, fought her way out of the bedclothes and picked up the clock. Eight o'clock! But it was her day off. What was he doing here at this time?

Grudgingly she pulled back the curtains. Warm summer sunshine flooded the room. She stretched slowly in the pool it made on the worn carpet.

'May!'

'I'm coming, Mam! For God's sake, just a minute. The house isn't on fire, is it?'

Downstairs Joe and her mother were sitting at the table, a silence hanging between them like guilt. May watched them, eyebrows raised. The two were no doubt in cahoots again. They looked just like they had before her birthday, sharing a secret, affecting nonchalance. The surprise party had taken years off her.

'Nobody died, have they?'

Her mother stood and patted Joe's shoulder, deliberately avoiding her gaze.

'I'd better go then. I've got some messages to fetch.'

'Thanks, Mrs Charlton,' Joe mumbled uncomfortably, his eyes flicking to May, then back to his cup.

Bemused, May watched her mother put on her coat and make for the door.

'But the shops aren't even open yet, Mam,' she called, feeling the first vague stirrings of alarm. 'And Alice said she would do the shopping anyway. Here! You've forgotten your coupons!'

But her mother had gone.

She turned questioningly to Joe. He was fiddling with his cup, fair hair flopping over one eye. Suddenly he looked up and grinned, his pale face splitting from ear to ear.

'Good grief, Joe!' May shook her head exasperated. 'I thought someone bloody well *had* died there for a moment. Honestly, you and my mother.'

With an exasperated sigh, she collapsed into the chair he pulled out for her. While he poured tea she unplaited her dark-red hair and spread it round her shoulders. As he had since he was a child, Joe automatically put up a hand and smoothed her hair down her back.

'You'd think I was a pet,' she'd joked some weeks before, suddenly made unaccountably uncomfortable by the action.

'A pet pre-Raphaelite,' he'd laughed, and later brought her a book of paintings. The woman in the picture it fell open at looked a little like her – big boned, pale skin, the same long waves of red hair. She'd been delighted, but he wouldn't let her keep the book.

It was hers now.

'Did you have a good day yesterday?' she asked, shaking her head free of his hand with an embarrassed laugh. She pulled her dressing-gown more tightly around her, but it was only Joe. 'And how was your aunt?'

'I didn't go.'

She looked up smiling, expecting nothing.

'I signed up, May. That's where I went.'

The cup paused at her lips.

'I joined the army,' he went on quietly. 'I start training next week.'

She stared, put the cup down and laughed. He was teasing.

'Joe! Don't joke like that.' But her laughter sounded hollow.

'This is my last day. I have to be at Catterick tomorrow afternoon.' His eyes were searching her face. 'And I don't know when I'll get home again—'

She shook her head. But this was nonsense! People just didn't get up and leave like that. And not Joe! Joe couldn't go. He was still too young! And he didn't even believe it was right! A bloody mess, he called the war.

'You're pulling my leg—'

But her smile faded in his silence.

'Why?' she asked, suddenly angry. 'Why couldn't you do something like Will? Will said there are jobs going begging at the Bladon pit. He could get you a job. Miners don't get called up. Reserved occupation. Important war work that is, so why can't—'

She stopped. Joe was looking down at his hands. Of course she knew why. It was because of Will he was going.

'Oh, Joe—'

She tried to smile, but the shock lay coldly inside her.

'What the hell will I do without you?'

May held herself stiffly as the tram started up again. What had he answered that morning?

The words suddenly rang in her head.

'*Well, you can give me today, at any rate*,' he'd finally said.

Weeks— months—? A lifetime ago.

They had gone to the fair on the town moor that day. She'd always loved the fair. It was the biggest in Europe and to miss it felt like missing Christmas. She'd been saving it up to go with Will. But she went with Joe.

The afternoon would always be fixed in her mind now, like a photograph. A photograph taken too quickly, with outlines blurred and shapes merging, but caught all the same. Their last day together.

Picking their way through the boggy ground, going in the back way, past caravans, thumping lorries, cables, diesel smells— then into the bustling jumble of canvas and carousels, the helter-skelter like a huge candy rocket thrusting up at the centre. Shouts and laughter, babies crying, demands and cajoles from the callers to 'Roll up! Roll up!' Children sucking rock to pencil points, faces already stuck red with candy floss. Lads in shirt-sleeves testing strength with hammers, impressing bold-faced, lipsticked girls whose loud shrieks all said: 'Look at me! Look at me!'

She'd seen a man they knew, in Sunday suit with a wide tie, she'd seen him look down into the upturned face of an anxious girl, who was not his wife, and kiss her for all the world to see. The war, Joe murmured, following her gaze. She hadn't understood what he meant.

She hadn't understood him at all. There had been an awkwardness between them, a silence – she and Joe, who had talked each other's lives away for years – so that it was a relief to walk through the

21

crowded fair, to let its hustle and bustle take away the need for conversation.

Past the boxing booth, they'd gone into a tent whose sign read, 'Greatest Show on Earth. The Mysteries of the World on View.' Inside, a two-headed snake, scarred from self-attack. Smug photographs of Siamese twin ladies with their husbands, begging delicate questions. An ordinary puppy, but miserably shaven. A three-legged sheep, leaning unsurely against the side of its pen.

'Hey, mister!' Joe called to the bowlered man, collarless and gold-toothed. 'Call this one Napoleon, do you then?'

She bent to see. Under its belly, a fourth leg was tucked up with a broad leather belt. Gold-Tooth had scowled and ordered them out. She'd thought Joe would fight, so she'd taken his arm and pulled him away.

He'd kept hold of her hand on his arm.

And then the bearded lady. A young girl with old eyes had taken their money. In the darkness it took a few moments before they could make out the burly, red-bearded man from the boxing booth sitting at the centre. ('Knock down Michael McGinty,' the sign had read under his picture, 'and take home ten shillings!') Bored, reading a newspaper, wearing a red and white spotted frock big enough to cover a battleship, he hadn't bothered to look up.

May tutted at the girl as they left the booth – threepence that had cost! But the girl just shrugged.

Joe had laughed. 'Canny one, pet,' he grinned, and the girl smiled back shyly. Girls liked Joe.

And all the while with his arm through hers, as if she were his girl.

He led her to the top of the helter-skelter, sat down behind her on the prickly coconut mat. He put his arms round her waist, his fingers warm through her thin print frock, and held her tightly, like a possession, so that all she was aware of, as they slid down through arcs of swirling colour, were his arms, and his breath on her neck.

Because she and Joe didn't touch. She and Joe had never touched. They had fought, kicked, nipped, pulled, poked, pushed and pummelled through the years. But never touched. Not like that.

'Read your fortune?' a woman asked as they were leaving the fair, and Joe's face had clouded. He'd put his arm round her shoulders (easily, as if it were always like that!), and led her quickly away.

Why? She wondered still.

For fear that he would see some grisly war lying ahead of him? Or a future in which Will and she lived happily ever after, a few bairns at their feet?

Both wrong—

They walked until they reached the edge of the moor and the fair was just a toy in the distance. She sat with her back against a tree and stiffened as he'd lain with his head in her lap. She didn't know this Joe who was staring up at her – except that the crumpled look was around his eyes. And she knew that.

He'd produced a book of poems written by men who had been in the First World War. Blunden, Sassoon and Owen their names were. She didn't know them then. The book was hers now, by her bed. All the books were hers now.

He read to her, frowning, as if looking for some secret that would help him understand, something to prepare himself for what was to come. Images of men like cattle to slaughter, the horrors of gas and death, the pain of a misplaced patriotism.

'But it won't be like that,' she protested. 'That was the trenches, our dads' war. You won't see anything like that.'

She couldn't remember what he'd answered. Just what he asked.

'But I might not come back May,' he repeated quietly, with a laugh to soften the words.

Still she hadn't understood.

'He'll have you for the whole of his life. This is just for one night.'

And she flushed with sudden understanding.

'Just tonight, May.'

She'd stood up, unable to meet his gaze. He couldn't ask her this.

'If I don't come back, May, I'll never have known what it's like,' he'd whispered urgently, as still she wouldn't answer. 'I'll never have made love—'

They journeyed back in silence. She wouldn't look at him. She didn't know how to. This wasn't her and Joe. *She loved Will.* He was asking too much.

She thought of the knitting class and the girls. It's doing our bit, they told each other, pleased and smug as helmets, socks and scarves appeared from wool and needles. Doing their bit for the war, they said.

The least we can do, they all kept saying.

But he was asking too much.

At home in her room she'd taken out the beige crêpe de Chine – only one more fitting was needed. Rose had sewn the pleats and tucks on the bodice by hand, and put yards into the flaring skirt. In a few months she would wear it and become Will's wife, which was all she'd ever wanted.

But she put it back. This had nothing to do with Will.

She sat at the dressing-table and took out the box. Inside, wrapped in white tissue, lay apricot silk, trimmed with cream lace. Stuff you dreamed about. Her sisters and the other girls from the class had clubbed together, pooling all their coupons.

'Camiknickers!' she'd laughed. 'For a wedding present?'

'For you both,' Alice had grinned. 'We reckon *he'll* get as much out of it as you.'

She unwrapped it remembering the words.

She'd walked first, through evening streets made gold by the smog that spoiled them, until the world had faded to grey and she was there, at the house. It was late. But the gas lamp still burned at the window, which meant Joe was still waiting, so she'd gone.

She'd thought there would be tenderness. There had been none. Undressing in silence, unable to look. And the urgent hands of the stranger who'd taken Joe's place laying her down— stop, she'd wanted to cry out. Stop!

But that was what she was there for. That was why she had come. So she closed her eyes.

She hadn't expected such pain, and the pushing and pushing, right through her pain— until finally she was at a small place deep inside her head, far away from her body.

Then silence, an awful silence, a stranger lying next to her, the back of one hand across his eyes.

'I'm sorry, May,' he'd whispered, his voice thick. 'I hadn't realised—'

His words hung in the darkness.

'I mean I didn't know. I thought you and Will—'

Then his voice caught, and he was Joe again, so she'd held him in her arms as he wept.

Afterwards the apricot silk was stained and the lace torn, so she'd thrown it away.

May shifted her gaze, focusing on the streets outside. The tram was slowing down. They were in Fenham. It was her stop. She stood and smiled at the clippie.

'Night, love,' the woman nodded back. 'Mind how you go now.'

Collar up against the cold, flashlight in one hand, the other thrust deep in her pocket, she walked quickly. She was late. The girls would have already arrived for the class, but Emily might be back by now, and her mother would help see to them.

Along Elborough Street, then Fenhamgate— She slowed a little. Joe's house.

Her fists clenched. But no regrets, she told herself. And no anger! She walked on. How could she feel angry, with Joe gone? There had been no grisly war for him after all; his boat was torpedoed on its way to the front.

She walked faster. So no anger!

After all, what did it matter? Any of it?

Virginity?

It was just a word.

And the doctor?

'It's doubtful you'll have babies, May,' he'd said, patting her hand to soften the words.

Yet how could she miss what she would never have?

And Joe's lie? Because this time he *had* lied to her.

'I'll never have made love—'

'Gonoccocal salpingitis,' the doctor said she'd had. An infection. Caused by gonorrhoea.

Joe's final lie.

Her fists clenched harder. But he couldn't have known. *He couldn't have known!* So no anger! What was he guilty of after all? Of loving her too much? Of wanting her?

So no anger!

Faster and faster, along Queensway, across the Lonnen— It was not a lie that should have mattered! There was only one lie that mattered! She'd found it in Joe's book, the familiar writing in the

25

margin, the words of the poem underlined: *Dulce et decorum est pro patria mori.*

'The Old Lie,' the poet called it.

The only lie!

She broke into a run. Because there were no rules any more! Not in a world where you could die for nothing! Where you could get blown out of the water for doing what you thought was right!

Through the iron gate, up the path, flashlight on the lock, the house dark-faced, but waiting.

Inside the living-room was brightly lit, the fire blazing. Most of the girls had already arrived. Knitting needles flashed and clicked, material tacked into vests getting pressed and folded for the London bomb victims, cups of tea already on the go.

'Oh, much better,' she answered Rose, catching her breath, hanging up her coat, composing a face to present.

And to Emily's question, 'Rumbling appendix, the doctor says.' She laughed a little. 'But more like grumbling if you ask me.'

Emily looked at her sharply.

'Well, you still don't look too well, May. You're terribly pale.'

A smile, accepting the tea to reassure, taking up her sewing, lest anyone think she wasn't all right. Because she *was* all right. Of course she was. Sitting back, listening to the chat of the girls. And smile, keep smiling.

Everyone is to put in threepence, Rose was saying. And then it could be spent on a parcel for a soldier one of them knew. This week it could be Lewis, their young cousin in Liverpool.

'May?'

She reached into her handbag.

Her youngest sister Alice suddenly arrived, in a rush of cold air and high spirits.

'And where have you been then?' asked Emily. 'Up to mischief? Lads involved, I'll be bound.'

The girl laughed, telling nothing, and everything.

'Is your dress ready yet, May?'

Turning to Alice, watching her speak, formulating a reply, but Rose interrupted.

'It needs another fitting,' Rose grumbled. 'If you lose weight at this rate, May, I'll have to remake the blessed thing. Mother!' she

26

shouted into the kitchen. 'You'll have to sort May out. She needs fattening up a bit before the wedding.'

'Bet she fattens up a bit *after* the wedding,' said Alice with a nudge to the girl next to her.

'And then a bit more,' the girl grinned back.

'And a bit more—'

'For nine months!' they laughed together.

'Alice,' Emily scolded, but smiling.

May turned away, no longer listening or watching, letting the chat wash around her.

'Seventy-two loops that scarf's got to have,' her mother reminded them. 'And two yards long. Mind you don't stretch yours this time, our Alice!'

Everyone laughed.

Her mother sounded aggrieved. 'The woman from the WVS accused me of cheating last week because of that girl,' she grumbled.

Everyone laughed again.

'May, are you all right?'

Concentrate on sewing, she told herself.

'They're off to the Lake District after the wedding. Isn't that right May?'

Her vision began to blur.

'What?'

Her throat tightened.

She pricked her finger, watched blood seep into a circle, crimson on white— stared, remembering apricot silk, once dreamed of, thrown away— there'll be things she'll not be able to say now, to Will— a distance that will always have to be there now— She closed her eyes. It's doubtful you'll have babies, he said.

No children—

Swallowing, her throat tighter and tighter.

'It's the wrong time of year for the Lakes, really. A bit too early to be warm, but I don't expect the two of you will notice that much, eh May?'

And no wedding. There can be no wedding. Not now.

Hands trembling, the material slipped to the floor. Her chair scraped back.

'I think I need to lie down,' she murmured, walking through concerned looks. 'Just for a while.'

She climbed the stairs, quietly locked the door behind her, and sat in the darkness. The pain was spreading, filling her body, burrowing deep. And it was there to stay, she knew.

Because to make it go, if only for a second, she would have to throw back her head and cry out.

And you didn't do that. You didn't scream.

In the darkness May held her arms tightly and silently let the tears fall.

3
Alice
1944

'You're going too fast,' May laughed, but Alice hardly heard.

Instead she pushed her glasses up the bridge of her nose and began scanning the page, quicker and quicker. The heroine had hardly met the hero – it was on a train pounding through the darkness in central Europe – and already they seemed to be falling in love! Without any of the difficulties and misunderstandings that usually have to get sorted out before lovers can first kiss. And she'd actually gone alone to his carriage!

> *'It's like a film,' Tara whispered, gazing at the heavy brocade drapes, silk cushions and exotic rugs.*
> *'But it's not— and I'm real,' the young Count answered, pushing dark, unruly hair from care-worn features. But the amusement vanished from his steely-grey eyes as Tara flushed and dropped her thick lashes, then unconsciously lifted them again in mute appeal. He felt his blood stir. This English girl had an enigmatic quality, a reserve that intrigued him . . .*

'Slow down, Alice. It's not *that* good.'

But Alice quickly turned the page.

'They're going to do it. I know it. She's gone to his bedroom—'

'Hey! I hadn't even read that.' May nudged her in the ribs.

Reluctantly Alice turned back the page.

'And it's *not* his bedroom,' May added wearily. 'They're on a train.'

The two girls were lying side by side on Alice's narrow bed, surrounded by the usual chaos of her bedroom: a chair lost under a heap of clothes, the strata of which revealed the history of what she had worn the previous week; small piles of library books gathering dust here and there; a tattered stack of film magazines, waiting to be rifled for romantic heroes as smouldering as the smoky-eyed Valentino who gazed down at them from above the bedhead.

They lay propped up on elbows, the latest romance by Bella D'Arcy open on the pillow before them.

May pointedly tugged the book more towards herself.

'Sorry,' Alice grinned, moving over from where she had pinned May to the wall in her excitement. 'But it's getting good. They're going to do it this time, I know.'

'Rubbish,' May said, pushing curtains of red hair behind her ears. 'Do you really think Mother would let you get this out of the library if they did? Of course they're not. They never do.'

'But they might—'

While May read on, Alice lay back and closed her eyes, picturing the lovers in her mind. The heroine, of course, looked just like herself. Lovely blue eyes. Silky dark hair (done up in rolls the way Emily had done hers in Rose's wedding photograph). But maybe she'd be a little taller. And not so flat-chested. And she wouldn't wear specs.

And she knew how *he* looked too. Right down to that tall, manly form, those handsome, care-worn features. Alice smiled to herself. She knew because she had met him the weekend before. He was one of the Italian POWs helping out with the hay at her uncle's farm.

'*Now* you can go on,' May finally said, after what felt like deliberate slowness. 'And if you race ahead again, Alice Charlton, I'm off to my own room and you'll be reading this rubbish on your own.'

Alice gave what she hoped was a suitably apologetic smile. It wasn't so much fun reading romance on your own. You needed someone to chat to about the good bits. Although May didn't seem so interested in these books any more. In fact, ever since she'd split up with Will, she'd become almost dismissive about romance. If May didn't look out she'd turn into a crotchety old spinster and no mistake.

'Sorry—' Alice moved the book nearer to May, then pushed up her glasses, eager to get back to Tara, the pretty English florist, and the handsome Count Georg. They *were* going to do it—

'Tara,' he whispered, pulling her towards one of the sumptuous sofas. 'Please. Come to me . . .'

'Alice!'

Alice looked up, surprised. May was backed up against the wall again, arms folded.

'For God's sake—'

Alice shrugged and sat up.

'They *are*, you know,' she insisted examining the book's cover as if she might find clues of confirmation. 'They can, you see, because of the war.'

May raised her eyes to heaven.

'Look, it says here—' Alice turned the pages and read in loud, melodramatic tones:

> *In cities all over Europe, the atmosphere was charged, the air heavy with a new realism. Men and women found themselves thrilling to the day, knowing that each moment might be their last. That at any second the situation could explode, overwhelming them with the inevitable debris of war . . .*

'Ooh to be overwhelmed by the inevitable,' she sighed, falling back on the bed with a bounce. She opened an eye and smiled brightly at May. 'They're all on the edge of a volcano, you see. Anything can happen. The old rules don't apply any more.'

'Really,' May said drily. 'Well, let's see then, shall we?'

Alice turned back on her stomach. She didn't understand how May could be so half-hearted about it all, about something as exciting as this. Just because her engagement hadn't worked out, May was getting positively old-maidish. Plenty more fish in the sea and all that, as the girls at college would say. Not that she had first-hand experience yet, but she would soon. She could feel it in the air. *'The atmosphere was charged,'* as Bella put it.

She waited carefully until May's eyes had travelled down the page and then she turned it over. With a bit of luck they might finish the book before they went out, after all.

*Caught fast in his arms, Tara felt all resistance drain away.
Aware of his heart beating against her breast, and of her own
joining it in strength, she knew then, that she was lost—*
*She was never to forget the next hour, or the touch of her
wonderful, wonderful lover. Nor was she ever to regret it . . .*

The two girls looked up and stared at each other. May's face had
turned pink, but Alice's eyes were shining.

'They *did* it,' she whispered.

May swallowed. 'Well I think she was bloody stupid. She didn't
even know him.'

She sat up and began searching under the bed for her shoes. 'It's
just rubbishy fiction. It won't be like that at all in real life. And,
my God. All those *wonderfuls*.'

'But they were in love, don't you see!'

Alice sat up eagerly, bouncing on the bed so that the book fell to
the floor. 'And it's *wartime*! It changes everything. She could never
have done it if it wasn't for the war. She ends up saving him from
the Nazis or something. One of the girls at the class told me.'

'Really.' But May sounded suddenly bored. She put on her shoes
and stood up. 'You'd better not let Mother catch you reading that
rubbish.' She picked up the book by one corner and dropped it on
the dressing-table. 'Especially as she reckons you're not taking your
studies seriously enough. She'd kill you.'

Alice shrugged. She doubted her mother would even notice. For
most of the time she barely noticed her existence, let alone took an
interest in her education. Her mother only had eyes for Emily. She
fingered the book regretfully. It was Emily who would disapprove,
Emily was for ever giving her 'better' books to read. Her mother
wouldn't mind Bella D'Arcy at all.

She glanced sideways at May.

'I know you don't like all this love rubbish as much as me any
more, May. You've got much better taste. But let's just finish it?'

She nodded for emphasis, anxiously watching May's tight-lipped
expression. Of course not for a moment did she consider it rubbish.
It was the most important thing she had discovered so far in her
sixteen years and she couldn't wait for it to happen to her. She
longed to be eighteen like May. Not that she would ever be like
May. May was crazy to refuse all the men who asked her out.

For a few moments May was silent.

'All right, all right, we'll finish it. But promise you'll also try to read some of those books Emily gives you.' May ruffled her sister's hair. 'Because real life isn't like this at all, you know.'

Zipped and corsaged, the two girls stood side by side before the mirror. Alice shifted uncomfortably. Maybe she had been wrong to insist on having her dress made exactly the same as May's. Maybe it did matter that they were different colouring, that they were different shapes. She glanced at May. May's dress clung to her in a way that hers didn't. And it set off the colour of May's hair. Next to May, no one would even notice her, let alone ask her to dance.

'Perhaps if you wore a belt with it?' May suggested tentatively.

'Nope. I think *you* should wear a snood,' Alice said, briskly picking up a net and piling May's thick hair into it.

While May obediently secured her hair, Alice surreptitiously opened the book lying on the dressing-table in front of her.

> *Tara stared up into the grey eyes melting down into her own. She loved him utterly, was shocked by the completeness of such a love. She belonged to him now, all of her. He could do with her what he would . . .*

She frowned and flicked over a few pages. There were always a few bits that she didn't like in these romances. She didn't see why Tara couldn't still be herself.

She'd read some of the books Emily had given her, and had to admit that they bore more resemblance to the real world. But the fact remained that Bella D'Arcy was fun, even if she didn't get it all right. And after a stultifying day at college, and coming home to talk of 'austerity and utility', you needed a little fun and glamour.

And that was exactly how she intended living her life when she was old enough. Not like Emily who was always working and, when she wasn't, lived in some quiet world of her own. Or May, who appeared determined to turn herself into a boring old maid. *She* wasn't going to be like her sisters at all. She was going to opt for fun.

Alice turned the pages until she found a bit she liked better and then closed her eyes and memorised it.

*   *   *

The music slowly faded, until finally there was only the sweet gentle murmurings of love, as heaven was revealed to a shy English girl, caught for ever in the strong manly arms of her foreign lover . . .

'*Foreign lover*,' Alice whispered, her mind once again returning to the Italian POW at her uncle's farm—

'I'll leave you two girls then,' Emily smiled.

'Thanks for coming with us,' Alice muttered, scanning the ballroom. The band was just warming up. There was hardly anyone there, and no one that she knew. Emily always got them there too early.

Although why she wanted to bring them in the first place, heaven only knew. It was the same every week. The band would play a song or two, then Emily would quietly disappear. She never stayed long enough to dance, she didn't even talk. She just listened to the music for a while, then left.

'Where are we going to sit then?' Alice began adjusting her corsage with nervous fingers. 'Over here? No— Maybe there would be better?' She looked anxiously at May. 'What do you think?'

May shrugged and indicated one of the fifty or so empty tables surrounding the dance floor. Alice sat down relieved. She was just a little tense in case no one asked her to dance. Although someone would eventually, she was sure.

Not that any of them would be the 'right sort', however. And she knew exactly what the right sort was; she'd read enough romances to know. To be hero material the colour of his eyes had to be steely-grey. (For a moment deep-brown and Italian came into mind.) He had to be tall, jutting-jawed, broad-chested with dark, unruly hair, powerful, sensitive, a little arrogant, and he had to go by the name of Rex, Grant, or something topographical, like Rock or Cliff.

There was a pile of books with heroes like that waiting to be read in her bedroom.

The hall was filling up. At the long bar behind them queues were forming, while at the other tables people were talking and laughing in the pink gloom, their faces occasionally dappled with the light bouncing off the silver ball above the dance floor.

'What the hell are they playing that for?' May grumbled, nodding at the band suddenly spotlit on the stage opposite. 'No one will ask anyone to dance if they have to start with something as slow as that.'

But Alice was watching Emily walk back across the dance floor, and the discreet and not so discreet glances her sister was attracting. She'd been talking to the band leader. Alice vaguely knew the words of the song. Very romantic. Something about moonlight. They were always romantic, the songs that Emily requested.

She watched her sister leaning back against a pillar, smoking a cigarette, her eyes half-closed as a trumpet began to pick out the melody. An enigma, that was what her Emily was. The music stopped, Emily slowly ground out her cigarette and then pushed her way through the crowded hall to the exit.

'Enigma,' Alice smiled. That was another thing she'd learnt from those romances. Any heroine worth her salt had to have an enigmatic side to her. It was positively vital to intrigue the hero. Which was where Alice thought she would maybe fall down.

As far as the other attributes were concerned she'd do as well as anyone. She was innocent – not that she thought that was any great shakes, no matter what her mother said. And she knew her lashes were long enough to be 'fluttered and lifted in mute appeal', because she'd practised in front of the mirror at home.

And lots of these heroines were plain, so that was all right too. Plain until they fell in love of course, and then they were transformed into something much more beautiful. Quite how this might work she couldn't imagine. But she was sure it would happen to her one day. It always did in the books.

But as for enigmatic—

She began chewing mercilessly at a hangnail, scanning the dance floor for potential partners.

'Have you decided what you're going to do yet, May?' she asked absently. Maybe no one would ask her to dance this time. May had already refused two invitations.

'Decided what?'

A soldier leaning against the pillar opposite caught Alice's eye. Automatically, she began to smile back, but then looked down. That was *not* how it was done. In the books, gazes had to be 'transferred', or glances 'cast'. And romantic heroines certainly didn't grin. Smiles had to hover, play about, or twitch at the corners of the mouth. Count Georg never grinned.

Her smile faded. And neither had the Italian at her uncle's farm.

She'd walked into the bottom field to tell the men their lunch was ready. She had noticed him at once. Younger than the others, bare-chested, tanned. He stopped pitching the hay as she approached and slowly straightened up, shielding his eyes with one hand, gazing at her for so long that she felt flushed and confused. She hadn't been able to say the jokey thing she'd prepared. Hadn't even been able to look at him. And as she walked back down the field, she hadn't needed to turn round to know he was still staring. She'd felt his eyes on her back all the way.

Alice bobbed her head looking for the soldier but he had disappeared into the crowd. She shouldn't be thinking about the Italian. The Italians were the enemy. There was a war on.

Feeling obscurely guilty, she turned back to May.

'Have you decided what war work you're going to do?'

She drummed her fingers on the table impatiently. Some soldiers had just asked the girls at the *next* table to dance.

'If you stay at the shop, you'll be drafted for war work soon. You could find yourself working in the munitions at Birtley in a few months. And have you seen the hats they have to wear?'

May laughed. 'There's nothing wrong with munitions. Rose doesn't seem to mind it and she says they all have a good natter. The pay's good too.'

Alice raised her eyes to heaven.

'But we said we'd do something together,' she said with mock patience, knowing this wasn't strictly true. 'And I thought we'd look at office jobs. You're qualified. And I will be too as soon as I've finished college.'

May pulled a face.

'Well, what else did we go to college for? Uncle Harry didn't pay for our education so that we'd end up in some stupid job. Your job at the shop was only supposed to be temporary. You used to say you wanted to work in the library before the war broke out. Now—'

With one eye on the dance floor, she took an eyebrow pencil from her bag and began to make a list on the tabletop.

'Factory inspector's office, shipyard office, pensions maybe—'

May was watching the couples dancing, looking bored. 'I was thinking I might go on the buses.'

Wordlessly Alice's mouth opened.

'Why not?' May asked.

'But you're clever!'

May shrugged. Alice stared at her. May couldn't mean it.

'Why not,' May repeated flatly, turning away.

There was a pause.

'Sometimes I don't think you're bothered about anything any more, May Charlton,' Alice said suddenly. 'You'll have to snap out of it soon. It's not good to go on like this! Ever since you and Will— You don't look as if you sleep, you're pale, you won't come to Uncle Harry's farm with me any more, and—' She stopped, feeling inexplicably near tears. 'It's not *good* for you, May,' she repeated.

'There's nothing wrong with the buses, Alice.'

Alice looked down at her hands.

'But you're cleverer than that,' she insisted in a low voice. This wasn't right. She could understand that some women might want to play down being clever. After all, romantic heroines in books were never clever. They could be attractive but dim, or unattractive and clever. Anything else was a paradox. Yet Emily had ended up in a classified job in the War Office— And May was her *sister*! Not some stupid woman in a stupid book!

'The buses are so common! There's nothing glamorous about them! It wouldn't be like an office job where you could wear smart clothes and meet lots of nice— It'll be all drunks and labourers and God knows what to contend with! Those sort of jobs are best done by men.'

May sighed. 'I really don't care what I do.' Then she turned and caught Alice's expression.

'Oh, Alice!' she laughed. 'It wouldn't be so bad. Jobs are up for grabs by both men and women at the moment. Look at Rose humping bomb cases around. Or our Emily at the War Office, *whatever* it is that she does there.'

May tried to look more interested in her surroundings and began drumming her fingers in time to the band. They were now playing a medley of Glen Miller tunes, the dance leader waving his baton at the audience, instead of at the musicians.

'Anyway, if you're worried about the munitions hats, *you* might

37

think about being a clippie. You'll be looking for a job yourself in a few months' time. You could look like Betty Grable in a clippie's uniform. Hat pinned to the back of your hair, take the trousers in a bit— They're all permanents and make-up, the ones on our route—'

But Alice had spotted the soldier again. Now she was sure that she knew the lad. She grinned before she could stop herself. She'd doubt he was hero material. His forearms were probably hairless. But you never knew.

He was picking his way through the dancing couples to their table. She *did* know him. What was his name? He was smiling at her, tall, fair-haired, good-looking. She composed her face as he approached. Try for enigmatic, she told herself, fingers crossed under the table. Don't grin.

But as he reached their table, her smile faded. It was Patrick Sullivan. He was at school in May's class for a while. Back row in the fifth year. He wasn't from the North-East. He'd left after a few months. There had been rumours—

'Want to dance, *May*,' the soldier asked, smug with the knowledge of her name. 'May Charlton, isn't it?'

Alice swallowed. So he hadn't been looking at her at all. He bumped her elbow as he leaned over the table towards May. He smelled of hair oil and whisky, although he was only a year or two older than May.

Now she remembered. May hadn't liked him.

'Patrick. No thank you,' she heard May say in a tone she seldom used. 'I'm not dancing. I'm with my sister.'

He stood up, mouth set, and stared at her. Then he turned his back pointedly to May.

'Well maybe your little sister would like to dance then.'

'Why don't you, Alice,' May said, standing up. 'I need some fresh air and you've been dying to get on the floor all night.'

The girls walked in silence, picking their way through the familiar streets by torchlight. For the first time she could remember, Alice hadn't enjoyed the dance. Vague feelings of discontent niggled. But she had enjoyed all the others—

It was because it was all so different from the books, she told herself. That was why. The soldiers had no glamour in their rough uniforms smelling of beer and tobacco. And the ones that asked her to dance seemed so young, and pimply, hardly out of school. All earnest faces and sweaty hands.

Only Patrick Sullivan had seemed mature in any way. Not that they had said very much to each other. He'd been a bit poker-faced. But at least he was handsome, and not bad a dancer.

Her cousin Mary in Liverpool had written that they were mostly Yanks at her dances, that they all looked like officers with their tailored uniforms, and sounded like film stars—

But here half the men weren't even in uniform! Miners probably, which, heaven knows, was no soft option, but as for glamorous—

She walked on, disgruntled. Not one man she'd really wanted to dance with! Not one! When Patrick left she'd spent the rest of the evening talking with a couple of lads drafted from the Hebrides to work in the pits, and then only because their island sounded romantic. She should have stayed at home and spent the evening with her book. It was preferable to real life if this was all there was.

She glanced at May's dim outline next to her. She could tell from the way she was walking that she was feeling sad again. She could always tell. Maybe a dance wasn't so important. Alice pushed her arm through May's and moved closer.

She didn't understand why May had parted with Will if it made her this miserable. But if she tried to talk to her about it, all May would say was, 'It wouldn't have worked.' Which didn't make sense. She could remember the way they were together.

'It's not always like it is in your books,' May would say, quietly closing the subject.

Alice squeezed her sister's arm. Well, when *she* met someone, she would make sure that it *did* work, and it would be terribly romantic, *just* like in the books. And it wouldn't be some sweaty-handed, poker-faced soldier from a dance.

In the darkness Alice smiled, and let herself think back to the weekend before.

So handsome— and the way he had looked at her—

It wasn't as if the Italians were enemies like the Germans and Japs, she told herself as they turned into their road. Everyone hated *them*. The Italians were different.

They'd given up quickly, it was true. But that was because they

39

weren't daft. Uncle Harry had said it was very sensible. Either that, or some hundred thousand would have been killed. And for what?

And everyone liked the Italians because of the last war. Her uncle and May's Will talked as if it were Mussolini alone who was the enemy, not the Italians—

So handsome—

It had been hot, the hottest weekend of the summer. She'd taken Rose's kids with her to help out with the hay. Such a beautiful day. The sky high and blue, just a few white clouds scudding over the corn, golden and swaying, everything peaceful. If it wasn't for the uniforms with their prison camp spot, you wouldn't have believed there was a war on. There wasn't even a guard. And the men certainly didn't look as if they considered themselves prisoners, laughing and relaxed, talking fast in Italian as they worked. They were all having a good war, Uncle Harry said.

Aunt Lizzie set up a long trestle table at the top of the field and laid on a real peacetime spread, pies, sandwiches, scones and jam, cakes with real butter. She said men who'd put in a hard day in the fields needed a good lunch, whoever they were. So they'd all sat down, the Italians, her uncle and the children.

Her aunt had given her the jug to pour the drinks. What had she said to him? Probably just would he like more lemonade, or was he full up. Alice grinned. Hardly the stuff of romantic novels. But then he'd looked up and stared into her eyes— for what felt like an age. With that look again. His dark eyes soft, unruly black hair blowing in the breeze, slight shadows under his eyes— just a little care-worn. Just the way the books would have it. Except that he was beautiful. And Bella D'Arcy would never describe a hero as beautiful.

He'd held up his glass, his voice low, as if it were for her ears only. '*Grazie signorina*', he'd said. Or something like that. It probably just meant thanks a lot. But the words had made her breathless, as if he'd said something entirely different—

'So Alice,' May said, breaking the silence, 'what about *your* job? What are *you* intending to do when you finish college? Only four months to go. Is it to be the Pensions Office with a smart frock for the benefit of those nice young men?'

For a while Alice was silent, her mind full of dreams, dreams firmly locked in the world of Bella D'Arcy where dark-eyed foreigners gazed down into the eyes of pale-faced English girls. Against a backdrop of golden corn—

'I'm not so sure, May,' she answered. 'I'm maybe thinking of something else.'

And in the darkness she suddenly smiled, because she knew exactly what she was going to do. She would join the Women's Land Army, become a land-girl. Uncle Harry at Stamfordham said he could do with someone at the farm to help out the POWs. And they might as well keep it in the family, hadn't they?

'Really? And what's that?' May laughed, for a minute sounding like her old self.

'It's a secret,' Alice said, in what she hoped was a thoroughly *enigmatic* way. 'I'll tell you when it's all arranged.'

4

Emily

1944

'Don't look!' her mother hissed as they walked away from the train in Liverpool Central Station.

Emily turned in the direction her mother was staring. Two girls of her own age stood giggling and whispering under the station clock.

'I said *don't look*!'

She grabbed Emily's arm under the elbow and forced her to quicken her pace.

'They're wearing— *nylons*.' She whispered the word with a shudder and walked on tight-lipped. 'Sluts—'

Emily flushed. Her mother's voice had been low, but not so low that the girls couldn't have heard. As was her way. Emily lowered her eyes as they passed, but her mother noticed. She noticed everything.

'Head up, girl. I didn't send you to deportment classes for nothing.'

'You're embarrassing sometimes, Mother,' Emily protested quietly. 'There really was no need—'

'You don't know about these things, my girl. And it's just as well. When I was your age—'

Emily closed her eyes. 'When you were my age, Mother, you were married.'

For a brief moment there was silence.

'Aye and look where that got me,' her mother continued briskly. 'Stuck in the back streets of Newcastle, a miner's wife. *And* widow. And I had looks like you, you know. I was considered a beauty myself in my day.'

She smoothed down a lock of Emily's hair, a gesture that had always spoken more of possession than affection.

'If I'd managed things differently— Well, it's not going to happen to you, my girl. Not with your beauty. There's better things in store for you.'

Emily flinched. Why did it always have to sound so much like a threat? She flinched again pointedly and her mother removed her hand. Emily looked over her shoulder. The two girls were still staring. They looked angry. She turned, the back of her neck pricking.

Her mother was getting worse, obsessive, suffocating even. She paid less and less attention to May and Alice, yet some days it seemed *she* was hardly allowed to breathe on her own.

'It's the war,' her elder sister Rose blithely said, laughing it off. But Rose was married and safely out of the house. 'The war makes her think of her own lost chances. She just doesn't want it to happen to you, that's all. It'll pass.'

But Rose couldn't understand how bad her mother was becoming.

'With your looks, I have to protect you for better things,' was her mother's continual refrain, and if Emily protested, there followed the inevitable chorus of 'My heart—'

As if on cue, her mother's brow creased.

'You shouldn't talk back to your mother in that way, Emmy,' she reproached weakly, slowing her pace. 'You know how easily I get upset these days. Flutters all over the place, it does.'

Emily watched her mother put her hand to her breast in the increasingly familiar gesture, and then deliberately looked away. Rose hadn't understood at all, because *she'd* never been stuck to like a leech, never had to have elocution lessons, attend endless night classes, music lessons, deportment— Even Alice had more freedom and she was only sixteen! Things had to change. And she was hoping her aunt could help during this visit.

They were nearing the end of the platform. Her mother came to a standstill. Emily waited while she went through a pantomime of heavy breathing.

In fact she was banking on her aunt. When her mother first suggested accompanying her to Liverpool she had protested, arguing that they shouldn't leave Alice alone at her age.

'Nonsense,' her mother replied, for once not resorting to the blackmail of her heart. 'May's old enough to be left in charge. She's become quite quiet and sensible of late. Alice will be safe enough with May. And you've seen how close the two are becoming. Thick as thieves nowadays, aren't they?'

Reluctantly Emily had to agree. Ever since May and Will parted, she'd been watching the two girls' growing closeness. But she suspected that both this, and May's recently acquired 'quiet and sensible' nature, had more to do with May being unhappy than anything else. Despite the face May showed to the world, she felt that the broken engagement was not the amicable parting of the ways May claimed it to be.

Which made her wish all the more that her sister had chosen herself, and not Alice, to move closer to. Alice was a good little thing, trusting and eager, but not someone to confide in. Emily stared at the train alongside the platform, suddenly struck by the thought that maybe that was how the world saw her too. Because in all her twenty years she had never been close to anyone.

The train was packed with servicemen from the air force, navy and army, a few still cluttering up the platform with their huge kitbags. Boys were hanging from windows smoking, spilling out of carriage doors laughing, while older men stood drawn and silent, wearing brave smiles for the benefit of pale-faced wives and children. Emily watched as a girl stood on tiptoe and put her arms around the neck of a soldier so tightly he seemed in danger of being pulled out of the carriage window.

'Safe journey, John,' she heard her say as the whistle blew. The man tried to smile, then he kissed the girl fiercely.

'Safe journey—' the girl whispered again, reluctantly dropping her arms. The train began moving.

Emily looked down. She had never felt really close to anyone. And certainly not like that, not to a man. Uncomfortably she turned away. She used to blame her mother. After all it was she who had found her the job – in an office with no men under forty. And stuck permanently to her side for the rest of the time, what chance did she have of meeting anyone? She couldn't even go to the knitting class without her.

The girl suddenly turned and pushed past Emily with a muffled sob. Emily looked away, but up and down the platform the same scene was being enacted. More tear-stained faces, more lives being wrenched apart. No, she'd never felt anything like that, for anyone.

And it wasn't just because of her mother. She knew that now. She watched as the train began to move out of the station, soldiers still hanging out of windows, waving, shouting final farewells, their faces wreathed in brave smiles. Or was it naïvety, a faith in their own immortality? But the truth was, although she had sympathy for them, even liked them as individuals, she wasn't much interested in them as *men*. She couldn't even imagine—

Her mother was fiddling noisily with a bottle of pills she'd produced with a flourish from her handbag. Emily patiently unscrewed the top and handed it back to her. They would only be aspirin. She looked back over her shoulder. The two girls under the clock were still there.

'Anyway, what's so wrong with wearing nylons?' she asked, hearing herself suddenly petulant. Chronologically she might well be twenty, but her mother had the capacity for reducing her to a ten-year-old.

Her mother swallowed the pills with conspicuous difficulty.

'It's who's been giving them—'

She jerked her head in the direction of a group of American soldiers coming into the station.

'Nylons are not given for nothing.'

Emily looked across to the group of young men. One of them caught her eye and winked. The girls under the clock had perked up and were sauntering across to the station coffee bar. Emily watched them, amused. Her eyes settled on another soldier smiling at her. He waved his hand in the direction of the café, as if in invitation. But she was probably mistaken. Men were usually no more interested in her than she was in them.

'It's because you're so beautiful,' Alice had once said, observing this, worldly-wise at sixteen. 'It scares 'em off, you see. Especially as you're sort of cool, and bit posh-sounding—'

At the time she'd laughed. Alice could be ridiculous. It was *she* who was the pretty one, petite, with her pale, heart-shaped face. And May with her glorious hair. A real bonny lass, her father used to call May. That *she* had somehow acquired the reputation of beauty was a constant source of surprise to her. When she looked in the mirror all she saw was a tall, fair, quiet woman looking back at her

46

through the eyes of the serious child she'd been. So what was the fuss? Two eyes, a nose, a mouth— just a face.

But whatever the reason, Alice was right. Men weren't comfortable around her. Even the boys she grew up with seldom spoke to her nowadays, freezing awkwardly in her presence.

The thing was, although she couldn't imagine it, although she couldn't imagine how it felt to be held, to be kissed— she didn't feel cool. *Not cool at all.*

'Common as muck,' her mother tutted, as the man who had winked at Emily draped his arm around one of the girls from under the clock. But Emily was watching the soldier who had beckoned to her. He was standing, palms of his hands upraised, an expression of mock despair on his face because she hadn't accepted his invitation. She turned away smiling. *He* didn't seem to be put off by any 'coolness'. Perhaps Americans were different.

She slowed her pace. The station suddenly seemed bursting with American servicemen. Ringing with their loud, confident tones. Different voices, drawling and smooth. James Stewart in *Destry Rides Again.* Gary Cooper in *Sergeant Yank.* Leaning back against station counters, not gangly and awkward like the boys back home, but relaxed and easy. Clark Gable in *Gone with the Wind.* Chewing gum nonchalantly. Dick Powell as Philip Marlowe. Smoking cigarettes in that special way. Humphrey Bogart—

'Riddled with them, this place,' her mother was muttering. 'No Yanks in Newcastle, thank God. If it's like this all over Liverpool I'm going to tell your aunt we're not stopping long.'

Her mother pulled her arm as someone whistled.

'And the quicker we're out of this place the better,' she snapped.

They passed another group of girls waiting outside the station.

'Don't look,' her mother hissed again.

Emily glanced down at their legs. Pencil lines bisected gravy-browned calves, in the hope of better things to come. Emily smiled at them.

Her mother knew the city well.

'Here, this way,' she said taking Emily's arm and ushering her down a side street.

But they stopped short. The street had been recently bombed, the road was covered in rubble. Five or six houses had been taken out of the terrace completely, like missing teeth, while others had their roofs and doors blown off. Emily stared, shocked. The house at the end of the terrace had lost the whole of its front wall, leaving it as open and exposed as a doll's house. Towels still hung over the chipped bath. The beds in the upstairs room were unmade. In the parlour pictures were hanging on the back wall, only slightly askew; the remains of a meal lay among the rubble on the table.

She had seen nothing like this. In Newcastle a shipyard had been bombed, a goods yard, a couple of empty factories— but not homes, not lives. Nothing like this.

A few people were wandering in and out of the houses that remained, a small boy with a runny nose wheeling a broken cart, a woman clutching a bundle of bedclothes, three men heaving an old piano into the street.

Emily made to turn back, reluctant to intrude, but her mother was already determinedly picking her way through the rubble. They passed an old couple sitting on chairs in the middle of the street, the woman asleep with her head on her husband's shoulder, while he just sat silently staring at the few possessions they had left – two neatly piled stacks of books, a suitcase tied with string, pictures and photographs with cracked glass, a headless tailor's dummy bizarrely standing guard at the other side of the sleeping woman.

Emily paused in front of him, trying to think of something to say. How hadn't she realised— What sort of a cocoon had she been living in? Radio announcements and black-outs and coupons and newspapers detailing military manoeuvres— But this? People buried alive, getting blown through their own front walls? The old man lifted his face to her. His expression was blank.

'It's not enough,' she murmured, turning away.

'What?' her mother asked impatiently, catching her leg on a piece of broken concrete.

'It's not enough,' Emily repeated. 'Tacking vests and knitting scarves— It's not enough.'

The words of a recent Ministry of Labour leaflet from work ran through her head: *The average woman takes to welding as readily as she takes to knitting, once she has overcome any initial nervousness due to sparks . . .*

'We must be able to do more than that,' she said, more to herself than anyone else.

'And what may I ask, do *you* think you can do, young lady?' her mother asked crossly. She'd holed a new pair of lisle stockings.

It was dusk before they reached the other side of the city. They hurried on, heads down, so that they almost collided with the group of soldiers coming round the corner.

'Whoa there!' One of them caught Emily's arms to steady her. Another American soldier. But not like the others. The moments passed. In fact he was unlike anyone she had ever seen before.

Voices behind her began laughing. She pulled her eyes away. Her mother was dusting down her suit as if it had been contaminated, accepting her handbag with a forced politeness from one of the men who had picked it up from the pavement.

She turned back to him. He was still smiling down at her, bowing his head slightly.

'Miss,' he said, releasing her arms. And then turning to her mother, he touched his cap. 'Ma'am— My apologies.'

Emily continued to stare. Such a voice— Deeper than any she had heard before.

'But they were very polite,' Emily protested as she was hurried on to the tram. 'I thought they were charming in fact.'

Her mother was checking to see that the contents of her handbag were all there. She'd heard about Yanks. And as for *that* sort of Yank— None of them in Newcastle either.

'All over the bloody place, I tell you. Here, check this purse. There should be four pound ten in there—'

But Emily's thoughts were elsewhere.

'Martha, Martha, you always were stubborn. I tell you, you can't treat your Emily like that.'

Emily was crouched on her cousin's bedroom floor, rug pulled back, her ear to the largest crack in the floorboards. She'd talked to her aunt – she knew she'd be sympathetic, even if she couldn't say the same for her peevish young cousin Mary – and tonight was the night designated for 'the chat'.

She'd persuaded a reluctant Mary to go up to bed early with her to give her aunt plenty of time. But so far it wasn't going well.

'The girl needs looking out for,' she heard her mother mutter defensively after a while.

49

'But that's just the point!' her aunt half-shouted back. 'She's not a girl. She's a woman!'

There was another silence.

'But young for her age. You can see that. Compared to Rose, or even May. And as for our Alice—'

'And whose fault's that then? You've never given Emily a chance. You'll have to stop suffocating the kid, or she'll be off.'

'Emily knows I just want what's best for her. With looks like hers she can get out of Newcastle, marry somebody with a bit of money, not waste herself like—'

'She'll pack her bags and be gone one morning, I'm telling you.' Her aunt was sounding exasperated.

'Rubbish, Dora. Not our Emmy.' The voice became wheedling. 'Not after all I've done for her— Not with my heart.'

Emily sat up and dusted her nightgown.

'Her and her bloody heart,' she muttered more to herself than her cousin. 'I should've known it wouldn't have done any good.'

Mary watched from the bed. Under the covers, she moved the second stone waterbottle from Emily's side of the bed and put her feet on it proprietorially. She was much too old to have to share a bed – especially with someone as stuck up as she considered her cousin Emily to be.

'My Mam can talk hind legs off donkeys,' she said, wriggling down the bed and rocking both bottles with her feet. 'But she's no match for yours, thank God.'

Emily sat at the dressing-table and looked at herself in the mirror. Her mother was right of course. She wouldn't go.

'Funny shade of blonde, your hair, isn't it?' said the voice from the bed. 'Neither one thing nor the other really.'

Emily picked up a brush. Where could she go, anyway? There was nowhere *to* go.

'Prefer warmer shades myself. "Golden honey" mine's called.'

Emily shifted her focus. Mary was lying on her side, staring at her with narrowed eyes. Emily looked back to her image. She'd always known the girl disliked her.

'And of course the thing about being a natural blonde,' Mary persisted, 'is that your eyebrows are so pale too, aren't they? I'd lend you my pencils, but what with rationing and all—'

Emily smiled and raised a too-pale eyebrow. Mary was a funny kid. She climbed into bed and picked up her book.

But her cousin wasn't finished.

'Because I find that *men* like strong features in a face, don't you think?'

For a few moments the girl's malice hung in the air.

'At least the men of *my* acquaintance do. And my friends' men friends. But maybe you don't know many men? Alice wrote and said you seldom went to dances—'

Emily remained silent.

'And now that there are so many Americans around, well—'

Mary gave a high, tinkling laugh.

'Loads of them come here, you know. They have to come here first to get sorted out, before being posted on. Those Yanks! Lucky Strikes, sticks of gum, scented soap, chocolate, oranges—'

She let her voice trail off, but Emily merely turned a page.

After a while, '*Bases*, I think they call them,' Mary said enigmatically.

Emily sighed and put down her book.

'All right, Mary.'

Her cousin sat up and put her arms round her knees.

'Well—' But now that she had Emily's attention she became suddenly doubtful.

'Go on. Bases?'

'Well, "first base" is what they call it when they touch your chest, you see,' the girl suddenly rushed. '*Over* your sweater, of course. Second base, the hand goes under. And third base—' Her voice trailed off. She giggled nervously, caught between a desire to impress and self-incrimination.

'Third base?'

She leaned over and whispered excitedly in Emily's ear.

'Until you get to fifth base, and then of course it's the whole hog. But you must know about that—'

Emily was searching out the stone bottle with her feet and rolling it back to her own side of the bed.

'Do you have any nylons, Mary?' she asked, turning off the light.

*   *   *

51

'I don't think the girls need the likes of us going with them,' said Emily's aunt as her mother began to put on her hat and coat. 'They're only going to the church social.'

Emily watched with a heavy heart as her mother grimly pushed a pin through her hat. It was grey felt with a pheasant feather and she must see that it made her nose look beaky, but she said she'd paid fair money for it and it had a few years left in it yet.

'Emily's always glad of my company, aren't you, pet, and it'll be late before they're back again. They'll be glad of some extra company in the black-out.'

'But we've got our torches, Aunt Martha!' Mary was sounding increasingly desperate.

'It's not a problem, Mary, and I really don't mind,' Emily's mother answered firmly, adjusting the feather in the mirror. 'No problem at all.'

Mary looked accusingly at Emily.

Emily flushed and cleared her throat. 'I don't mind staying in, if Mary's allowed to go alone, I'll—'

Mary glared at her then raised her eyes to heaven.

'Nonsense,' her aunt said. 'Mary can't go on her own and of course you must go.' She paused. 'Listen, Martha,' she began slowly. 'I didn't like to say so before, but I think I've got one of my heads coming, and I could do with some company with our Jack on warden duty. You wouldn't mind?'

She winked at Emily. She knew her sister never could resist the direct appeal. Especially one that involved an ailment, an ailment that could be ministered to with demonstrably superior skills. And more importantly, one that could be outdone in the recalling of more horrible ailments.

But Emily's mother still looked undecided. Her aunt put her fingers to her temples, then began massaging the back of her neck pointedly.

'Well, if you really think you *need* me—'

'I do, my dear, I do.'

Her mother reluctantly took off her coat.

'Have a nice time, girls,' she said in a strained voice. 'And do be careful with yourselves, won't you?' she added, looking straight at Emily.

*   *   *

The hall was packed, but not with the card-playing men and women of the church social Emily had expected. It was full of girls, powdered, painted and pinned, and uniformed servicemen. Some, she could tell from their accents, were local lads on leave. But unlike the few dances she'd taken Alice to, the majority here were Americans.

'I'm going to join my friends,' Mary declared as soon as they arrived. 'I don't think you're— I mean I don't think they're really your type, but you can join us if you want.'

Emily felt annoyed. She hadn't wanted to come in any case. She'd only agreed because she'd thought it might give her aunt another opportunity to speak to her mother. A band was arriving. She certainly wouldn't have come if she'd known it was going to be a dance. She glared at Mary. The kid wasn't sixteen yet. She was younger than Alice! She didn't know where she got the nerve. Her mother would kill her if she knew.

Mary shrugged at her expression. 'Well, you don't have to stay. I can always walk home with one of the other girls.'

Emily watched the girl flounce off with a smug grin. She had a good mind to let her aunt know. She thought of Alice at home alone with May, who in comparison was so sweet and trusting and yet totally neglected. It wasn't right.

She was getting jostled. The hall was crowded, but still filling, the air already smoky and full of the smells of cheap scent, hair oil and expectant perspiration. Well, she wouldn't stay. She would get her coat. Tell them at home that she'd developed a headache too. She would let Mary keep her secret.

He caught her arms in the same way as he had the day she arrived in Liverpool.

'Whoa there,' he said, laughing, as she struggled to make her way out of the hall.

She recognised him at once, even in the gloom, even before she looked up into his face. That voice. And she could see from his face that he recognised her also.

In fact he had spent the whole of his first day's leave combing the streets of Liverpool, shops and all, just trying to get a glimpse of her. He told her this on the next night they met, when she was supposed to be at Mary's sewing group. She laughed politely, knowing she wasn't expected to believe it. And then, finding she wouldn't talk, he told her about his home town.

His name was Matt. And although he came from New Orleans, he now lived in New York, he told her the following night, when she was supposed to be taking some air with the connivance of another of her aunt's 'heads'. He was a musician, he said, played the trumpet. He used to be with a musical comedy touring company, but it had folded. He had played the clubs on the West coast, he told her. CAL-I-FORN-I-AYE. Emily listened quietly, shyly, half-mesmerised by his voice, as well as by his descriptions of far away places.

And on the night she was supposed to be at the whist drive he told her of his ambitions, of how he wanted to move back to the West coast, and start up his own band there. But being black it would be especially difficult, he said. At the moment he only played cheap clubs; he was just another horn. But he had dreams, he laughed. And she nodded. Because she too had dreams. She knew how that felt.

And on the night she was supposed to be at the bingo he spoke of more serious things, and there was less laughter. He spoke of the difficulties of living in a society in which he felt he didn't really belong. And she listened with growing shock, as he gave words to feelings she'd lived with all her life. He laughed at the expression in her eyes, tried to lighten the moment, telling her that here in the forces, for the first time in his life, he didn't feel set apart. Now he *belonged*, he insisted. But still she remained silent. Because she wished she knew how that felt.

And finally, on the night she was supposed to be at the pictures, she began to tell him about herself, surprising herself by what she said, as if something inside had been released. Half-formulated thoughts were dragged into being, vaguely perceived feelings crystallised into truths.

About how she felt she didn't belong, had never belonged, and now felt irredeemably set apart. The fact that her very existence puzzled her. How she could find no rhyme or reason for a life that was mysterious in its tedium.

How she longed to escape from Newcastle, from the North-East, from England with all its smallness. She wanted to be somewhere with space. Somewhere with a sense of freedom.

And she told him how she knew she would never find it. Because she was a woman, and she didn't know any women who had escaped.

'There's no man in your life to help?' he asked quietly.

She shook her head. She had looked at the lives of her sister Rose and the married girls at the class, and she could never in her wildest dreams imagine herself having such a life. Husbands? Children? It all seemed as alien to her as life on another planet.

There had to be something else. But she was trapped, she said. And in the saying, she realised the reality.

He listened gravely, not trying to touch, or even take her arm, and she felt that here at last was someone who cared, at last someone who understood.

Of course, she told herself later in bed, staring up into the darkness next to a sulking Mary, going over Matt's every word in her head, she knew it was just because of the war. She had seen the intensity it could bring to people's lives. The whole ball game had changed, as he put it. Rules were no longer relevant, life was more vivid. The edited highlights. *Lamb's Tales* instead of Shakespeare. You could leap straight to the core. As they had done, she believed.

So no matter that he was leaving in a week, she told herself, trying to ignore the painful feelings created by the thought. It would be enough, she told herself. To have felt so close to another human being— it would be enough. *It would be enough*, she kept repeating, trying to convince herself.

On their last night he walked her home in the black-out. She had her flashlight, but as the third warden yelled she switched it off, joking about the army of officiousness the war had brought out of the woodwork. Inevitably someone bumped into them. There was a male 'oof' and female giggles. Emily was thrown off balance. And again, for the last time, he caught her.

They apologised to each other, but his arms stayed around her, and hers around him. He pulled her towards him. She didn't draw away.

It's just because he's leaving, she told herself, as the unfamiliar wave of desire shot through her. Natural that she would want to hold him.

Friends needed to exchange affection too, she told herself, as the desire grew.

And even friends exchanged kisses, she told herself, shaken by the urgency of her response, as he put his lips to hers.

And even kisses like this, she told herself, lips parting.

'Emily,' he whispered.

But she closed her eyes, and in answer kissed him again, pulling him closer, back into the shop doorway. She was trembling, but she felt alive.

First base— she heard her cousin Mary's voice, in a far-off place at the back of her head.

'Don't stop—' she heard her own voice say.

Second base—

'Don't stop,' she murmured again, her voice low, strange to her ears.

Third base—

Fourth base—

And she felt she was falling, dissolving, her body warm and boneless.

He took hold of her hips, and lifted her, right there, in the shop doorway.

Fifth base.

As the butcher's door rattled behind her, Emily had a fleeting thought of her mother and of her grand hopes for her, and for a split second wanted to laugh out loud as she heard the closed sign fall to the floor.

But instead she cried out, all thought gradually disappearing, until the moment she cried out again, burying her face in his neck. And then she knew.

This could make sense of it all. *This* was a reason to exist.

As his own breathing quickened and he cried out himself – a strange sound she had never heard a man make – and the rattling grew louder, waking the shopkeeper upstairs who opened the window and yelled at them to clear off, she told herself that if this was all there was, it would be enough.

And this time she was convinced.

5
Alice
1946

'Come to tea at four thirty,' May had whispered to her at the class, the week before. 'I have something to tell you.'

So on a warm afternoon in early September Alice Charlton checked her watch and stepped off a dusty country bus that had seen better days. She brushed down her clothes anxiously. Ten past four already. The driver had taken his time, stopping to chat in the last village. She was going to be late. It would take her a good half hour to walk to the farm.

She hesitated a moment and looked over to the fields opposite. Then, mouth set, she walked purposefully in their direction, a slight figure, dark curls framing a small, pale face marked only by frown lines between carefully pencilled eyebrows. It would have to be the short cut. There was nothing else for it.

Checking no one was around, she hitched up her lilac summer dress, climbed the wooden stile and jumped into the field on the other side. Her heels immediately sank into the ground. Brambles snagged at the hem of her dress and caught in her best white cardigan.

'Bloody countryside—'

Flushed, she picked herself free, and smiled wryly. Maybe it was as well that she hadn't become a land-girl. May seemed much better suited to it, sitting at the class the week before in an old dress, without a scrap of make-up, not minding that her hands were red-rough and her face nut-brown from working outdoors all week. Patrick had been quite shocked.

But May looked well, almost like her old self again. Uncle Harry

57

had known what he was doing persuading May to live at the farm. There was no doubt that two years in the countryside had done May good. But maybe now— maybe now she would come home.

Alice picked her way precariously along the edge of the field, her new high heels sinking at every other step. She wished May would come into town more often. She barely saw her for months, except at the class. She missed her. Another bramble caught at her cardigan and snagged her hair. Patrick said she was crazy to come out to the farm, 'traipsing around in muck and clarts', as he called it, when the new coffee shop in town would have been much more civilised. Then he would have been able to join them.

But gradually the ground rose and the earth became harder, and Alice could concentrate less on the path and begin to look around. The sky was cloudless, the breeze soft. To her left beech trees and silver birches swayed and rustled, alongside huge chestnut trees, their conkers hanging ready to fall. The undergrowth was thick with briars and dogroses, fat orange hips, blackberries ripe for picking. To her right, most of the corn had been cut, so that the pale field was dotted with triangles of sheaves airing in the sun. But further on she could see a broad strip of wheat still growing, golden and swaying, splashed crimson with poppies.

She rummaged in her bag and produced a handkerchief in readiness. No doubt it would start off her hay fever, then her eyes would water, then her make-up run, and then what sort of advertisement for city life would she be?

She hurried on through the patchwork of yellows and greens, woods and hills, but at the top of the field she stopped again. She leaned on the familiar five-barred gate and breathed deeply. The air even tasted different from the sooty streets of Newcastle.

She'd always loved this place, no matter what Patrick said. In her memory the days had always been like this, sweet-scented, warm-breezed, and lying on their backs exhausted by the bike ride May and she would gaze at a sky that was always this blue. So deep you could dive into it, May would say.

She couldn't remember any rainy, wintry days, only swimming in the river, swopping secrets in the orchard under apple blossom, picnic lunches with the farm hands—

You're doing it again, Alice Charlton, she reprimanded herself, tugging sharply at the bolt of the gate. Eighteen years old and already you're living in the past. All her life she'd longed to be older, and now that she was old enough to do all the things she wanted, she found herself dwelling more and more on her childhood. She'd tell May about that. May would laugh at the irony. Patrick didn't like her to talk about the past. He said you had to outgrow that sort of thing.

With a struggle she locked the gate behind her. The rusty bolt had stained her hands orange. She bent down, rubbed them on the grass, pushed a curl back in place, then walked resolutely on. She'd tell May about Patrick too. May would know what to do.

She walked faster, with growing excitement. It had been months since she last visited the farm. She'd heard a couple of the Italian POWs had stayed on— 'Alice Charlton,' she whispered to herself with a smile.

But more importantly she was excited at the idea of seeing May alone. Because then she could ask her to move back home. She could tell her how much she had been missing her. Now that May was looking so much better, no longer so thin and depressed, now she *could* tell her. And now that Emily had announced she was taking a high-flying job down in London, May wouldn't want her to be left living all alone. She'd thought May might have moved back home when their mother died. Or at least when the war ended. But 'not yet' was all May would say. Well, now it was time. Surely May would have to see that. She would show May how good city life could be, with a job in an office and all.

The next field was pasture, sloping quite steeply to where the farmhouse stood, and harder to walk through than the last. Alice was beginning to feel hot, and her legs weary, but she walked more quickly. She would bring it up the first opportunity she got. She'd wanted to say more at the class the week before, but everyone had been too stunned by Emily's news about her job in London.

Patrick had been quite shocked by that too. He'd come right out and said it at the class (or 'gossip shop', as he called the knitting class, with a pat on her cheek so she couldn't be offended). It would make Emily appear most unattractive to do a job like that, he'd said, after questioning her closely about what she was going to do. He said it sounded like a man's job, or else was Emily exaggerating? And which was worse, he had asked everyone.

Alice stopped a moment to catch her breath. She didn't want to think about the class. It was the first time Patrick had been invited in. Usually she made sure she was ready when he came to pick her up. Not everyone understood Patrick as well as she did.

Everyone had fallen silent at his speech. She'd seen May and Emily exchange a look, then Emily had been coldly cutting with Patrick. So she'd *had* to stand up for him, hadn't she, even though she didn't really agree. Perhaps women *ought* to move aside now that the war was over, she'd said quietly, hoping no one would hear but Patrick.

But Emily had looked up and shook her head sadly at her, and then turning to Patrick she said, 'Home again, home again, jiggety-jig, eh?' Which didn't mean anything, and had made Patrick go pink with annoyance. So that afterwards—

Determinedly, she put on a spurt. She was nearly at the top of the field. Anyway, when May came home she wouldn't have to see so much of Patrick. Patrick could get annoyed so *easily* nowadays. She would talk to May. May couldn't have properly understood what she meant about moving home the week before, because she'd only smiled. Come out to the farm, was all she'd said. Come and see how things are. Come to one of Aunt Lizzie's Sunday teas.

Suddenly something moved in the corner of Alice's eye. She fumbled in her handbag for her glasses. A dozen curious bullocks were slowly making their way in her direction.

Oh, God— Cows— She tried to walk more quickly.

'Alice! Alice!!'

Looking up, she saw May running down the field, bounding, legs flying, her long red hair streaming out behind her like a flag in the wind. She arrived breathless and smiling.

'You've come!' she said delightedly.

Alice accepted the hug and jerked her head in the direction of the animals. The bullocks were almost up to them. They were going to block their path. She could feel her cheeks burning.

May took her arm and laughed. 'They won't harm you. They're just nosey. Hey you!' She slapped the broad flank of one of the animals. 'Off with you now.' The animal turned and ran a yard or two, the others following, then stopped and swung its head around to stare again at the two young women, as if awaiting further instructions.

'If I thought you'd be taking the short cut I'd have warned you. You're hardly dressed for it now, are you?'

Alice looked down at her mud-covered shoes and her best dress pricked with bits of briars. She'd wanted to look so sophisticated, an advertisement for city life.

'And you look ever so warm. Aren't you hot in that?'

But Alice pulled her cardigan more tightly around her and shook her head. This was not how she'd wanted to arrive at all.

The farmhouse was a low, solid building of honey-coloured stone, built around two sides of a paved yard with a barn making up a third side. A few chickens and geese wandered in and out of the barn, pecking at the stone flags. One of the geese waddled over, put down its neck and hissed. May waved it to one side and, just in time, stopped herself laughing as she saw Alice's expression.

'Aunt Lizzie's watchdogs, this lot,' she apologised.

'Fine land-girl I would have made,' Alice laughed, quickly moving out of range. 'I'd forgotten how nervous the wildlife made me.'

But she turned with pleasure to the house. Hydrangeas were growing either side of the front door, turning a deep red, while above a late-flowering clematis scrambled purple through an old and bony wisteria. There was a small hedge of lavender under the window, but no other garden. The Boltons' had always been a working farm. No time for frills. Alice glanced at May's dirty work clothes. A bit like May, she thought, amused. It was definitely time to take May back to the city.

Inside it was thankfully cool. As Alice picked her way through the jumble of weatherproofs and wellingtons that were always in the hall, the smell – wax polish mingled with baking, apples and pot-pourri – caught her off balance in another wave of nostalgia. The Sunday afternoons of her childhood.

'Alice, you're doing it again,' she muttered, briskly turning to check her face in a mirror that was obscured by a huge arrangement of copper beech. She moved her head this way and that until she saw herself looking back hot and flushed. No, this was not how she'd wanted to arrive at all.

61

'Aunt Lizzie's in the kitchen. She's waiting for you,' May said. 'I won't be long.'

But at the foot of the stairs May suddenly turned, ran back and impulsively gave Alice a hug.

'Just like old times, eh?'

Alice smiled back at her.

'Just like old times,' she nodded happily. May had obviously been missing her, just as much as she had been missing May.

Alice watched her sister take the stairs two at a time like an excited child. May could move back next week if she could get her room ready in time. She'd been planning to redecorate it, as a surprise. But maybe she could even come back with her today! She didn't really have to tell Patrick everything, despite what he said. She could wait until everything was settled. In fact once May was back, maybe she wouldn't have to tell Patrick *anything*.

'Alice? Alice! Is that you arrived, hinny?'

Feeling happier than she had been for months, Alice made her way to the kitchen.

'More tea?'

'No thanks, Aunt Lizzie.'

Alice's stomach was a hard knot. She felt foolish, embarrassed, and something akin to betrayed. On the other side of the table her sister May and a dark young man, a *foreigner*, *Francesco* they called him, were talking and laughing about something May had done wrong that morning in the threshing.

May had rolled and piled up her hair in a way Alice hadn't seen before. Nor had she seen the white lace blouse May was wearing, nor the pearls at her neck and ears. Alice looked away confused. She didn't seem like her May at all.

'No, my May,' the Italian was saying in his sing-song accent. *His* May. Alice's face burned.

'Corn with ears goes in, not hay lying in the barn.'

He couldn't even speak English properly! She looked up as May laughed. And touching her all the time! All the way through tea. Staring at her in silence, as if no one else was sitting at the table!

'How was I to know? I didn't look at the bale that carefully. I was in a hurry.'

'You won't make a farmer's wife like that, our May,' her uncle teased.

Alice stared at her cutlery. Everyone was talking so easily. As if it were nothing unusual. Aunt Lizzie smiling, pouring the foreigner tea, while he helped himself to more scones. *Helped himself.* Not waiting to be asked. *At home.* Why wasn't he eating with the other men in the yard?

'Well, in that case it's just as well then, Uncle Harry, isn't it?' May said with a laugh.

Alice picked up the napkin in her lap and began twisting it. How could she! Why hadn't May told her? Had he been there since the war?

'May?' Her aunt was looking at May with raised eyebrows, an expectant smile on her face.

'Well—'

Alice suddenly looked across at May too. The atmosphere at the table had changed, become tense. As if everyone were waiting.

'Yes, my dear, yes—' her aunt encouraged impatiently.

But May was looking straight at Alice.

'I wanted my favourite little sister to be here for this announcement,' she said, almost shyly, not the May she knew at all.

Alice could hear her own heart beating. She watched May turn to Francesco. He took her hand. They smiled at each other. The room suddenly felt oppressively close.

'Francesco and I are going to be married,' she heard May say calmly. She closed her eyes. When she opened them, May's left hand was outstretched on the table before her.

'I send to my mother for it,' Francesco explained as everyone's eyes went to the diamond and pearl ring. 'We wait until it arrives until we say anything to anyone.'

'May Charlton!' Her aunt jumped to her feet so that her chair fell back with a clatter. She rushed around to the other side of the table. 'I'm *so* happy for you, my dear.'

Alice stared at them all, breathing rapidly, as the next few minutes passed in a confused blur. Her uncle thumping backs, a bottle of elderflower wine produced, a handkerchief to be dabbed at her aunt's eyes—

'Pet, you've been like a daughter to us these last two years. It couldn't happen to a nicer young couple.'

Alice put the glass to her lips along with everyone else, but her throat was choked. She felt numb with disbelief. So May hadn't been excited to see her at all. She hadn't been missing her one bit, not like she had been missing— Alice's eyes began to blur.

'Alice—?'

May's hand reached across the table and held hers.

'Aren't you pleased for me? Isn't it a grand surprise?'

Alice smiled as widely as she could. 'Of course. It's wonderful May— It just takes a bit of getting used to, that's all.'

The two young women walked arm in arm across the yard. Behind them the farmer and Francesco had joined the other men, while their aunt stood at the kitchen window, still beaming widely and dabbing at her eyes.

They walked in silence through the lane between the open barns, past the cow sheds, in the direction of the orchard.

'How?' Alice demanded suddenly. She didn't understand. She and May were so close. Why hadn't she told her?

'Well, I first met him when I came to work on the farm,' May explained easily. 'And you know what sort of state I was in then.'

A piglet ran squealing across their path. Dropping Alice's arm, May ran after it, laughing. She came back with the small pink animal wriggling furiously under her arm, scolding it with mock anger.

'Sweet, aren't they? Such a pity they grow to be such ugly great brutes and have you seen the size of—'

'May!'

May smiled and stooping over a low wall, deposited the piglet back with its mother, then kicked the sheet of corrugated iron that acted as a gate to the pen back in place.

'My uncle will have to start spending some money on this place if he wants to get it back to how it was before the war. Honestly, you should see the state of some of the machinery—'

'May!' Alice repeated desperately. It all had to be some sort of mistake! He didn't even speak proper English!

'Well, it's quite recent, really. It's only these last few months that we've become close. All those smouldering looks of his, I guess—' She laughed uncomfortably.

'Months! You're getting married and you've only known him a

few months!' Alice repeated in disbelief. 'But you'd known Will all your life. And what *about* Will! You always said you'd never love anyone else and—'

May dropped her arm.

'And he's a labourer!' Alice went on. 'And foreign! And—'

May sighed.

'It's not always like it is in your books, you know,' she said in a low voice. 'Francesco loves me and— well, I like him. That's enough isn't it? Francesco's all right. He's a decent man.'

'But you can't even talk to him! You and Will used to talk all the time! And he was the enemy, for God's sake! A prisoner!'

May turned to her impatiently, but stopped when she saw Alice's tear-stained face. For a moment she was speechless.

'Oh, Alice— Yes, he's a foreigner,' she went on more gently. 'And yes, his English is poor, but he'll learn.'

There was a pause.

'And Will's gone,' she added quietly. 'You know that. He's in Australia, he might not even come back, his mother says. And he wouldn't want me back if he did. He never answered any of my letters.'

Alice stared at her. 'But he probably never even received your letters! You read about that happening all the time in books! And he only went because of you. You know that! Giving up his job, pretending to get himself all riled up about the war. *You should have stopped him, May!'*

Alice swallowed back her tears. Will had always included her, always talked to her, let her join him and May. If May married this man she would hardly see her!

May was silent for a while.

'Will joined the RAF because he thought it was the right thing to do,' she answered in a controlled voice. 'It had nothing to do with me. If he wanted to, I'm sure he could have stayed in England, just as he could have written. Anyway,' she was suddenly brisk, 'Francesco and I are getting married.'

Alice looked at her bitterly. 'You don't even love him.'

May turned away.

'You'll get to like him, Alice,' she said after a while. 'And the Italians weren't really the enemy, you know. Not in spirit. The war is over, and anyway the Italians liked Mussolini no more than we did. Look what they did to him! Killed the bugger and strung him up on a lamppost!'

She squeezed Alice's tense arm. She needed to change the subject, needed to see her sister smile. 'They're a very passionate people, you see, the Italians.'

But Alice froze again.

'Passionate? You haven't, May—'

May rubbed her eyes. 'Oh, Alice—'

Of course she hadn't. Not when every time Francesco held her she thought of Will, when every time he kissed her— But the memories would fade with time. And when she married Francesco, Will's memory would *have* to fade.

'D'you mean you and Patrick haven't?' she teased, forcing a smile.

Alice felt hot and light-headed. She wished she hadn't drunk so much elderflower wine.

'Of course not. You have to save yourself until you're married. Patrick and I are waiting.'

May looked surprised a moment, then frowned.

'Alice? You and Patrick Sullivan! But you never said!'

Alice wiped her forehead, struggling to feel in control. She felt as if the ground beneath her feet was turning out to be not at all what she thought it was. Quicksand, instead of concrete.

'Well, neither did you,' she answered, using all her efforts to smile.

Alice waved again and bolted the gate to the field. The two men immediately began walking back to the yard, the short, stocky figure of her uncle, and the foreigner her favourite sister had announced she was going to marry. May and her aunt remained waving outside the farmhouse. Alice turned and began to make her way down the field. She'd told them she had to catch the seven o'clock bus, even though she'd been hoping to stay.

She walked quickly, this time heedless of the bullocks or of her best shoes. The breeze carried the women's voices towards her. She heard her aunt say that from the look of her, she could do with more days out in the countryside. Alice pursed her lips. Well, if it made her as brown and buxom as May, that was the last thing she needed. She turned round again. May raised a hand anxiously. Alice waved back unsmiling. If they were going to talk about her, they could at least go into the house.

'Well, more fool May,' she thought stumbling through the long grass. Tears stood in her eyes. 'And bloody hay fever,' she mumbled, pulling out her handkerchief. 'Bloody, bloody, hay fever—' She walked faster. Well, it wouldn't last. She would put money on that. She didn't believe all that stuff about friendship. She'd *seen* May in love. It wouldn't last.

Out of sight of the house, she suddenly stopped, leaned against the fence, and put her face in her hands. But maybe nothing did last. Including the closeness of sisters.

Tears rolled down her cheeks. *She'd wanted May to come home.* The thing was, she whispered to herself, she cared much more about May, than she ever could about Patrick Sullivan.

She looked up, suddenly cold. And now— now she'd as good as said she was going to marry the man. Alice straightened, wiped her face and walked on.

He had asked her of course. She just hadn't actually said yes. But now— well, why shouldn't she? What else was there? She was lucky to have a man. Someone to take her to places.

From over her shoulder came the whir of the thresher machine starting up, followed by male laughter. Alice turned and looked back up the field. She'd hoped she might join in the harvest work herself today, just as in the old days when May and she— She shook her head.

Patrick even resented that, resented her memories. Sentimental nonsense, he called them. She was having to learn to keep her thoughts to herself.

But he would be different when they were married, he would get less irritated with her then. And everyone probably had doubts about getting married— For a moment Alice stared into space, remembering the day when May and Will had made their announcement.

It isn't like it is in your books, May now said.

Hot and uncomfortable, Alice impatiently took off the cardigan she had worn all day, wincing as she pulled it over the black and purple bruises that covered the tops of her arms. Yes, she was sure Patrick would change once they were married. After all, wasn't that why people got married? To get closer and understand each other better?

A sob escaped from the back of her throat and Alice broke into

67

a run, so that she didn't hear the warning shout from the farm behind her. She ran on, oblivious to the threshing machine that had suddenly stopped with a creaking groan, as it jammed. On and on, not hearing the cries, unaware of any commotion—

But she did hear May scream. The sound was shrill and long, piercing the air. Alice froze. Shouts and yells floated down the field behind her. She looked over her shoulder.

May—

She began to hurry back, faster and faster up the field.

May!

Through the gate, not bothering to lock it again, so that later the bullocks would trample what was left of the unharvested corn. Elbowing her way through the herd of animals, their low protests mingling with the shouts coming from above. Finally, kicking off shoes and running, legs heavier and slower than in a nightmare— And then a sudden silence.

But that had been May's voice that had cut the air.

Alice was never to forget the scene. Her aunt running wide-eyed towards the house to telephone for help. Uncle Harry ashen-faced, putting a blanket under the head of a man lying beside the threshing machine, something trapped in its jaws. Checked cloth, a hand . . .

And May on her knees, slowly straightening, her white blouse smeared red, staring at Alice with unseeing eyes— letting out a low moan, followed by the awful begging, the choking, the imploring as she tucked the blanket around the shuddering body, Francesco's body, holding him tighter and tighter, her cheek next to his, until finally the body became still.

6

The Class
1965

'More haste less speed,' my mother says, screeching to a halt outside
Gran's front door. I glare at her in the driving mirror. So much for
her short cut. Now I'm late for the class.

'But better late than never, Megan,' she says, ushering me out
of the car. I swear my mother has a proverb for everything. It's a
family trait, like the Hapsburg jaw or an inherited family tic. Gran
and my aunts are just the same, full of sayings. Whole conversations
can take place without anyone contributing any original speech.

'Too many cooks spoil the broth,' Aunt Emily will say with a
nod.

'Aye, but if you can't stand the heat stay out of the kitchen,' May
will reply darkly.

'Because the bread never falls on the buttered side,' Alice will add,
a beat out as usual nowadays.

My contribution is to muddle them up and see if anyone notices.
'Too many cooks stay out of the kitchen,' I said with a nod and a
knowing look to them all the other day.

Aunt Emily looked at me reprovingly and informed me that 'child
is father of the man'. This is one of her favourites, that we all grow
up to be products of what's gone before. She explained this to me
a couple of times, and I think I understand, but I'm not sure I
believe it to be true. I mean, I can just about see how doing my
homework might decide how I turn out – the Wimpy Bar or doctor's
surgery – but I can't see how teasing my aunts can 'determine my
character', as she puts it. (I'm already determined anyway. 'She's a
very determined young lady, our Megan,' as May is always saying.)

Anyway I reckon they only come out with this stuff when they don't like what I'm doing. It's like 'if the wind changes you'll stay that way', May's favourite, and usually said when I'm sulking (as if she's a one to talk). Or 'if you don't eat your crusts you'll never get curly hair'. Aunt Emily's, but said with a wink, because her hair is long and straight like mine and she knows I hate curly hair.

Alice's sayings are a little odd. I had tea the other day with her and my Uncle Patrick, and she told me to eat up 'because spinach puts colour in your cheeks'.

'Why should I want green cheeks anyway?' I teased.

'Because he who hesitates is lost, Megan,' she replied, and I know she wasn't joking, because then she went to lie down. I hope she'll be at the class today. She missed the last one.

'Now you be good, mind, with Gran's ladies,' my mother says, getting back into the car.

'And nice and quiet when I have to be,' I finish, kissing her cheek. My family and I do a lot of double acts.

She hands me my overnight bag which I'm about to forget.

'Tell Gran I'll be here in the morning and I'll catch her then.'

I haven't been to the class for ages, and I love playing cards, but I wish it wasn't the class.

For two reasons.

Number one, I haven't seen my grandmother for a while, and so I would like her to have *me* all to herself. If no one was coming we would bake, sit on cushions on the back step, chat and shell pea-pods.

And number two, at Aunt Emily's class during the Easter holidays some of the other girls' husbands were there. And apart from my grandfather (whom I'm not speaking to anyway), they spoil the class. The girls are different with them around, more snappy, less fun. Of course Alice and May can be like that with each other anyway, which is pretty odd considering they decide to meet every week and twice in those weeks when it's the class. Sometimes I think they *have* to be kidding.

My mother drives off. Purple and yellow velvet pansies show their faces as I walk up the path. Tiny, dark-red roses are climbing up the front wall in the sun. I hope no one has arrived yet. I want to see the back garden.

Aunt Emily and Alice have already arrived. But as they're real aunties and not 'girls', I root around in the sideboard cupboard, grab a handful of raisins and go out to the garden anyway.

The clump of montbretia is coming out round the drainpipe, but the lily of the valley next to it is over, which is sad, because it's always so cool, and the flowers grow inside the leaves as if in secret, and it smells of Alice.

But the peony roses are still out, huge, fat, dark-crimson things, so full and so heavy that their stems can't keep them up. God gets things wrong sometimes. Clumps of marguerites, flat, climbing roses so pale they're hardly pink, spikes of midnight blue.

Our garden at home has roses, which I quite like because they're pink and lemon at the same time and they smell of sherbet dabs, but everything else is neat in rows and quite low to the ground. Here everything grows in wild clumps, great splashes of colour that bump into each other, some nearly as tall as me.

My grandmother calls me, which means the girls must be arriving and Gran is hot on my manners now that I've reached double figures. 'Manners maketh the man, Megan.'

I hesitate and look through the rose arch to the vegetable patch. There'll be loads of caterpillars because I haven't collected any for two weeks nearly. But it doesn't matter. Because I won't be collecting them again. *Not ever.* Not after the last time.

'Ee, Megan, you're getting a big lass,' May says as I stand in the centre of the room preparing to be patted. Then Aunt Emily says it. Then one by one the girls join in. It's as if they're all fixated on my growth. ('Fixated'. I've just learned this word and try to use it at any available opportunity.) I smile the same smile for all of them, my good girl polite number, even though I know for a fact that I haven't grown. I've been making marks on the kitchen wall. I haven't grown since Christmas. I get kissed a lot and have to do a bit of kissing in return. I don't do lips. I taste face powder and smell Max Factor lipstick. The men aren't here yet.

I get eleven cards nowadays, which can be tricky, but today I manage to spread them into a fan, no problem.

'Will she come, do you think?' my grandmother asks May.

I look up expectantly. 'Who?'

They always include me in their conversations. They're the only ones who don't treat me like a little kid. They even swear in front of me, especially May, although it's only 'bloody'. (Still, my mother would have a fit. I'm not allowed to say 'bloody'.)

'Who?' I repeat, but no one seems to hear.

May shrugs. 'I don't know. She's not doing too well.'

They both look a bit poker-faced, so I go back to my cards. It's only recently I've been given eleven cards for rummy. I used to get only seven, but this is much better because you can make lots more runs and sets.

We start to play. I'm waiting, but no one asks me about school. Usually I make them laugh telling them about what I've been up to (usually no good).

There's a knock at the door.

'Thank God, that'll be Alice,' says Gran, relieved, and I think thank God indeed, because Alice always cheers things up, even when she doesn't mean to. Recently she's been smelling of sherry, and the more she smells of it, the more the girls tut and shake their heads at her, which is funny, since she's a grown-up.

But Alice forgets to kiss me, so I can't tell whether she smells of sherry today or not. But when she sits and gets dealt some cards, I can see that her hands are very shaky. And I know sherry can do this. 'Wise beyond my years', that's me.

My grandmother goes and gets Alice a cup of tea without being asked, even though no one has tea until the first few hands have been played.

Then I see her arm stay around Alice's shoulders as she puts the cup down next to her. I notice this because the girls hardly ever touch one another. There's none of that kissing the air beside cheeks that my mother and her friends go in for.

'I think you might want that,' Aunt Emily murmurs, picking up the Jack that Alice has just thrown away. I look up, surprised. She's right – Jacks *are* out – but they don't even help me any more, let alone each other.

And then later, 'That's a two, Alice. Twos float, remember.' And this from May! May never helps anyone!

I decide it's because of the men. They must be due, that's why everyone's acting odd. Or maybe someone's fallen out. The girls can fall out with each other even more than we do at school.

And they're much better at keeping up the huffs. I look sideways to May. But she's *still* helping Alice.

And then something happens. Alice's fan of cards collapses, even though she only had about six or seven left in her hand, and she has bigger hands than me. They fall to the table with a clatter. I look to everyone expectantly. She must have had lots of sherry. I wait, but the usual tuts don't come.

'It's all right, pet,' May says, getting up, walking round the table and putting her hands on Alice's shoulders. 'You let it all out.'

I stare at her. I've never heard her talk like that. Apart from a sixpence she once gave me when I was little, I've never seen May be kind to anyone.

And I'm so busy watching May, I don't notice at first that Alice has started to cry. She's sort of slumped forward and isn't making any sounds. But her pink-lipsticked mouth is moving, making odd, soft shapes, and tears are standing in her eyes. She always draws turquoise shadow round her eyes, and little blue-green lines are collecting at the sides and running down her cheeks. Then I notice that only one of her cheeks is rouge-pink; the other is reddish-blue.

My heart beats faster. I look down at the cards in my hand. They're muddled up. I'm waiting for my grandmother's voice, someone to tell Alice to pull herself together as they usually do. But instead, I hear Alice moan, breathing quickly as if she's been running. My heart pounds harder.

And then she's *really* crying. And no one is saying *anything*. I know it's because they're all looking at their hands, embarrassed, pretending it's not happening, the way grown-ups do. I swallow and glance up. They're not. They're all looking at Alice, and their faces are sad and worried. My grandmother is sitting next to her, holding her hand. May is still standing beside her chair, holding her shoulders. Aunt Emily has leant across the table so she can stroke her arm.

'As if life wasn't bloody well hard enough,' May mutters, walking to the window. She looks really angry, but her voice is low and quiet.

'You'll have to go this time,' she says over her shoulder. 'This time you'll have to leave the bugger.'

Alice is silent.

73

I look back down at my cards. My vision blurs and I blink. I don't want to be here any more. I wish my mother were here. I stare down at merging hearts and spades, Queens and fives. I can hear myself breathing, and I don't want anyone else to hear, so I start to hold my breath, and gradually things start to go sparkly.

Suddenly my grandmother has hold of my hand.

'I've got some buns to come out of the oven,' she says, quickly taking my elbow and forcing me to stand.

I breathe again.

'You come and put a spot of icing on them, Megan, eh?'

And then in the kitchen she looks at me hard, then sits me down with cake and a drink.

After a while she says quietly, 'Your Aunt Alice isn't feeling well today.'

I nod and think about whether or not I want to go home still. I think not. My mother will be under the drier at the hairdresser's now, anyway. I wash my hands ready for the icing. I like to make each one different. After the third bun is covered with blue icing and an off-centre cherry, I look up at my grandmother.

'Because she hurt her face again?'

'Yes,' my grandmother nods. 'Probably.'

But I'm *still* not going to think about it, even though there's a thought pushing and pushing at the edge of my brain, trying to get in. I get very busy with the icing. I look through the half-open door. Alice is blowing her nose and May has sat down again. I don't want to understand. It's all patterns and puzzles. When I grow up, it'll be like finishing some huge jigsaw puzzle. But then what do you do?

My grandad arrives. He nods and says hello to all the girls, but he looks really pleased to see me.

He lifts me up and twirls me round a bit like he always does, even though I'm nearly as tall as Gran now. Then he sets me down and pats the backs of my legs as if I were still five.

He hasn't remembered.

'How's my twopence?' he asks, and before I can answer, he starts to sing, even though this embarrasses me nowadays.

> *'Dance fer Grandaddy, ma little lassie,*
> *Dance fer Grandaddy, ma-a little lass.'*

It's not even the right words. It's obvious he hasn't remembered. How could he? *I* will never forget.

I don't hug him as I usually do, but instead just offer my cheek, like my mother and her friends. But he kisses it and doesn't seem to notice anything's wrong.

'I *haven't* been up to the vegetable patch,' I begin pointedly, but then Gran comes in and says it's time to set the supper things out and off he goes to help. I've been waiting to say this to him all day, and now I feel flat.

The other men begin to arrive. May's husband, my Uncle Will, is nice really. He's a funny man to be married to May, because she's got a rough, loud voice, and he seems quiet and gentle. They're such an odd couple that I've been watching them recently, and I've discovered something, although I'm not sure exactly what it is I've discovered.

It's got something to do with pretending, though, I know that much – I do enough of *that* myself. I mean, they're like my mother and father, they like each other a lot. But when they talk to each other they pretend that they don't. May usually has a bit of a snap in her voice, and Uncle Will sounds weary. But that's not the way they look at each other, when the other one's not looking. I've seen them. Patterns and puzzles.

Another two men arrive and they're all right too. In fact I decide that they're all not too bad really, as long as they just come for tea and don't play cards.

'Megan, say hello nicely,' says Gran, mouthing the word 'manners' as I move behind the table because there's been more than enough kissing. But just then Patrick, Alice's husband, arrives and I'm spared, so I give Pat a really big smile.

Patrick's all right. He's tall, with nice sandy-grey hair and very blue, twinkly eyes, but not like my grandfather's, which are the bluest eyes in the world, a really strong, light blue with a navy-blue rim. I paint them in all the faces I do. But Pat's all right. He winks at me a lot, like one of those nodding dogs in the back of cars that has gone wrong, and he comes out with a bit of rubbish, but at least he doesn't try to kiss.

'Let me see you,' he begins, holding both my hands out in front of me so that my arms are outstretched. 'Now would you look at the sight of her,' he says with a wink.

I think he only pretends to be Irish. I think he's really from Liverpool.

'Not like our plain Jane at home. God, Megan, but you've grown,' he says twirling me round. 'A young lady almost.'

Oh my Gawd, I say in my head, but outside I do my good girl polite smile.

'She'll knock a few hoists this one, eh?' he says to no one in particular, because suddenly, even though you could have heard a pin drop a moment ago, everyone is now busy talking to everyone else, and if *I* ignored someone who had just arrived, it would be 'Manners maketh—' and no mistake. Alice just nods silently at him. Alice is always quiet when he's around. She must be a lot in love with him. I hope that when I'm old my husband looks like him, although, as I say, my grandad is the best. But I don't want to think about him at the moment.

I'm in bed. I've got Gran's old stone water-bottle which you can roll backwards and forwards with your feet, and I've got all my mother's books with those girls with their baggy frocks and funny haircuts, and I didn't have to kiss goodnight to *anyone*, so I should feel happy, but I'm not.

I can hear them all talking downstairs. I can tell the fire has been lit because I can smell smoky coal, so it must just be taking. I also know from the gaps in the conversation that they're playing cards. I don't mind missing this, because I know they won't be scoring because the men are so hopeless. They're *so* slow.

There's a chink of glass. I imagine the girls all drinking snowballs, with lemonade and a glacé cherry on top like I'm allowed on New Year's Day. The men will be having whisky.

I told Grandad I didn't want a story. And he did notice this time. He looked sort of sad a moment, and then tried to look cheery and said something like, 'Well, I suppose you're starting to grow up, twopenny, eh?'

Then *I* felt sad. I wish he would remember.

Occasionally people come upstairs to use the toilet. Alice comes up and gives me a kiss and a tickle. I can tell the next one's

May because she always stomps heavily and humphs a lot. I turn off the light and play a game to guess who the next one will be.

'Check Megan's asleep, will you?' I hear someone say as the door downstairs opens again.

'He's a right one to ask,' comes another voice.

I hear the footsteps come upstairs. I hear the toilet being used. Then the sink in the bathroom. Then footsteps across the landing to my room. They wait a few moments, then my door creaks a bit and the blackness behind my eyes goes red. I lie as still as possible with my eyes tight shut.

The door is opened wider and he comes in. He sits on the side of my bed, which makes me roll a bit. A hand begins to stroke the hair off my forehead, and then I *have* to open my eyes, because they're flickering all over the place and it must be obvious that I'm not asleep.

'Such a young lady,' Pat says, still stroking my hair. 'You'll knock a few hoists, you will, lass,' he says.

Again, I wonder what the heck a hoist is, but I smile my good girl polite number at him, even though it is an effort.

'And such a pretty young lady,' he mutters, stroking my hair down to my shoulders.

I don't mind Pat, but I wish it had been Grandad who had come up. I was ready to tell him.

He bends down and kisses my cheek. I can smell whisky. OK, so now he'll go, I think to myself. But then he kisses my other cheek, and then my forehead, my eyes, my chin, my lips, and then the kisses are raining all over my face, hundreds of them, over and over again. I've got my eyes tight shut and under the blankets my hands are clenched. This is awful. He stops a moment. I let out my breath.

'Such a pretty young lady,' he mutters again, but I don't open my eyes and instead I concentrate really hard and think *now will he go!* And after another age I feel his weight leave the bed and I breathe again.

He looks down at me but I can't smile, because I'm too embarrassed, and instead I say goodnight and try to turn over. But he's kneeling on the side of the bed and before I realise anything, he's lying on top of me! Right on top of me! I freeze,

I'm so shocked, and he takes my face in his hands and begins to do the kissing stuff all over again.

'Such a pretty girl,' he whispers, and I close my eyes tight, wishing I wasn't pretty, because I'm not at all interested in being pretty, and it's a stupid and useless thing to be, and I feel trapped, and I'm not good about being trapped, because once I got stuck in a lift and— and I want to shout at him to *GET OFF ME!*

But he's my uncle, so instead I clench my fists really hard and tell myself that everyone gets kissed by their aunts and uncles and you just have to put up with it *but it's going on for so long.*

And then something even more horrible happens. By accident, because he's drunk, or because he's talking at the same time as doing the kissing, his tongue falls out and a bit of it goes into my mouth. I squirm, because it's really revolting, even though I know he didn't do it on purpose, and that *I'll* be old one day and maybe not in charge of *my* tongue.

And he starts to squirm too, which hurts because he's heavy, and I try to speak, but I can't because my throat feels clogged, and instead I can feel something gushing up inside me and at first I don't realise, but then I know what it is, and I panic and try really hard to breathe, because if I *do* scream, everyone will come running up and be angry with me and my mother is always saying I'm a drama queen—

I feel a hand on my leg. His hand is inside my bed. And suddenly I'm cold and frightened, and he's stroking my leg, pushing my nightie— So then I just stop breathing altogether.

The blood pounds in my ears as I will it to get sparkly, quickly, quicker—

'Go up and see what's keeping him,' I hear someone say from far, far away.

Pat rolls off me and sits up. 'Sleep tight, pretty girl,' he says, calmly kissing my cheek as if nothing unusual has happened. He walks quietly across the room.

I start to breathe again. I'm trembling. Not just a bit, but hard, like I was freezing cold. I hold on to my arms.

The door closes only seconds before I hear Grandad's voice.

'She off yet, Pat?'

'Not quite. You know kids,' Pat laughs, easily, unconcerned.

My teeth are chattering. I want to cry, even though I'm trying not to be so babyish these days.

78

My grandad tiptoes into my room. 'And are you not asleep yet, twopence?'

He crouches down by my bed so that he can look into my face.

'But you're cold, Megan!' he exclaims, rubbing my arms under the blankets. 'No wonder you're not asleep. Here. I'll heat up the bottle.'

'No!' I grab his arm as he starts to leave. 'You killed my caterpillars!' I shout, sitting up and glaring at him. 'My bloody caterpillars. Bloody, bloody—'

A strangled sound comes from my throat. And the next moment tears are running down my face and I'm hitting his arm angrily, shouting, 'You killed them! You bloody killed them! You *bloody*!' over and over again.

I rock myself back and forward but I can't get rid of the feeling of the heavy body on mine. I rock and rock but it won't go.

'How could you!' I scream between great shaky sobs. I close my eyes tight.

'They were my pets!'

I can still feel the hand on the top of my leg.

'Gran told me,' I choke. I can smell sickly whisky kisses on my face. 'She said you found them in their matchbox and you threw them on the fire!'

This last is hurled at him. I want to throw off the covers and run somewhere, where no one will ever find me.

'*You— killed— my— caterpillars!*'

I fling myself into his arms.

'Megan, Meg—' he says, surprised, hurt.

I bury my face in his neck. I'm never coming to the class again!

'I didn't realise they were your pets, Meg. I'm sorry, I couldn't have been thinking—'

He untangles my arms and makes me look at him.

'And they would have died in the matchbox, you know,' he says gently. 'I couldn't put them back on the cabbages now, could I? You're a collector and I'm a gardener, you see. Understand, Megan?'

He gives me a handkerchief. I blow hard.

'So that was what this was all about? You were in the huff with your old grandad?'

79

I nod, then hold on to him tightly, which makes the heavy-body-feeling less, but I still need to spit. But I won't leave the room, so I try not to swallow instead.

'I rang up,' I say into his neck. 'Gran said you'd put them on the fire.'

When she'd told me this, I imagined them sizzling as they hit the coals, giving small caterpillar screams. I was going to tell him that I would never forgive him. But instead I say,

'Stay here until I go to sleep. Please.'

He unclenches my hands and tucks me in.

'I'll refill the bottle first,' he says, because I'm still trembling. 'And you can go and sit downstairs with the others while I do it, eh? Would you like that?'

'No!' I shout. Then more softly, 'No, thank you,' because he's frowning and no one must ever know.

'You're a funny wee thing,' he says, and I can see he's upset, but I can't say anything more.

I'm lying face down in the pillow when Aunt Emily comes in. I know it's her because of the swish of her silk dress. She's brought my hot water-bottle. I can hear it glooping. She sits on the bed. I don't move, but she knows I'm not asleep. Even though I'm not close to her like I am to Alice, Aunt Emily always knows things about me. She even knows what I think sometimes. She once said it's because I'm a bit like her, with being an only child, but this doesn't make sense because she's got loads of sisters.

I know she'll wait all night if need be, so finally I turn over.

'You're sad, Megan,' she says, telling not asking.

Sad's not quite right, I don't know how I feel, but I nod. She motions me to move along, then plumps up my pillows against the wall and sits with me on the bed.

'Your grandad told me,' she says quietly.

I nod again. I like Aunt Emily, and I did want to talk with her, about why she moved back to Newcastle, about why she didn't like London any more. But not now. Now I don't want to talk. I look down at the bedclothes.

She sits in silence as if she's in no hurry, but I don't mind, it's not uncomfortable. Then after a while she says,

'It'll hurt less tomorrow, I promise, Megan.'

And she takes one of my hands and presses it between her own beautiful cool hands.

'It always hurts less with time,' she says gravely, so gravely, I look up at her face. Aunt Emily never talks to me like I was a kid anyway, but now she sounds *really* serious. She looks back at me and from her eyes I know she's talking about herself, about how *she* was hurt. We sit together in silence for a long while and, eventually, I do start to feel a bit better.

'Now you sleep, my pet,' she says, as if she's read my mind and she brushes my cheek with her lips, so that a warm spicy scent lingers over my face.

I lie hugging the bottle. I can't sleep, but I don't want to think, it's important not to think, important not to think about *that*.

So I lie and think about my aunts instead. I think about May and Uncle Will and why they pretend that they don't care about each other, when really I know that they do. Patterns and puzzles.

I think about Aunt Emily, how I once overheard Gran's neighbour say that Aunt Emily never cared about anyone or anything, because all she's bothered about is her career. And I know that they're wrong.

And I think about Alice. My lovely Aunt Alice. And it's not all patterns and puzzles. Because I know why Alice is sad. And I know why she's got a blue face. And I even know why she drinks sherry, now.

But I don't know how she could have married him.

'I don't like cards any more,' I whisper into the darkness. 'So I'm not coming to the class again.'

7

Emily
1955

Awakening, Emily stretched out her limbs, but deliberately kept her eyes closed. There was luxury to be had behind closed lids. Safety, privacy, and the power of imaginings— She lay, the back of her hand over her eyes, prolonging the darkness a little longer.

In darkness, everything could be imagined, anything be possible. She could be in Venice, Paris or Rome. Not in a small mews in Bloomsbury. She could even be in California, by an ocean she'd never seen before, listening to waves crashing and murmuring on the shore, in a house with palm trees in its garden, while a child slept peacefully in the room next to hers—

'Ten years ago today,' she whispered aloud. 'Ten years already.'

The shape next to her stirred slightly. She opened her eyes and the apartment instantly became a bubble of daylight, uncluttered and spacious. For a moment she looked fondly at the tousled head on the pillow next to her and then she turned away. She would have to be quick. She must get up and leave silently before he woke. That way was best. His words last night, the question he asked, left her with no other choice.

From the street below came the chink of glass on glass, the clatter of the milk cart, the first tentative birdsong. She would have to be quick. She could walk, arrive at the office an hour or two before anyone else showed up. Today she needed time alone. Today it was time to remember. As she had on this day every day for the past ten years.

Carefully she slid from his arms to the edge of the bed.

'Emily—'

She paused, but he was awake. He laid an arm heavily across her body.

'Not yet,' he murmured into the pillow, pulling her back with gentle force. 'Come back.'

For a moment she tried to resist. She had wanted simply to leave the note that she had been composing in the darkness. That way was always best—

'James. I have to go.'

But his hands moved over her, slipping straps from shoulders, pulling her closer to his warmth, and as she knew she would, she softened.

'I must,' she whispered, and was silenced.

James Goldman, eyes closed, but very much awake, buried his face into the offered neck, confident that Emily would be going nowhere for quite some time yet.

'I don't understand you.' His voice was low, a mixture of hurt and anger. He was sitting in bed watching her dress, watching her effect the transformation which at first had stunned him: that this woman, in private so beautiful, could appear in public as sombre and plain as a prison guard.

He had met her twice at the Ministry before he had even noticed her, before he had seen past the barely-needed spectacles and severe all-concealing suits. He had been shocked at such deception, but she'd only laughed. She'd said it might well be a cliché, but in a world dominated by men, where women seldom got further than secretarial status, it was also expediency.

She'd insisted their affair be secret. Over the course of its six months he had come to love this secrecy, in the same way as he loved her duplicity of image. It made him feel rich, as if he owned a plain box that contained a jewel, the more precious because only he had seen it.

She couldn't mean this.

'So when did this change of heart happen?' He pushed back his hair and laughed shortly, more hurt than he was prepared to let her see. Women didn't do this to him. And he'd been so sure that she felt as he did, so sure, that last night he'd asked her—

'You certainly didn't feel like that a short while ago,' he said bitterly before he could stop himself.

84

Emily looked up quickly, then looked away. Earlier, arms entwined, each urgently absorbed in the other, her eyes had widened, her breath caught, and then the words of love had poured.

'I'm so sorry.'

Suddenly, and bewilderingly, James Goldman, youngest and newest Deputy Secretary in the Foreign Office, found himself near to tears.

'But I don't understand!'

Emily slipped her feet into sensible shoes. She began brushing her hair, staring ahead, avoiding his gaze in the mirror.

'Please. Don't make it any more difficult than it has to be.' The over-familiar words sprang to her lips; always the same clichés. 'I need more space, that's all. Some time alone—'

From the corner of her eye she saw a violent movement in the bedclothes and he was suddenly behind her. Eyes on a level with her own, his face young and relaxed with sleep, his dark hair soft. Her other lovers had all been tall, strong, much older than herself. But not James. With James she could swing dizzily between a physical attraction that often overwhelmed, and an almost maternal protectiveness.

She tried to pin up her hair but her fingers were trembling.

He saw, and moved closer.

'Emily—'

She could smell his warmth, his skin, their shared scent of the past hour. She closed her eyes.

'Christ!' He grabbed her shoulders, forcing her to face him. 'A break? What the hell do you think I am? Some bloody machine you can turn on and off? I love you, for God's sake. You can't just turn round and say that's all for now. I'm not a fucking gigolo.'

She flushed. 'It was going wrong— an affair— no commitments, we both said—'

So why did it feel so hard this time? Impatiently she pulled a jacket from the wardrobe.

'I told you. I don't ever get involved.'

'Don't? Or can't? Have you ever asked yourself why, Emily?'

Her face felt hot. She was struggling to feel in control. She needed to get out quickly.

'I'll call you sometime and—'

She swallowed, and looked up at him. His arms hung helplessly by his sides, his face a mixture of pain and bewilderment. She'd seen the expression on many other faces, there'd been many other times like this, so many— Except that this time was different. Because this time she felt the same.

'James— listen—' But the clichés had deserted her.

'I'm coming back, Emily,' he called after her as she hurried down the stairs. 'You won't get rid of me as easily as that.'

She looked back. His tone had been defiant, but his face was that of a child.

'I'm so sorry,' she whispered, and closed the door behind her.

It had rained for most of the night, but the day was fine, the damp coolness of the morning air giving it an illusion of freshness. Emily leaned against the door, breathing deeply for a few moments, then carefully picked her way around the shiny puddles that dotted the cobbles of the mews.

She should have simply left a note, as she had intended. That way was always best. She turned and looked back over her shoulder. He was still standing at the window, bare-chested, his face pale under the shock of dark hair. She half-raised a hand, but he continued to stare, motionless.

James—

She felt a sudden impulse to run back. Half a dozen steps. That was all it would take. 'You're right,' she could say. 'Yes!'

God, James—

Deliberately she turned and walked briskly on towards the main road. She had let the relationship continue for too long. That's all it was. She was stopping things just in time. She couldn't afford to get close to anyone. She knew the danger of that, how much it could hurt.

She turned again. This time the window was empty, and for a moment she was gripped by panic, and by a fear she couldn't name, but whose shape she knew. Heart pounding, she walked on. She had let it continue for too long, that's all it was.

But James had been special. Clever and funny, with a wry and gentle way of looking at the world that made her laugh, that suggested life didn't have to be taken so seriously. She'd even felt that she might have been able to be with him as she really was, and as an equal, not just a decorative possession.

Her steps faltered and she turned back again. But probably not—
And if you let yourself get too close, you got hurt. That was the way
of the world.

A taxi slowed down as it approached her. She shook her head at
the driver and walked on more briskly. The way of the world. *So
no regrets.* She was stopping things just in time.

Early morning London was coming to life. Emily made her way
through the back streets of Bloomsbury to Tottenham Court Road,
past pubs and restaurants where staff were washing down pavements,
lorries making deliveries. On into Charing Cross Road, past dead-
faced theatres with littered foyers, smells of Chinese cooking already
drifting over from the restaurants of Chinatown, and on into
Trafalgar Square. She checked her watch. She still had over an hour.

She would sit in St James's Park. She would use the time to
remember. That would focus her mind, that would blot out the
image of James's face before her eyes, take his touch from her
cheek—

The park was almost empty, the hoots of buses and taxis distant.
She could see early morning commuters hurrying along, heads down,
beyond the railings. She sat on a wooden bench at the side of
the lake, as brown and white ducks, moorhens and swans began
moving over the water towards her.

Think, she told herself. Remember.

She watched a pair of Canada Geese, sinuously moving their long
necks, heads down, calling out to each other, absorbed in their
courtship ritual. Geese pair for life, James had told her—

Think!

The black swans slid gracefully from under a willow in front of
her. A foreigner was arrested last week for killing a swan for his
Sunday lunch, James had read—

Think!

She closed her eyes.

Remember!

Ten years ago today. Ten years exactly. She had behaved badly
that day too. The midwife had almost walked out—

'For goodness sake, Mrs Charlton, pull yourself together. Just
breathe normally. No, don't pant like that. And please, *please* will
you lie down!'

'It's Miss,' Emily hissed through clenched teeth. She pushed away the midwife's arm and turned herself over so that she was on all fours. There was another one coming.

'Miss, Mrs, you're all the same to me,' the midwife muttered, trying vainly to prise Emily's hands off the bedstead. Emily closed her eyes. She had to concentrate. How did it go? How did it go? She searched in her mind for the song.

'*Pack up your troubles in your old kitbag,*' she began to sing as the contraction took hold. '*And smile, smile, smile. While you've a Lucifer to light your fag,*' she shouted at the peak of the pain, drowning out the midwife's protests, '*Smile boys that's the—*'

It was beginning to recede. She let go of the brass rail and collapsed back on the bed.

'*—style.*'

The midwife tutted.

'You're making it much worse for yourself, you know,' she said, folding her arms across her chest.

Emily breathed deeply. Her mouth was dry and her face wet with perspiration. She couldn't take much more of this.

'You young girls with education are all the same,' the midwife went on in a Liverpool accent. 'Either shouting blue bloody murder that you've changed your mind half-way through— And the language! You wouldn't believe such well-spoken girls could come out with them things! Or else you're trying to wander around and have the baby on all fours as if you were in the bloody jungle.'

She moved Emily back into a lying position and began to examine her.

'Well, my girl, this isn't Tarzan and you're not Jane. We have our babies lying down in a civilised manner here.' She paused a moment, frowning. 'And you, young lady, are ready! And the doctor's not even here yet!'

She turned away, disgruntled, her expression implying that Emily and her education had planned it this way on purpose.

Emily looked at the woman properly for the first time.

'Really? I'm ready to push now?'

The midwife nodded grimly. 'And we'd better do it my way if you don't mind.'

But Emily was already pulling herself up the bed into a sitting position.

'Anything I can do?' Her aunt's face appeared around the door.

The midwife sounded exasperated. 'You can try and persuade this headstrong girl that she'll be much better off co-operating with me. I don't know what kind of books she's been reading but—'

She was suddenly silenced as Emily gripped the bedstead and began to push, face screwed up with concentration.

'Good girl—'

Good Lord—

Good grief—

No, just pant—

No, don't push any more!

Just sing your bloody song then! Don't push! Pant!

'It's a long way to Tipperary,' Emily panted. 'It's a long way to go.'

She was aware that the room had more people in it, that her mother had joined her aunt at the foot of the bed and was trying to give instructions.

'Our Rose never took this long,' she heard her mother grumble.

She gritted her teeth. Another was coming—

'Goodbye Piccadilly, Farewell Leicester Square—'

'That's right— one more—

Now hold— good girl, good girl—

Again—

It's coming—

I can see the head— lots of lovely black hair—'

'Black?' her mother whispered, just before Emily pushed, with one huge effort, for the last time.

'And here we are,' the midwife said, gently, softly, in a different voice altogether.

There was a moment's total silence.

Then a moan. Followed by a heavy thud at the foot of the bed. She heard her aunt calling out her mother's name.

And then she heard a baby's cry.

Emily was only vaguely aware of the activity at the other side of the room, couldn't see her aunt trying to revive her mother. She remained oblivious to the mounting concern as it was realised that her mother's long feigned heart complaint had finally become a self-fulfilling prophecy.

Even when it became clear that her mother was not going to regain consciousness, and had chosen rather to pass silently away than meet her new grandson, Emily seemed unable to take it in. Or unwilling, as if it were a final piece of maternal disapproval to be ignored, some posthumous attempt to divert attention.

Because she only had eyes for the tiny baby boy, who was held up, pronounced perfect by a now beaming midwife, wrapped in a soft sheet, and placed in her arms.

His crying stopped the instant she spoke to him.

'And so it was you in there all the time, eh?' she whispered, offering a finger for a miniature hand to clasp. She smiled down into his eyes. They were dark, like his father's. So was his hair. Only his skin was lighter, more coffee-coloured than black.

And as his unfocused eyes gazed back at her, mesmerised by her voice, searching her face for its source, Emily felt herself falling in love for the second time in her life. With Matt's son.

Emily pushed her coat more tightly around her. The promise of the morning was fading, the sky darkening. Ten years ago today. A new life— and a death.

She had called the baby Matthew, after his father. She took the worn photograph from her handbag. Swaddled in blankets, he could have been anyone's, but he had been hers. For two weeks, anyway. She'd only been allowed to keep him for two weeks. But she'd made sure, in those few days, that no one could have loved him more, so that he might grow to know instinctively how much she had cared.

She never told Matt about his son, although he had written many times. She hadn't written back. She hadn't been able to. What could she have said to him? We made a child, but I gave him away? She had been right not to reply to his letters.

So no regrets.

Better that Matt be left with the good memories of their affair. Those few weeks had been the most intense time of her life too. She hadn't been surprised to discover she was pregnant, as if a love that strong had to have resulted in new life.

Gently she smoothed the photograph between her fingers. But she couldn't have kept their child. She'd fought and argued, but everyone was right. No money, no job, and bringing up a baby alone— Alice had said she would help, and Rose, and even May, despite her pretended aversion to children— But it wasn't enough.

Society could be cruel. The mother and baby home she'd run from was proof of that. Examining her first for venereal disease, making her feel like some sort of pariah, shunned by the other married women— She wanted a better life for her son than that kind of society would give.

She slipped the photograph back into her bag, beside a faded bundle of airmail letters.

So no regrets, she told herself, yet again.

A few drops of rain had begun to fall. Emily shivered and walked back along the path, the ducks and geese following by the lake edge, still hopeful for bread. Ten years old today. How tall would that make him? Would he be celebrating?

The people who adopted him would care, she'd seen that. They were hoping to move abroad, they said. To Australia, or even America. Which had seemed like fate. And so she had let them take him, let them take her son to a better life, so that he could grow up somewhere with space, with the sun on his face.

That was how she thought of him, as she lay alone in the early mornings— Except she hadn't been alone in the mornings for a while, because James had been with her.

Briskly, Emily walked on, but the chill and fear were back.

Emily's career rise had been slow, but steady. After witnessing the bombings in Liverpool she'd applied to do more than clerical work for the war effort in Newcastle, where it was discovered that she was not only quick and intelligent, but also quiet and discreet, a profile which eventually earned her a posting to the London War Office.

Here, for the first time in her life, Emily found a sense of identity, a place where she fitted. She was good at her job, efficient and effective; she could make things happen, get things done. So she threw herself into her work, and didn't mind the fact that it left her no time for friends or family. She could cultivate friendships and visit her sisters more often when her career was fully established, she told herself. At the moment her work was more than enough. A series of deliberately short affairs were all she needed to fill out her life, she came to believe.

So no regrets.

She knew there was talk at work, that she was not popular, but she accepted this as the inevitable jibing that follows successful women. She could ignore the murmurs beneath the clatter of the typewriters as the women criticised her appearance, and shut her ears to the cruder whisperings from the men in the corridors. It didn't have to concern her. She didn't need their friendship. She was good at her job. This was recognised, and that was all that mattered. It was a good enough life.

So when her secretary informed her later that morning that her head of department had asked to see her for an unscheduled meeting, Emily thought nothing of it. Nor did she catch the drift of a colleague's well-meaning hint about a proposed promotion of someone who happened to be the nephew of her superior.

Her concentration was poor and the morning consequently long. At lunch time she pushed the door of her office closed, instructing that she wasn't to be disturbed.

The vague stirrings of panic were still with her, still that nameless, yet familiar fear—

Finally she put her work to one side. She would think of her son instead, she would think of Matt.

But when she tried to remember how Matt looked, all she could see was James's face. When she tried to remember Matt's voice, she could only hear James's voice. And she only knew James's touch.

She put her face in her hands. But what else could she have done? She had to end it. She knew the pain that loving someone could bring.

So no regrets!

A sudden gale of laughter outside the office startled her, and as she turned, unguarded, in its direction, the chill and fear that had been with her all day suddenly grew to such force she felt physically hit. From nowhere tears began streaming, as she gripped the desk, bewildered, confused— Crying was not something she did— yet more and more, as the pain she'd been fighting against for years, whistling in the dark against for years, took hold.

Loss washed through her. Matt— her son— her mother— and now James. Now she had let James go too. So afraid of loss, she had recreated it, over and over again.

So *many* regrets.

*　　*　　*

Gradually Emily became aware that the laughter and whisperings behind the door had ceased. She lifted her face from the desk. The clock on the wall said that somehow an hour had passed.

She stared at the intercom on her desk for a few moments. Then, hands trembling, she pushed the button. She felt drained, but she felt sure. We create our own reality, James had once said. Her heart beat faster.

'The Foreign Office, please.'

She didn't even know his schedule, knew little of his life, in fact. Ignorance of the details was one of the means by which she kept herself distant.

'But Miss Charlton,' the intercom whined back, followed by a silence which eloquently conveyed the message that lunch hour wasn't over yet. 'Isn't it almost time for your appointment on the fifth floor, ma'am?'

Emily walked quickly through the corridors. She would call as soon as the meeting was over. Track him down. Drag him out of the office if necessary! And she would say yes! *Yes*, to what he'd asked the night before, to the question he thought she hadn't heard. Ten years was long enough. She quickened her step, half-laughing. Such a curious freedom realising this! Such a freedom, she could hardly keep from running.

They couldn't marry, the department forbade it, it would mean giving up everything she had worked for over the last ten years, but they could still be together. And the hell with society! She would shout YES!

Emily was still smiling as she walked into her superior's office. It took a few seconds to register what he said.

'Cyprus?' she repeated in disbelief.

The Colonel nodded, attempting to look amiable.

'Giving the fairer sex a fair go,' he said, 'sending a woman out to a listening post, what?'

'You do have a choice of course,' he said less comfortably when Emily didn't answer, patting the papers on his desk.

The words her colleague had spoken earlier suddenly took on their intended meaning. Emily slowly sat down. She knew what her choice was.

'Hell of an opportunity for a woman, of course,' he went on airily, walking around and sitting on the edge of the desk so that he could look down at her. 'Important position, what with the current hoohah over Suez, Nasser thumbing his nose, and all this trouble with those EOKA chappies.'

Emily swallowed. She knew exactly what was being said. Her 'choice' was to take it, or leave it.

The Colonel waited, taking in Emily's heightened colour, her overbright eyes, and the blonde strands escaping from the usually tightly rolled hair, and used it all as justification for his decision. The woman appeared to be slipping anyway. He'd always maintained it wasn't a good idea to have females in senior positions. Especially not civil servants. Women's problems, and all that. But abroad, well that was another matter. Out of his jurisdiction then.

Emily stared at her hands in her lap. Ten years she'd worked to get to this position. Ten years of working weekends and evenings, of making her job her whole life. Ten years of total commitment—

And ten years of being alone. Ten years of punishing herself.

'It would only be for a couple of years, you understand. We wouldn't want to let you go for longer than that.'

James's face swam before her. *Cyprus.*

She composed her expression.

'I'll let you know my decision by the end of the week, sir,' she said, sounding cool and professional. But in her heart, the chill and fear were back.

8

May
1955

May poured Alice tea and pushed the cup towards her. Still Alice didn't speak. May waited uneasily. Alice's kitchen was a mess, for Alice's kitchen. The remains of the breakfast things lay in a heap in the sink, the wooden table was covered with crumbs and smears of butter, and the floor hadn't been swept. May's kitchen looked like that for the best part of the week, but Alice's never did.

Something crashed to the floor in the front room. May could hear Rose's children beginning to shout and argue. On the days Alice looked after them the kids were usually so well organised there was hardly a bad word between them. 'As good as gold,' Alice described them. Alice was every child's favourite aunt. Unlike May.

A small boy with fair hair and the round cheeks of recent toddlerhood opened the door and stood looking at them both. Beyond him May could see his two elder sisters squabbling, hunched over a table covered with papers and pencils, a jam jar of water, pots of paints. Alice didn't usually allow painting in the front room.

'Auntie Alice,' the boy began in a wheedling tone. May looked to Alice. She sat absently swirling her mug round and round in her hands so that tea was slopping over the side. She looked as if she'd dressed in the dark, her hair hadn't been done. Alice was usually meticulously turned out. The child waited, but Alice didn't even appear to have heard.

May began to feel more uneasy. Alice's tone when she'd rung earlier that morning had been hesitant, embarrassed, *asking* if May would come over, as if it wasn't a normal occurrence for her to drop in throughout the week.

'Auntie Alice!' the child repeated insistently. 'They're not letting me have the crayons!' He gazed at his aunt, puzzled. 'And our Betty says—'

'Out, Tom,' May said quietly. The boy was only five, but his sisters were more than old enough to look after him. The child's eyes widened and he turned on his heels. None of them argued with their Aunt May.

Alice looked up as the door slammed. She took a gulp of tea.

'I've gone and got myself caught,' she said, with a tight smile. 'Pregnant—'

'And after I was being so careful,' she ended in a whisper.

'Alice! But that's marvel—'

'I'm not ready for a baby yet,' Alice interrupted quickly. 'I couldn't cope with it. Not now.'

There was a heavy silence. May laughed uneasily. Alice was joking. Alice loved children!

'Nonsense!' she said as brightly as she could. 'Of course you can cope! And not ready? We've all been wondering what was keeping you!'

But Alice's tone was bitter.

'I can't now. It wouldn't be right.'

May stared at her in disbelief.

'You've just got the early pregnancy blues, a bit of the jitters, that's all. It happens to most women, doesn't it?' She was guessing, she knew little of this. 'That's all that's wrong—'

Alice laughed shortly. 'Not very clever of me, eh? And after Rose had lent me that Marie Stopes book. Given me the clinic opening times. Even *shown* me her blessed cap. But I thought I was doing it right. Except recently Patrick's been— more insistent.'

She went back to swirling her cup.

May looked at her anxiously. It must be Patrick. He was making her say all this. A baby would dint his precious savings account, spoil his plans for buying the next new gadget— This wasn't Alice at all.

'Alice, you'll manage,' she said, willing her younger sister to believe it. 'And as for coping, we'll all help—'

She paused and flushed. She'd never helped with any of the girls' children; she'd made a point of keeping out of their way where kids were concerned, in fact.

'The girls will all help, you'll see. It'll probably even bring our Emily back home!' She tried to laugh. 'And that would be something!'

Alice stood up.

'It wouldn't be right,' she repeated flatly. 'Not now. So I've fixed up to do something about it.'

'Alice!' May's anxiety was turning to something more chilling.

'That's why I called you. I need someone to come with me. You're the only one I could ask.'

May shook her head. 'God, Alice—'

'I thought I'd be all right. I thought I could manage on my own.' Alice laughed bitterly. 'But I've been waking up with night sweats just thinking about it. Patrick thinks I've got a bug. Some bug.'

'You haven't told him?' May stared at her. None of this made any sense. Alice had always insisted that Patrick and she had the perfect marriage, were so happy together— The perfect couple! To the extent that she and Emily had to keep quiet about how they really felt about Patrick Sullivan. Yet Alice hadn't even told him! And was actually contemplating—

'Alice, what the hell do you mean? *What* have you fixed?'

'I mean you're so clever,' Alice went on as if she hadn't heard. 'I know what you think about kids. So you make sure *you* never get caught. I must be as stupid as he says.'

Alice turned to the window. May watched her in silence, still searching for explanations. This wasn't her sister, her eager, cheerful sister. Admittedly Alice had become more quiet, more subdued over the past year, but May had assumed that was because Alice was settling down, growing up at last. Had she and Patrick argued? Was that it? Had Alice discovered that he was seeing another woman?

But even so, a *baby*— Alice had always wanted a baby!

'You were a real turn up for the books, you know,' Alice said, suddenly turning. 'I mean I always thought that you and Will were planning to have masses of bairns. Before you broke off your engagement with Will the first time— before— well, you always said—'

Her eyes drifted back to the window. The garden was neat and tidy. As usual. Rows and rows of orderly flowers. Tall dahlias at the back, geraniums in the middle, dwarf marigolds at the front. All standing to attention. Not a leaf out of place. Only the rose bushes she'd planted when they first married had any wild feeling, and they were trapped in the middle by the serried ranks.

And if she had this baby, she whispered to herself, she would be just as trapped. And so would the child.

May cleared her throat. 'What have you arranged, Alice?' she asked again quietly, praying that she was wrong, that she had misunderstood.

'When did *you* decide, May?' Alice swung round, smiling brightly, much too brightly. 'I mean not to have kids. Loads of women would have succumbed. But not you. I admire you for sticking to it and all.'

May swallowed. *Don't, Alice.*

'I remember at the knitting class, you know,' Alice said with a forced laugh, an imitation of her old self. 'When you were on honeymoon, Emily and I organised a sweep on whether you would come home pregnant or not. Now that the two of you had finally got together, after all those false starts, we were sure it would happen straight away— We all lost, I seem to remember.'

May closed her eyes. *Stop, Alice.*

'When you were younger, you and Will could hardly keep your hands off each other. I used to think you were like a couple out of a Bella D'Arcy romance. Remember those daft romances we used to read together?'

She laughed again, the sound high and false, echoing round the room.

'And remember those camiknickers we gave you? Or was that when you were first engaged— before—' Alice's eyes drifted back to the garden.

May looked down at her hands. Before. Yes, that was before.

But aloud she said, 'It was on our honeymoon. In the Lake District. We decided then. I'm just not the maternal type. Even Will could see that. So we decided—' She looked up, despairing. 'Alice, this isn't right. You can't mean it!'

But the lines had reappeared on Alice's brow and she was no longer listening.

'Well, I can see now that you're not the type— But at the time— We'd always thought—' Alice's voice trailed off. She had better see to the children. Rose would be here soon. She'd told her she had to go and have a tooth out and would probably need to rest when she got back. But she'd already made Patrick's evening meal, it just needed the gas lighting, and his clothes were already pressed for tomorrow. And May would take her. Thank God for May.

'I can see that now,' she muttered, and went off into the other room.

May heard the children protesting, then Alice's voice brightly soothing, followed by the clatter of pens and pencils being put away.

She sat motionless. *A child.*

'It was on honeymoon, that we decided not to have children,' she said aloud to the empty room. Eight years ago. On a cold spring day—

'Are you pedalling, May?'

'Yes.' She shivered and took her feet down from where they had been resting – on the frame of the tandem they had hired to tour the Lakes, for a laugh, Will had said. 'Of course I am.'

They were reaching the brow of a hill. On either side of them sheep grazed on the rough grass, while further back pine woods sloped down towards the village they had just left.

'Sure about that?' Will laughed as the bicycle began to move lightly and easily again.

There was a silence.

'No. You're right. I suppose I wasn't.'

'May—'

He'd meant it as a joke. To lighten the silence. Now it would be worse.

He slowed and stopped the bike. Spread out in front of them were hills and valleys, a panoramic postcard with the silver strips of the southern lakes glinting here and there in the distance.

'What is it, May?' He turned to her, hoping this time she would answer, that this time she wouldn't avoid his eyes.

'You can talk to me, you know.' He waited. 'It's me. Will. Your husband. *Husband!*' He tried to laugh. 'Now how does that sound?'

But she was gazing into the woods at the side of the road.

He climbed off the bike and took her arms. 'May— Tell me what you're thinking, at any rate.'

She glanced at him, smiling vaguely. 'I was just thinking, that when you look at the grass, with the evening sunlight slanting through it that way, you can see thousands of spiders' webs. Look. Millions of strands of gossamer. All glistening.'

She could never tell him, never tell him the reason why she lay frozen in his arms, night after night. Even though she knew it filled both their minds.

She stared ahead. Clumps of pale primroses gleamed at the base of the trees. A little deeper, she could see violet-grey hints of early bluebells. When they had first talked of going to the Lake District she had looked forward to it so much. But that had been before— when she was younger. When she had been someone else altogether.

There was a silence. 'Yes, it's beautiful,' he murmured after a while, joining in her lie.

The tall, red-brick house was on the outskirts of Newcastle, in one of the more affluent areas of the city that neither May nor Alice had much cause to visit. A tall, dark-haired woman of about fifty, unsmiling and aproned, opened the door. She stared blankly at Alice for a moment, then her face relaxed.

'Mrs Sullivan. You're early. But what's she doing here?' she asked, lips tightening as she saw May. 'You said you'd be coming alone.'

Alice held out her hand. The woman reluctantly shook it. 'This is my sister. I thought I might need some company on the way home, Mrs Smallwood,' she said firmly but soothingly, rather as she might to one of Rose's children.

'Well— you'd better come in then,' the woman said with a pinched smile, as if it were against her better judgement.

The hall was gloomy, dusty, red velvet curtains hanging over the front door, a dark print of the 'Monarch of the Glen' on mustard-coloured walls, vague hints of antiseptic mingling with smells of frying. Mrs Smallwood nodded them towards a room on the left. Alice looked the other way as she passed by her. The woman seemed to have egg yolk at the corner of her mouth.

'And you're early,' Mrs Smallwood repeated, closing the door on them both. An accusation.

The mustiness of the room suggested no one had been in it for quite a while. A clock on the mantelpiece ticked importantly. A vase of plastic tulips stood at the window gathering dust. But apart from these, and a photograph of Mrs Smallwood suggesting that the woman had not aged well, the room was featureless. They could have been in a boarding-house lounge.

May sat next to Alice, glancing at her with concern. Her sister's usually pale face had turned very white. May took her hand. It felt cold. She tried to steady her breathing, fighting her instinct to get up and hurry Alice out of this place. Maybe she should—? She wished Emily were there, Emily was always calm, Emily would know what to say.

But Emily was abroad now. Alice was relying on *her*. She held Alice's hand more tightly. The day was bright, but she felt chilled.

Alice— Alice— What the hell are you doing? What's that woman about to do?

Don't think about it, she told herself. Don't try to imagine—

She closed her eyes, searching for other images to fill the silence.

On the last day of the honeymoon they set out to walk from Elterwater to Skelwirth Bridge. All around were glassy meadows, rivers, woods and waterfalls. The river had burst its banks, forcing sheep to graze on higher ground, surrounded by huge mirrors that reflected the hills all around.

They had to pick their way carefully through the flooded fields and May stumbled. Will caught her arm, but for a moment her foot was firmly stuck in the mud. They both laughed as she yanked it free, and the tension that had been with them all week was momentarily gone.

'It does get better, you know,' he suddenly said, keeping hold of her arm.

Her heart quickened, even though she had been waiting for the words, knew them to be inevitable. Lying tense beneath him that first night, she had seen his bewildered expression. Before she had been so eager. Before it had been an effort to wait. Before—

She removed her arm. 'But it's beautiful here, Will,' she answered, waving her hand at the scenery. 'It doesn't have to get any better. I think I prefer it to Ullswater in fact,' she said, her cheeks flushed.

'But it *will* get better,' he repeated quietly, sure that she understood.

*   *   *

'I got Mrs Smallwood's name from the hairdresser,' Alice said, removing her hand from May's tightening grasp. She stared directly ahead, trying not to look around, trying not to take in the dust, the sour smell, the anonymous atmosphere. 'She was different last time.'

The week before, she had been shown into a room at the back of the house that had looked like a doctor's consulting-room. There, in her white coat, Mrs Smallwood had seemed authoritative and professional.

'How late are you, Mrs Sullivan?' she'd asked, expertly feeling her stomach. 'Four weeks late? Six?'

And Alice had nodded, reassured. Mrs Smallwood had answered all her questions. She'd even shown her the steel dilator her doctor friend had made for her, especially for the purpose. She would use lots of warm water and just gently dilate the womb, she'd said. It might take a few visits before it would really come away, but she would make sure that it did.

Alice had felt reassured. It was either this woman, or the woman Rose knew, who had just used soapy water and some powder. And after half a dozen times Rose still hadn't come away, even though she'd had to pay twelve pounds by then. Little Tom, that had turned out to be. Although when he was born, you would have thought that Rose had won the pools—

Alice stared at her feet. But she had to do this. And Mrs Smallwood was just fine, with her white coat and her friend who was a doctor. She just wished they hadn't been so early. She let go of her arms and tried to relax.

When Mrs Smallwood reappeared she brought with her a smell of carbolic, and she wore a freshly-laundered white coat. She was also smiling, which May didn't consider an improvement.

'You wait here,' she said with a formidable array of teeth in May's direction. She took Alice's arm and helped her to stand as if she were an invalid. 'We'll call you if we need any help, won't we, Mrs Sullivan. It might be a little unpleasant, but it won't take long.'

Alone, May stared into space.

Oh God, Alice, Alice. *A baby.*

If only things had been different— Will would have made such a good father.

*   *   *

They walked into the woods to the sound of water rushing, she still talking too quickly about scenery, Will silent. They sat on a rock jutting out into the river, above a waterfall with emerald in its depths, while a mist blew cool on their faces, smelling of peat and leafy earth. She glanced up at his profile, luminous under the spring foliage. She would have to say something some time. She owed him that much. She would have to give some explanation.

But what? She could never tell him the truth, that she lay tense beneath him because she was frozen, transfixed by memories.

She stared at the rushing water, thinking of the landlady's delight at having honeymooners, of the pretty room in the boarding-house, of the double bed in which she lay, trying not to flinch at his touch while a jumble of images crowded her mind, blocking out whose arms it was that were holding her. A fairground, a gas lamp in a window, a stranger lying with the back of one hand across his eyes, a friend she lost, a doctor's words— and pain, so much pain.

'We don't have to if you're not ready,' Will said as she'd tightened against him the first time. 'We can wait,' he whispered, gently stroking her arms.

But instead she had closed her eyes.

'Just do it,' she'd urged, willing the memories to go.

'May?' He touched her arm. She continued to stare at the rushing water.

'God, May—' And his tone was suddenly so desperate, his voice such a plea, that she turned and held out her arms to him.

'I'm sure I'm clumsy. I will get better,' he promised quietly. And she was stung.

'But it's not you!' That he could think that— 'It's *me*! It's because— it's because I'm afraid of getting pregnant,' she suddenly rushed. 'I hate the idea. It must affect the way I feel about making love.'

He stared at her, bewildered. 'But we've talked about children. And before, you always said—'

'I couldn't have known my own mind then,' she said flatly. 'I was wrong, anyway.'

He shook his head. 'I don't understand. I remember what you said, May. I *know* you, I've known you all my life.'

He suddenly looked down at his hands. There was silence.

'It's the Italian, isn't it,' he said after a while. 'You were in love with him. And you're still grieving for him.'

He took her arms, suddenly earnest. 'I know it must hurt. But it'll hurt less with time. And in the meantime turn to *me*! Talk to *me*! I'll be there for you, I promise. If we're open and honest with each other, then in time you could learn to love me again!'

'But it's not that, Will,' she repeated quietly, willing him to believe, but instead saw his pain, and his shame.

The clock chimed the quarter hour. May looked up startled, for a moment not knowing where she was. She stared ahead, listening to the clock ticking loudly in the forbidding, silent room. Too silent. Alice— God, Alice.

She sat back, folding her hands tightly in her lap, trying to be calm.

What else could she have said to Will, that day? Maybe she could have told him the truth, that she had never loved Francesco? That she lay frozen because she had betrayed him with Joe, that as a result she would never give him the children he wanted—

Maybe he would have forgiven her.

But maybe not. And she couldn't have risked that.

After the war ended and he came back from Australia, appearing before her like a dream, just when she'd feared he was dead, miraculously still wanting her, wanting to start all over again, she hadn't been strong enough to say no a second time. She loved him too much. She'd decided then that he must never know about Joe, about her sterility. She couldn't risk losing him a second time. Better a marriage based on a lie than none at all.

She'd always known that the secret would hang between them, that there would be a distance, as a result. Will knew her too well for it to be otherwise. But she hadn't realised how hurt he would be by this knowledge that she kept something from him. And she'd seen his pain grow over the years.

So at last she had decided to speak, so that it could all be over— not realising that she was too late. Even though the bad memories had faded, even though she was no longer physically afraid, even though she'd discovered with Will a side of herself she thought she would never know, a passion whose promise had been extinguished that night with Joe, even so, she was too late.

Outside there was the sound of screeching tyres, a horn blaring, but May didn't move, didn't appear to have heard. She stared ahead unseeing. Too late— And after there had been so many moments when she could have spoken! Moments locked naked and vulnerable with love, moments when eyes at least couldn't lie, moments in which Will's touch and warmth all pleaded, *tell me, be honest with me—*

And she had always looked away.

But now she was ready! The next time, she had silently promised, as Will turned from her in the darkness. The next time she would speak, the next time she would tell him *everything*, Joe, her ridiculous pretence with contraceptive pessaries, how she had only ever turned to Francesco to lessen the pain of losing Will— *The next time!* Not realising that when Will turned from her that night, he would not be turning back again. That there wouldn't be a next time.

Instead he began spending more and more time away from her, and his eyes no longer asked questions, as if he had given up and resigned himself to the way things were. Or perhaps he simply no longer cared.

May held her arms tightly and looked around. What was she doing here, in this horrible musty place? What the hell was her sister doing such a dreadful thing for? What were any of them doing? She stood and began to pace quickly round the room. Sometimes life felt like a cruel game. If you didn't get the timing right you were punished. You had to be in the right place at the right time, and you had to choose the right words at the right moment, and if you lost the moment—

She laughed bitterly, thinking of the film she had seen the week before, the heroine, at last realising her feelings, only to be met with the hero's *'Frankly, my dear, I don't give a damn.'* If you lost your moment, then you lost your chance of happiness.

And she appeared to have lost her moment.

'No! No!'

May turned to the door.

'May!'

Alice's voice came louder, more urgent.

'May!!'

She stood hesitating by the doorway.

Unpleasant, but it won't take long, the woman had said. Poor Alice. May opened the door, then paused again. Women cried out in childbirth— maybe this was the same.

'God, no— May!' Panic rang through the house.

And hardly realising she had left the room, May was racing down the corridor, trying all the doors: a back room with the remains of a meal on the table, brown sauce, a greasy plate; a store room with bottles and linen; a kitchen, frying pan propped up in the sink; and finally the consulting-room, and Alice.

She was lying on a table with her head to the door, her legs stretched rigidly out in front of her. Red-faced, Mrs Smallwood stood holding a pad of cotton wool in one hand, while her other arm was anchored across Alice's body.

'Don't make such a fuss, woman,' she was saying as May burst in. 'This is just to calm you down a bit.'

'Mrs Smallwood!'

May crossed the room quickly and put her hand on the woman's shoulder. 'I think Mrs Sullivan is trying to tell you something.'

There was a chemical smell in the air, a sickly mixture of hospitals and anaesthetic gases.

The woman turned to her in surprise, her mouth tightening.

'There's no need for your help. I said I'll call if I need you.' She removed her arm from Alice's body and stood stiffly. 'This often happens. But Mrs Sullivan will thank me in the long run, I can guarantee you that.' She glared at May, the pad of chloroform still in her hand.

May took Alice's arm and helped her to stand.

'No she won't,' she said firmly.

'Get me out of here,' Alice whispered. 'Get me home.'

May stood close as Alice put on her underclothes and adjusted her skirt with trembling fingers.

'As I've been trying to say for the last ten minutes,' Alice said shakily, turning to Mrs Smallwood. 'I've changed my mind.' She took an envelope from her handbag and handed it to the woman.

'I'm sure it can't be the first time it's happened. And this should cover your trouble.'

Mrs Smallwood's expression changed. She stared at them both a moment, then shrugged.

'Well, if you should change your mind *again*, Mrs Sullivan,' she said, counting the money. 'You'd better let me know quick. Easier now it's early days. Any later, and aye well— It gets a bit messy.' She nodded. It was all there.

'And I shouldn't worry about today,' she said, smiling widely at the front door. 'I didn't manage to get much done.'

May sat in silence on the bus, as pale-faced as Alice. This time she would help, she told herself over and over again. She wouldn't turn away from this baby. Alice would see. Emily would want to visit more often, Rose would help. They'd *all* be there for Alice.

'Bloody enormous,' Alice suddenly muttered, staring out of the window.

'What?'

'Size of a cucumber,' she mumbled.

She made a strange noise in the back of her throat. May reached out for her hand. Poor Alice.

'And who said that size doesn't matter?' Alice went on under her breath. 'It does when it's that big.'

She suddenly turned to May with a grin.

'I lost my nerve. I raised my head, saw it coming at me, and I thought, hell's teeth, Alice!'

She made a noise half-way between a laugh and a snort. May stared in disbelief.

'Alice!'

'I thought to myself, it might be all right for the street girls down Pink Lane, but you're never going to let her put *that* inside you!' She giggled.

'Alice! You daft bugger. You had me that worried. I thought you were in shock!'

'At the sight of it from that angle I nearly was, I can tell you!'

The woman in front turned and frowned at them both.

'But you should have seen the fight I put up,' she went on in a stage whisper. 'I got her a good right kick at one stage. That'll fettle her, I thought.'

May laughed explosively and then clapped her hand over her mouth. Maybe Alice *was* in shock. But Alice was laughing openly now.

'I kicked the silver brute right out of her hand. I said to her, if she thinks her and her silver dick are getting anywhere near me—'

The woman in front tutted loudly.

'So she didn't get to do *anything*?'

Alice smiled and shook her head. 'Not an inch.' Her eyes widened. 'And there were plenty of inches, I can tell you. That long, the bloody thing was! Well—' She reduced the space between her hands from three feet to one. 'It looked like it from where I was lying.'

The woman in front got up and changed seats.

'I mean, Patrick's bad enough when he's in the mood,' Alice went on, vainly trying to keep her voice low as her laughter became more hysterical. '*If* you know what I mean. Sometimes I think, God, I'll never manage all that— But a bloody silver one? And one that makes him look like a Swan Vestas? Good grief!'

'Anyway,' she said, when they had both stopped laughing. 'I reckon there's probably a bit of life left in Rose's old pram yet, eh May? And you know Rose and her sayings, how does it go? "He that has children knows what is love".'

There was a long silence.

'Everything *will* be all right,' Alice whispered, looking down at her hands.

'Sure to be,' May answered, turning away to the window, so that neither saw that the other's eyes were wet.

When John MacIntyre arrived to pick up his wife Rose and his three children that evening, he was greeted by an unusual sight. It wasn't that his sister-in-law Alice was in bed in the early evening, although this was peculiar enough, as everyone knew that Alice Sullivan wasn't a one for relaxing. Nor was it that Rose and the children were all perched on Alice's bed, having tea in such high spirits you'd think they were on a Sunday school picnic.

No. What struck him most of all, was the sight of May Armstrong, the formidable May Armstrong he'd always thought such an unlikely sister for his affectionate wife, with tears of laughter rolling down her cheeks, hugging a thoroughly bemused-looking Tommy on her lap.

And he'd swear that he even saw her plant a kiss on the top of the bairn's head.

9

Alice

1959

Alice lay on the top of the bed, feet together in polished shoes, dress smoothed out and her hands folded tidily in her lap. She was staring at the crack in the ceiling. It went from the light at the centre, right to the far corner, a jagged grey line on white paint. Her eyes travelled up and down its length, meandered along its offshoots and tributaries, and came back to its beginning.

The attic was above. No one else used the attic except for her. Only her weight walked above this ceiling. She swallowed. But that didn't mean the crack was down to her. Perhaps it just needed a lick of paint? She'd tell Patrick. He would want to see to it straight away. Patrick liked things to be nice for her.

'Have to make the house look nice for my girl,' he'd say.

The clock ticked loudly in the silence of the morning. No one could say the crack was her fault.

Outside there was a shout, distant, but echoing round the terraces in the still air.

'Wo-a-wo-oh!'

A slow clatter of horse's hooves getting nearer, the rumble of wheels, words becoming more distinct.

'Rag and bo-ones!'

The cart rumbled by below the window.

Alice continued to stare at the ceiling, imagining the crack growing wide and black, its paint peeling back, gaping, dust falling, then bricks and mortar, until she would be left covered in rubble, with only her eyes visible, staring up into the little room above.

She would have to tell him.

'Wo-a-wo-oh!'

The call was receding, already in the next street. She had something to give the rag and bone man, the old mangle, cluttering up the garden, spoiling the effect of Patrick's carefully planted marigolds. But it couldn't be helped, because she'd missed him now. Too much to do. She continued staring at the crack.

Now tiles were falling, whirling down in slow motion on top of her, the house opening up to the sky.

'Sorry, darling,' she'll say. 'So busy today. You know how it is.' And he'll ruffle her hair and laugh. 'Always so busy you are. Never known a woman like it!' said with just a hint of pride.

Slowly she took her eyes from the ceiling. She must focus on something else. Something clear and defined. She looked to the window. The day had become silent again. But she could always catch the man next week.

She swung her legs off the bed, neatly, as if following instructions on how to get out of a sports car, and stared myopically in the mirror. Her face looked pale and indistinct. She patted her hair. Patrick was proud of the way she looked. She knew this because he said the other girls at the class were sluts.

If she asked directly, he'd laugh and tilt her chin. 'Such a bonnie lass,' he'd say.

She put on her glasses, slid them up her nose, and deliberately didn't look in the mirror again.

Tuesday. Tuesday was ironing day. She might as well make a start.

She spat on the iron. The bubble whitened and fizzled away, and she began the pushing and pressing and smoothing. Her shoes pinched and their heels were high, which would cause her back to ache after a while. But it was impossible to know when Patrick would be popping home through the day and it was important always to look one's best. It was the least he deserved, working so hard for her and the child.

'A well turned out lass, my wife,' he'd confide to his friends at that pub.

She began on the pile of shirts, aware of the scene she would present, should he drop in unexpectedly. Straight from a magazine. New-look flared skirt, hair recently permed, everything gleaming.

Modern wife in a modern kitchen. Patrick liked her to have new things. Washing machine *and* the new blue Frigidaire.

'Nothing but the best for my girl,' he'd say to those friends.

And the girls at the class were so envious.

Each shirt took a long time and there were several. Sometimes Patrick liked to wear two a day. You had to look smart, he explained, if you were going to get past the front doors. Selling insurance wasn't a job just anyone could do. She began with the top back of each, and meticulously worked her way round to the front, just as he had instructed. Twenty minutes a shirt, he'd said, or you can't be doing it right.

'A real treasure for a wife,' he'll boast to those friends at the pub.

The clock ticked and the new refrigerator hummed and at last the pile was finished. Only her daughter's clothes remained in the basket. Tiny gingham dresses in blue and green, gaily patterned circular skirts, with satin ribbons of red and blue and yellow at the hem. All made by herself. Only right that the clothing money should be spent on him. He had to go out in the world.

'My wife keeps the bairn looking perfect,' he probably says, behind her back, to whoever those people are he drinks with.

The child's clothes were pressed quickly, but with love. As she ironed, a slight scent of the five-year-old rose from each garment, lingering in the air, hovering like a ghost. She smiled and inhaled deeply. *Sugar and spice and all things nice.* Jane would be having lunch at school now. She always knew what she would be doing; her mind followed her through her day like an invisible shadow.

'A silent little thing,' her teacher had said. 'And rather grave for her age.'

The telephone suddenly rang, making Alice jump as it filled the house with its violent, demanding call. The iron caught the side of her hand. You needed butter, quickly, for a burn, but it might be Patrick. She ran into the hall.

She grabbed for the receiver before it had time to ring again. Patrick pulled her leg if she took too long answering.

'Got a fancy man with you,' he joked last time, when she'd had to run down the ladder from the attic. But it would have been said with a smile, with a wink.

'Alice? It's May.'

She closed her eyes and steadied her breathing. Of course it was May. It was ten o'clock. Rose rang at twelve, and Emily from London at six, when she could. Everyone's little sister.

'May— How are you?'

'Why weren't you at the class yesterday?' May went on immediately. 'I had to partner that bloody Lily Dodds and she's clueless. She calls clubs "the curly ones", I ask you!'

There was a pause.

'Where were you?'

'I had to pop in and see Jane's teacher,' Alice lied, knowing that May would know. She always knew.

'What's the matter with your mouth,' May asked suspiciously. 'Have you been to the dentist?'

Silence. Trying to be bothered to formulate the reply, knowing that she wouldn't be believed.

'You're speaking funny,' May said shortly.

'I banged it. Walked into the side of the door.'

She looked up at her face in the hall mirror. A woman wearing glasses, with softly waved black hair framing a pale face, stared back at her. Her top lip was swollen, a dark cut down its centre. Tentatively she put her tongue to it and tasted blood.

'You know how careless I am—'

'Oh Alice— Not again— Jesus!'

Alice waited patiently for what would follow. In her mind's eye she could see May's expression, had seen this particular expression often enough over the past five years. May didn't understand. She was sure she must be very provoking at times. Patrick wouldn't act that way otherwise.

'Oh Alice— The bastard!'

And always in the same shocked tones.

'Look. I'll be back from the library at five. Pack a case and come over. Don't even think about it. Just do it.'

'Oh— there's no need for that,' Alice said calmly, airily, watching herself speak in the mirror. Her top lip hardly moved.

'Jesus—' May repeated.

Alice continued to stare at herself. The hall was dim, but she could see that behind her glasses one eye was dark, the skin discoloured, her right cheek bone a livid purple.

'I'm fine. Really May. You know how careless I'm getting.' She attempted to laugh, the sound shrill and high in the empty hall. 'Maybe it's time for new glasses again.'

'For God's sake!'

But she knew May would leave it now. The conversation usually stumbled at this point.

'Maybe I could come over to you? He doesn't scare me, and—'

'I'm fine, I'm really fine, May,' Alice whispered, and put down the phone.

She took off her glasses. The woman opposite became blurred and featureless again. She folded them and put them away in her pocket.

Leaning back against the wall, she thought of May at work. She knew exactly where she would be standing. She closed her eyes, picturing the scene. She did this for all her sisters, imagining their days; May at the library, Rose with her house full of kids, Emily at some big swanky desk in a smart London office— It helped pass the time.

May would be in the centre of the circular room, under the clock, with the aisles of books radiating out around her. The phone was on the right of the main wooden counter. She would have a book under the ledge, and she would be glancing at it in between attending to customers.

It would be a romance, of course. May always read romances. Herself, she didn't have time for that kind of thing. She preferred crime. Whodunits. An Agatha Christie, Francis Durbridge, Raymond Chandler. Even accounts of true-life crimes. Romance she found unconvincing somehow. Strange when it was all she read when she was young.

Edward Hepple preferred crime too. It was the first thing she discovered about him. They met reaching out for the same book at the same time. She'd been dreaming and was startled, pulling her hand away as if stung.

'Didn't see you there myself,' he smiled, slowly taking his hand off her own.

A gigolo sort, was her first impression. Darkly handsome. If you liked that particular type. Which of course she didn't, being happily married. Handsome men were only interested in themselves as a rule. Apart from her Patrick, of course. Although strangely, when she thought of Patrick nowadays, it was of someone heavy, and broad, and grey. Yet when she looked, there he was, as slim as ever, his fair hair hardly touched.

Edward Hepple had taken her hand again and introduced himself, although really there had been no need. She thought him very forward and had felt flustered. She nodded and moved quickly on, so that he would see she was not someone who could be picked up, but a respectable married woman.

But he followed her, talking all the while in a huge stage whisper, despite the 'Silence' notices all over the place, so that eventually she had to move to another area of the library altogether.

'I found this for you,' he suddenly whispered, loudly, popping up in a gap in the books in front of her. She'd had to laugh.

And then, with a coincidence that made her shiver, that made her think of fate, he handed her the very book she'd been searching for. *Crime through the Ages*. The very book. And she'd been waiting months for it!

She had to speak to him then, to thank him. It was only appropriate to explain the coincidence, and having discovered their mutual interest, it was surely only polite to have coffee with him in the café on the corner.

He said he usually came to the library on a Wednesday. The store where he said he was manager – yet he was so young! – had a half day then. And she felt a mixed relief, because Wednesday was May's day off, and so Alice rarely visited the library on that day. So why not stay and have a second, and even a third cup, as he suggested. They would never meet again, so where was the harm?

The coffee bar had been noisy, smoky, full of teenagers. The waitresses all seemed to know him, hovering around as if they expected him to chat. But he only had eyes for her. After a while he stopped asking her questions. They sat in silence, she toying with a cream cake, while he smoked, watching her through narrowed eyes, with always the same amused expression.

'Audrey Hepburn,' he finally said, breaking the silence. 'That's who you remind me of. From that film *Funny Face*.'

She laughed, confused. She hadn't seen the film. Patrick and she didn't go to the cinema any more.

*   *   *

Alice walked back to the kitchen and looked in the new refrigerator. There was nothing in it. Patrick still liked her to buy fresh food daily. But he would understand that she couldn't go out today, even though everyone knew by now how clumsy she was. She would have to concoct something from left-overs.

'A great little manager,' he'd say to his friends. 'Meals like you wouldn't believe.'

And of course she had the time, because she didn't have to work. She was lucky. Emily and May both had to work. And even Rose was thinking about starting a part-time job. It made her feel special that Patrick preferred her at home. And she didn't think going out to work could really be as much fun as it sounded.

She began washing down the kitchen walls. Patrick liked her to clean the paintwork every two weeks. There was real pride to be had in housework, he said.

Before they married she had worked for Patrick's company, in the insurance office. He got her the job himself. He liked to know where she was through the day, he'd said, and that it was she who did his typing. She had liked it too. Routines, schedules, agendas, neatly typed stacks of papers to file— what's more, she found she was surprisingly good at it, creating a world of calm and order.

But when she'd been promoted from filing and typing to organising the men's rotas, and then put in charge of collecting their money at the end of the week, Patrick had suddenly become adamant.

'No wife of mine is going to work. She shall have the life of a lady,' he would say down at that pub.

Alice went out to the coal bunker and began to shovel in the new sack waiting for her. Her back hurt. Ironing in high heels, she told herself, rubbing her side. She winced. The skin felt bruised. But she wasn't going to look. He hadn't meant it. He never did.

The metal grated on the concrete. She lifted a shovel of coal and threw it, pulling her face back from the cloud of black dust. She mustn't think of it. She was sure she could be irritating at times. He wouldn't behave like that otherwise. He had said so himself.

'Do you think I want to treat you this way?' he'd shouted at one point the night before, when she tried to defend herself. They had woken Jane. Better to apologise and get it over with. Except sometimes, sometimes that only seemed to make him worse.

Tentatively she felt around her back. He couldn't have realised what he was doing. It must have been the drink. Because later in bed— She closed her eyes, swallowed. Because later in bed—

She mustn't think of it. He really couldn't have known what he was doing.

She moved mechanically. Scrape, lift, throw. Scrape, lift, throw. She should have been more sensitive, talking about her trip to the library like that, when it should have been obvious that he had a headache.

She'd thought at first his anger was due to someone seeing her with Edward Hepple yesterday. Someone had perhaps seen them together, got the wrong idea and mentioned it to Patrick. Yet she'd only agreed to meet Edward because he telephoned to say he had a book for her. And she would probably never see him on a Wednesday again anyway, even though Wednesdays had turned out more convenient for her after all—

Because afterwards, in the coffee shop, they had bumped into a neighbour's son. And the boy had given her a cheeky look. It was a fact of life. People could get the wrong idea about such things.

She'd said as much to Edward and then told him it wouldn't be a good idea to meet him at the library again. He'd gone silent and looked into her eyes for so long she'd felt herself colouring.

Then he'd taken hold of her hand, and just whispered her name. So softly. '*Alice* . . .'

'Alice!'

Startled, Alice looked over her shoulder and quickly pushed the shovel into the bunker. Straightening, she smoothed down her skirt and patted her hair.

He was in the garden in a moment.

'What the hell are you up to!' he said, striding towards her. 'I've been knocking on doors all bloody day to keep a roof over your head, and when I get home it's to an empty house, no fire lit, and is it too much to expect a cup of tea, then?'

Flustered, she prepared her face into a smile.

'Of course, pet, I was just—'

'Just look at yourself,' he said scornfully. 'Just look at the bloody state of yourself.'

Confused she looked down. Coal dust streaked her skirt. She turned her palms upwards. They were black. Tentatively she put a hand to her face.

'Yes,' he said smiling humourlessly. 'All over your ugly mug as well.' He looked more closely, as if just noticing her bruised cheek, then turned away.

'A slut. You look like a slut,' he mumbled, walking back to the house. 'Honestly, if the boys in the pub could see you— It's no wonder I won't take you.' He threw the words over his shoulder, avoiding her face. 'Couple of them reckon they have seen you, and well—' He laughed. 'You should hear the comments.'

Following behind, she flinched, stung the more because she knew nothing would have been said.

'Life of bloody Riley—' he muttered, putting his coat back on. 'Nothing to do except sit around the house, all mod cons provided, and I have to come home to something that looks like this?'

'It's just that the coal had come and— I'll get washed. Not be a minute, pet, and then—'

'Don't bother yourself,' he said, picking up his trilby and checking his reflection in the mirror.

'I'm not staying. I can get *decent* company at the pub.'

At the door he turned and shook his head wearily.

'At least try to make sure there's a meal ready when I get back?'

Alice stared at the door a while after it slammed, her mind returning to the crack in the ceiling. She'd forgotten to mention it. Then stirring herself, she gingerly applied make-up to her bruises, attempted to lipstick her swollen mouth and tied on a headscarf.

She had better shop for his supper after all.

Jane was waiting for her at the school gate, standing apart, not talking and laughing like the other children. Alice's heart sank at the child's separateness. A grave and quiet little thing for her age, the teacher had said. 'Perhaps too quiet?' the woman had added, as if implying there might be something wrong at home. Well, there wasn't. And Alice would make sure there never was. After all, they talked together, laughed a lot. And Patrick was always good to the child.

'My little girl's a right peach,' he probably says to those friends.

She hurried the last few steps and bent down to the child's level, partly to be closer, partly to avoid the inquisitive eyes of the other mothers at the gate. Jane didn't smile back.

'Are you all right now, Mummy?' she asked quietly, almost politely. The voice of a small adult. Alice's eyes blurred. She wanted to pick her up and hug her, swing her around so that the lines which had no place on her young forehead would disappear and be changed into laughter.

But Jane said the other children didn't do that, now that they were growing big. So instead Alice took the child's hand, talking brightly as they walked.

'Had a good day? Want to tell me what you've been up to?'

But the child continued to stare anxiously up at her face.

'I'm all right now,' Alice said softly, bending down so that only she could hear. 'You're not to worry. It's not as bad as it looks. And I'm going to get some new glasses so I don't do it again, eh?' She laughed. 'Good idea?'

The child looked down at her feet. Suddenly Alice swept her up in her arms.

'I can see it's been a hard day for a little girl,' she said, putting her face to the child's neck and blowing against her skin. 'So it's off for an ice-cream and then to the swings. The supper can wait. Now how's that for my girl?'

The child held her arms tightly round Alice's neck and allowed herself to be carried to the park.

Alice sat on the wooden bench watching her daughter wandering around the playground, hovering on the edges of the different groups of children. When she looked at her she saw a miniature version of herself, pale and dark, small boned, slight. 'Petite', Patrick used to call her, when they first met. Insubstantial, was how she thought of herself nowadays. Invisible even, until she got in the way and provoked his notice.

But Jane wasn't invisible. She was the most important thing in her life. She *was* her life. It would be different for her. She would protect her. Emily had said that to look at Jane you'd think Patrick had no part in her making. Parthenogenesis, she'd called it. Alice had laughed. But she felt proud and oddly comforted by the fact that there didn't appear to be a trace of Patrick in Jane. She was *her* daughter.

By the roundabout Jane had found a friend, then another, and another. And suddenly they were all talking animatedly, leaping on and off the iron disk as it spun round and round, laughing, Jane's face lit up and carefree.

Alice felt the chill inside her begin to thaw. She smiled. Her daughter wasn't grave and silent at all. And it *would* be different for her. She would make sure that it was.

Alice cleared away the remains of the meal. The child was asleep in bed.

'I'll read your story tonight then, shall I?' she'd asked earlier, as if it were unusual, as if she didn't read the story every night. But it helped create the idea that Patrick was part of the family, surely a healthy thing. 'Daddy is trying to get home in time to tuck you in,' she said most nights.

'Lovely little lass at home, waiting for me to say goodnight,' she could imagine him saying, drinking up and waving goodbye to those friends who weren't lucky enough to have a wife and child at home waiting.

But she always made sure Jane was asleep before he returned. The child would find the smell of alcohol unpleasant, she told herself.

She stood, hands in the sink, aware of him sitting behind at the table. He hadn't drunk as much as usual. Pay day was due. He still wouldn't look at her face. He'd kept his eyes down throughout the meal. But now she could feel him staring at her.

'Here,' he said gruffly, when she'd almost finished. 'I'll do these for you, if you like.'

She let him take the blue cloth from her hands, recognising the apology. He was a good man, really. She couldn't have married him otherwise, could she? She leaned towards him, expecting a kiss on the cheek, but he backed away.

'You go on up and get on with your scrapbooks and bits,' he mumbled, concentrating on the plate in his hands. 'I'll manage down here.'

She nodded, knowing he was probably embarrassed because his breath smelled of alcohol. She would have kissed him, to show that she didn't care, but her mouth was still sore.

She went up to the attic. A good man really, she repeated aloud. So it must be a real curse having a temper like that. It was the Irish blood in him, he said. She should try harder to understand.

'My wife is such a great support to me,' he'll tell his friends.

She walked across the attic floor carefully, the image of the crack on the ceiling below again in her mind.

The room was cold and bare, apart from a large wooden table under the single light bulb which was fixed to a beam of the sloping roof. On the table were notebooks and large scrapbooks, stacks of newspapers, paste and scissors. And at the centre, the pile of books that Edward Hepple had helped her find over the last few weeks.

Patrick liked the house to be tidy and uncluttered. Jane's toys and games had to be kept in her room; her own hobby materials up here. But she liked somewhere where she could work undisturbed. Patrick never came up here. He said all the dust made him sneeze. Although it was she who was prone to sneezing and wheezing.

She picked up the book on the top of the pile. *Famous Crimes of the Twentieth Century*. This wasn't a library book. Edward had said it was an old one of his he wanted her to have. But when she'd got it home, she'd seen it was obviously new. She wouldn't have accepted it had she known. She laid the book down and put her head in her hands.

'Just meet me once more,' Edward had begged. 'Let's have lunch somewhere. Spend some time together. And *then* tell me you won't meet me again. Alice, I want to be with you.'

She'd listened, twisting the ring on her finger, realising she had been expecting this from him, ever since they had first met.

But she couldn't go. She knew what lunch would mean. She knew what they were doing. She couldn't see him again. She was too afraid.

'You can, you know,' he'd said softly, as if he could read her thoughts. 'You can do anything you like if you put your mind to it. You needn't be afraid.'

And she'd looked up at him, surprised at his perception. How could she ever have thought him a gigolo, ever doubted his sincerity? So what if he had an eye for the girls, if his eye sometimes wandered and his hands occasionally strayed behind the waitresses' uniforms? It didn't have to mean he was any the less sincere with her, did it?

'I understand you. Words aren't necessary between us,' he'd whispered, taking her hand, linking his fingers through hers and staring into her eyes. 'Alice, I *know* you.'

And she'd looked back at him, tears threatening, wondering at how he knew, marvelling that he did. No! She couldn't meet him again.

There was a creak on the stairs below. She looked to the hatch in the floor. Patrick was coming up, probably to look in on Jane, to check she was sleeping. She smiled. He could be a good father, when he wanted to be.

She suddenly heard his voice, low and angry. She stared at the hatch. Jane was asleep. He must be talking to himself. But then she heard the child's voice, piping and tearful. The stairs creaked again. Quickly she climbed down the ladder.

Jane was buried under the covers.

'Janey?'

'He woke me up,' the child said emerging tearfully. 'He said I'd made the bathroom messy.'

Alice swallowed. She'd forgotten to clear the toys out of the bath. But just a couple of rubber ducks—

'And then he shook me!'

The child's face was pale, but she was tense with outrage, her tiny body rigid. Alice tried to smooth her forehead. She had never seen her daughter like this. Angry, furious even, eyes flashing, not remotely quiet and submissive. Jane wasn't like her at all.

'Never mind,' she said soothingly. 'I'll clear up. It'll only take a minute. And then we'll have another story, eh?'

The child lay back against the pillows, preparing to listen.

'He shook me hard,' she repeated, her mouth still set in anger, as Alice was about to start reading.

'Well I'm sure Daddy didn't realise it was hard,' Alice said, stroking the girl's arms. The child winced. Alice stared at her, then slowly she lifted the sleeves of the child's nightgown. Purple bruises had already formed on the white skin.

The chill hit the pit of Alice's stomach like a familiar ball, hard and round. But worse, more sickening than those moments in which she realised the inevitability of Patrick's anger towards herself. *Her daughter. He had hurt her daughter.* She stared at the child's pale limbs. For a moment she couldn't say anything. Jane nudged her impatiently.

'Go on Mummy,' she ordered, waiting.

Slowly Alice turned the pages, unaware of what she was reading.

*   *   *

121

Back in the attic she worked for a while, automatically copying out details from the book Edward had given her. She was compiling an anthology of true-life whodunits. May had joked that she ought to get it published, after all the work she put in. But it was just a hobby.

'I like the wife to have an interest. Shows she's got a good brain, an interesting person,' Patrick probably says to his friends.

She put down her pen, hardly aware of what she had written. A decadent bunch of people in Kenya, an affair, a shooting, a Lord— She sat in silence. He shouldn't have done that to Jane. He really shouldn't have done that.

She moved the books to one side. Perhaps she could concentrate better on the scrapbooks. Patrick thought she collected recipes. But inside were newspaper cuttings, stories of jealousy, despair, figures caught in eternal triangles, mostly clipped from the foreign sections of newspapers.

A French government minister, shot four times by his wife on the day he was appointed to office. The public had at first sided with the dead man. Until they heard the woman's testimony. She was acquitted.

A young Italian teacher who murdered her lover with a claw hammer, when she found out he'd been unfaithful. She too was acquitted.

Another Frenchwoman, provoked beyond endurance. Another shooting. Frenchwomen seemed to have an easy access to guns. Not an acquittal this time, but a nominal sentence.

Slowly Alice turned the pages. She didn't talk about this aspect of her hobby. It wasn't important. It was just a collection, like any other. It could just as easily be stamps.

But still she couldn't concentrate. She closed her eyes. *Patrick shouldn't have done that.*

She picked up a newspaper from the top of the pile and began scanning its pages. Most of the papers May collected for her from the library contained little of interest. But after a few minutes she paused, surprised to find a story so quickly, and a local one at that. Most of her cuttings referred to France and other Latin countries, as if the English weren't hot-blooded enough for the *crime passionel*. Or perhaps it was because there seemed to be relatively little leniency in Anglo-Saxon courts. Too much *sang-froid* for sympathy, perhaps.

A year ago they'd actually hanged a woman in London, a nightclub manageress who had shot her lover. Alice had deliberately chosen not to clip this story. But she could remember every detail. The woman, Ruth Ellis, was only twenty-eight, younger than herself. Standing in the dock, making the law even more hostile with her proud peroxide rinse and lipsticked mouth. They would have preferred her to look broken, of course. They had not understood at all.

'He only used to hit me with his fists and hands, but I bruise very easily,' the girl had said. No one could have heard. No one had read between those lines. Hanged her by the neck until she was dead.

Briskly Alice reached out for the scissors, cut around the local newspaper article and pasted it on to a new page in her scrapbook. Then, feeling cheered, she tidied the table, put away the glue and neatly stacked the pile of books with her present from Edward Hepple at the top.

She smiled. She must remember to thank him for the book when she met Edward for lunch on Wednesday.

10

May
1959

May had discovered two new things that morning. The first was a crumpled receipt from a restaurant she had never been to. The other was a lump, a small painful nodule, midway between her armpit and her right breast.

She'd found the former amongst the loose change, emptied from her husband's pockets on to the dressing-table (on to her best scarf, blue silk, Italian, a gift from Francesco), along with a dirty handkerchief, some toffee papers and a leaking ball-point pen.

She'd found the lump when she was soaping herself in the bath.

She smoothed out the receipt. It was from two nights ago. But Will had said he was at a union meeting that night. She stared at the piece of paper, her mouth drying as its implications sank in.

She was only shocked, she told herself after a while, not because he was being unfaithful to her, and perhaps *again*, but because he could be so casual about it. Or was it a Freudian slip, his leaving it lying around? Three pounds he'd spent on whoever she was—

May threw the receipt contemptuously back on the dressing-table. She would leave it there. Let him see that she'd found it. Let him sweat. And this time her blind eye would be reluctant to turn.

Her fingers moved in a circular motion over the tender area at the side of her breast. It was the time of the month. That was all it was. There was no need to worry. It felt nothing like the lump she had the last time. And even if it did, they had said she was clear.

Briskly she began to tidy the room, moving faster and faster, cramming Will's ties into the drawer, stuffing his trousers in the wardrobe, hurling heavy shoes in after them, until there wasn't a masculine trace left visible. Panting, she stopped and looked around, momentarily satisfied. Will wouldn't be able to find a thing now, of course. But after this, she glanced again at the crumpled paper, she would be asking him to move out of the room tonight, anyway.

She checked her watch – still an hour before she had to leave for her hospital appointment. And slowly the panic began to creep up again. She noticed a pair of his armbands lying on the dressing-table and quickly threw them in the drawer, slamming it shut. Ridiculous. There was nothing to be afraid of. Her breasts had been tender before. It was just the time of the month.

She sat on the edge of the bed. Opposite on the dressing-table stood her wedding photograph in its carved mahogany frame, showing Will in what looked like a demob suit, herself wearing a long white dress, tiara and veil, half-hidden by a huge, trailing bouquet. The dark flowers she carried were roses, her favourite flowers. Will had said he would always give her roses from that day on. There had been none in the house for over a year now. Red roses, dozens and dozens, surrounded by long trails of ivy—

You could tell that the photographer had taken too long taking the picture. Her darkly-lipsticked mouth was stretched into a smile, yet her eyes looked blank. But he had caught Will turning to her with that special look, a look he reserved for her alone, soft with tenderness. It was this look she had chosen to frame. But like the roses, it was a look she hadn't seen for a long while.

I won't bother you again, May, he'd said. It's up to you now.

Her eyes blurred and she picked up the photograph. But what could she say to a back that was always turned to her in bed? She'd tried to be a good wife. Yes, there had been things she could have spoken of, and should have, she knew that now. But she had always loved him! They had companionship, a mutual respect. Surely she had a right to expect his fidelity!

She looked down at the photograph. Blank-eyed, like a doll whose eyes open and shut as you pick her up and lie her down. But that was not how she had felt that day. After all that had gone before, the wedding had seemed magical, too good to be true. As make-believe as the games she used to play with Alice, pretending to be princesses, slipping into their mother's high-heeled shoes that with a whisk of the imagination became golden slippers, donning huge, faded print frocks that instantly swirled into silk ballgowns, old curtains tied round their necks transformed into velvet evening capes— But the wedding vows had been real.

'Now you really look the part,' Alice had whispered, trailing behind in peach satin, as the wedding march struck up. 'You're so lucky, May—'

And so she had thought. So she had thought.

May began to rock herself gently at the edge of the bed. Well, Will Armstrong was acting like no prince now and the hell with him! If she didn't have his support, she didn't need this. Not now. And not, despite his protestations, again.

'But you're talking nonsense!' He had affected shock, when she confronted him the last time, a year ago, just after she found the first lump in her breast. He denied having an affair, had an explanation for everything.

'There's only ever been you and you know that, May,' he finally said, refusing to discuss it further.

She put back the photograph and her fingers automatically returned to the side of her breast. No need to worry. The doctor would probably laugh at her concern. And in another hour she would be laughing about it as well.

She picked up a book from the bedside. She would refuse to give Will, or anything else, another thought. She turned pages, words swimming before her eyes, trying to concentrate, but the plot was thin, the dialogue painful, the heroine annoyingly pale and surrendering. Her eyes scanned the pages, unseeing. She would confront him tonight! She would tell him to leave! The last time he'd said she was using her accusations as an excuse, that something else lay behind them, that something else was upsetting her. 'I know you,' he'd said. 'You're panicking over something, May.' But he would have said anything to wriggle out of his guilt!

She put down the book. She should stop reading these romances. They only upset her. It used to be Alice who read romance, not her. She only read them because they were light and easily put down, she told the girl she worked with. But the truth was, the hero often reminded her of Will, and the descriptions struck echoes, so that sometimes, just sometimes, there'd be a trace of something she remembered from before the war, when Will and she had been happy, before Joe, before secrets, before—

She put a hand over her eyes. She should stop reading them,

would stop. She didn't think she knew what love was any more, anyway. She could remember years ago, a feeling that made her so happy it had also made her afraid, as if such intensity, by definition, had to end. And so it had.

She held her arms tightly. Crazy to think back to that time after all these years. Crazy to feel the need for Will she was feeling right now, when he might well be out with some other— She didn't want to know! Their relationship had to be over!

No need to worry, she told herself. No need to panic. The doctor would tell her it was nothing. The doctors had said she was clear. She hadn't told Will when she'd found the first lump. In fact, he had known nothing of the operation. Instead she'd said she was going to spend a few days with her cousin Mary, in Liverpool. He had been surprised, knowing there was little love between her and her cousin. But she hadn't wanted to worry him. She had been thinking about *him* when she lied, trying to protect *him*.

Yet it was when she returned home from the hospital that he'd turned from her so completely.

'It's up to you now, May,' he'd said after she related a few half-hearted tales of Liverpool. And there was a note in his voice she hadn't heard before.

I won't bother you again, he'd said. It's up to you now.

May closed her eyes. The last time the doctors had just removed the lump— If he loved her so little now, how would she feel if worse were to happen? If this time it had to be more?

It had to be over. *Then he would never have to know.*

She touched the area of the lump again. But maybe it would just go away of its own accord? And maybe it wasn't so hard and defined as it had felt earlier? For a while May just sat, staring ahead in the silence.

'Take off your things, put them on the chair, and the gown opens at the front,' the nurse instructed, brisk and capable, a maternal smile, for all she couldn't be more than twenty.

May obeyed automatically, as she had obeyed the previous three hospital staff she had seen.

Complete this form.
Roll up your sleeve.
Fill this bottle.

Obeying each without question. It was the doctor she would question.

She folded her clothes and placed them on the chair, neatly, as she never did at home, like a dutiful child, as if the antiseptic smells and anonymous green walls stripped away adulthood, along with personality. She put on the gown and sat on the bed, swinging her legs, studying the pattern on the cubicle curtains. Or was it the attitude of the staff that made her feel regressed into childhood each visit. The nurses with their *there, there nows*, as she retched painfully coming out from anaesthetic. Or the doctors with their *good girls* as they took blood from her veins.

She turned from the curtains to the mirrored cabinet above the sink. She had forgotten to put on any make-up. Her clean face was palely freckled, her dark-red hair loose around her shoulders. She even looked like a child. She should be wearing plaits.

But she was thirty-three years old. And yet too young for all this! This wasn't right. Her body looked little different from when she was younger, so how could this be happening inside it? It felt like a betrayal.

No need to panic, she told herself again. No need to panic—

But it wasn't fair! It was like being told that you'd passed an exam and then someone coming along and demanding a re-mark! You should be clear now, they had said!

The doctor was surprisingly young, fresh-faced, seeming just past the pimple stage. But the needle he wielded was large, of comic-strip proportions, looming in front of her so that she had to turn her head away, shocked.

'Well done,' he said withdrawing it carefully from the painful area in her breast. 'All done now.'

All done. Words Rose and Alice used for the children, lifting them off a potty, drying them after a bath. *All done.* God, was she all done?

They would study the cells he'd just taken from the lump, he explained. Then they would know whether they should operate or not.

'Find out whether or not we want to go in and have a look,' he said with forced jollity.

She flinched. He made her sound as if she were a museum of dubious interest.

'And the cells will tell us if it's benign or not.'

'You mean it might wish me well?' she said with a small attempt at a laugh. The doctor looked at her, alarmed. She smiled to reassure him. He was only young.

But of course it would be benign. It had to be.

She put on her clothes and then quietly asked him her questions, looking him directly in the eye. See me as a person, her look ordered. But he answered her shortly, uncomfortably, as if she were prying into something that didn't concern her, and referred her instead to the consultant who would see her next time with the results. Then he took refuge in his notes, scribbling indecipherably.

The library was quiet. There were only ten minutes to go before it closed.

'You'll lock up?'

May nodded.

'Sure you don't mind being on your own?'

May ushered her colleague to the door with mock exasperation. The girl had left at this time every night for the last two weeks, ever since May first started doing the night shift at the library, but each time they went through the same conversation.

May smiled. 'I'm quite sure. You know how things are. There's not a great deal to go home to at the moment.'

The girl gave her a sympathetic look, but quickly left before May had a chance to change her mind. She had a date.

May returned to the main counter. She liked the library in the evenings. It felt calm and peaceful compared to the afternoon sessions, and working both shifts meant she had less time to think. There was still another week before she would know the results of the test.

The library was also infinitely preferable to the silence that existed at home. Will had refused to leave. He'd moved out of their bedroom eventually, reluctantly, but he'd said he wasn't leaving the house. As before, he denied having an affair. And as before he had seemingly plausible explanations. He even professed to be worried about *her*, said that she was acting out of character. He said that something else must be bothering her. He pretended such concern! Holding her hands, saying she could tell him anything. But it was all tactics. He was just trying to turn the tables, to divert the focus from his own guilt. He'd even suggested she was acting hysterically, she, who hardly raised her voice!

Their relationship was over. It had to be. Will had to see it. And if he wouldn't leave, well, maybe she would have to find a way to make him go.

A book was slid over the counter towards her. It was late, almost time to close. She hadn't seen anyone approach. She looked up, surprised.

Him again, the Jack the Lad with his smooth, slow smile, showing his nice, white teeth. He hadn't missed an evening at the library for the last two weeks.

'I'd like to take this out, please,' he said, his voice warm and insinuating, as if everything had another meaning. A master of the *double entendre*. He'd been flirting with her in an increasingly open fashion over the past few days. She smiled and took the book. She'd met his type before, many times. At first she'd ignored him, but then she'd thought, why not? He helped to pass the time. Over the last few days she'd even encouraged his banter. He made her laugh.

She looked at the title of the book. And what would it be tonight? *Early Greece: The Bronze and Archaic Ages*. She looked up at him questioningly.

'An archaeologist,' he whispered, in confiding tones.

She laughed.

Yesterday it had been *Snakes and their Habits*. Much more appropriate. A real snake if ever she saw one. A herpetologist, he'd said he was, as she stamped that book out. She'd seen him using the dictionary before he brought it to the counter.

The day before it had been *A Geological Exploration of Rock Formations in the Yorkshire Dales*.

'Speleologist?' she'd asked and he'd looked at her blankly, but then swiftly recovered, nodding wisely, so authoritatively she'd had to laugh. Quick, as well as handsome. A real Jack the Lad.

He leaned over the counter towards her.

'I'm a cultured well-read man of catholic taste,' he announced in a thickly fake Yorkshire accent, as if his broad Tyneside wasn't convincing enough.

She pressed a purple-ink stamp on the sheet in the book.

'Well, you have two weeks to add this to your "culture",' she said, copying the accent, knowing the book would be back tomorrow, to be replaced in favour of some equally obscure title she had no doubt he would find. And she would look forward to it. He was becoming a bright spot in her day.

'You're a fast reader, I'll grant you that.'

'As fast as they come.' He gave her a pantomime wink.

She shook her head and turned away. He'd asked her out the night before. And the night before that. *And* he'd seen her wedding ring.

Aware of his eyes following her around the room, she began to check the aisles. There were only a couple of people left in the library, elderly men who smelled in need of a bath, both asleep in the newspaper section. She was reluctant to wake them, but they would have to go, and no doubt back to empty and probably cold little rooms. But they would be back tomorrow. They always were.

She shook them gently, and began to gather up the scattered newspapers as they stirred themselves awake. She collected the papers for Alice, who had recently taken up an interest in current affairs. Poor Alice. Things must be bad. Guiltily, May made a mental note to call her younger sister. They had seen little of each other recently.

'Time to shut up shop,' she said with a smile to each of the men. They both looked slightly lost and befuddled with sleep. They rose stiffly and made for the entrance, each going a different way. They never spoke to each other. Each evening she intended to introduce them, but there never seemed to be the right moment.

There was a cough behind her. She turned and saw him standing by the cookery section, watching her. No doubt he would be a chef next. She tapped her watch pointedly and nodded in the direction of the door. Time to lock up, she mouthed. But he pushed back his long hair and leaned against the shelves, arms folded, one leg over the other, looking as if he had all the time in the world.

'Time to go!' she whispered loudly.

Frowning, he put his fingers to his lips and pointed to the 'Silence' notice above her head.

She turned back to the counter, smiling despite herself. Well, maybe she would let him walk her home after all this evening. He was funny and young, he made her laugh, and, God knows, she could do with a breath of fresh air.

She sorted through the tickets in the long wooden boxes, watching him from the corner of her eye. She knew nothing about him. They had communicated in a series of whispers, silences, raised eyebrows and funny faces. And book titles. The night before it had been *Be Mine Tonight*, snatched away before she had time to stamp it, and when she didn't respond, *The Long Night of the Soul*.

He was out of work, she knew that much. She'd seen him scanning the jobs pages when he thought he was unobserved. And despite his hints suggesting a white collar job, she could tell that he wasn't an office worker. The hands that pushed those unread books across the counter were calloused, their fingers nicked. Nor the mines. His skin was tanned, setting off those seductive blue eyes, and didn't he know it. The shipyards she reckoned as the most probable. The Swan's yard had laid off a stack of men recently.

She gathered up a pile of books to be returned to the basement. All the same she would let him walk her home. And if Will didn't like it, well, that couldn't be helped. In fact if Will didn't like it, then so much the better.

The basement was dimly lit and dusty. May made her way carefully through broken desks and other assorted pieces of furniture that never got mended but the council wouldn't allow to be thrown away, stepping over boxes of cleaning materials, a vacuum cleaner, a floor polisher, and began arranging the books on a shelf on the far wall.

There was a click behind her, followed by the sound of footsteps on the stairs. She stood waiting, unsurprised. A real Jack the Lad.

Hands touched her shoulders. She turned. He was smiling down at her with his toothpaste advert grin.

'Mrs Armstrong,' he whispered with mock gravity, taking pins from her hair and shaking it free. 'My, but you're beautiful.'

She laughed out loud, shocked yet amused. He was outrageous.

'Mrs M. Armstrong,' he murmured, emphasising the initial shown on the nameplate, and bent his face to hers.

May still felt amused. No other man had come close to her since she married Will. She'd forgotten what it was to flirt, to enjoy the sense of complicity.

'M for Mary— or is it Margaret—' he whispered, kissing her lightly.

Still with the smile on his lips, still the mischievous child, carefully watching her face, waiting for any rebuff, kissing her ear, her neck— She laughed, but now she would stop him.

She tried to speak, but he pressed his mouth over hers. For a moment she hesitated, then softened. She owed Will no loyalty, not after what he had done. It was over. *It had to be over.*

She allowed him to kiss her again. And if Will wouldn't leave— she let him pull her closer— well maybe she should show Will that she had left him.

He picked up her arms and placed them round his neck.

'We must go,' she said, not moving, as his hands slid over her body.

'We shouldn't,' she said, as his fingers pushed up her skirt.

A few deft movements, a pull of her hips, before she realised, before she even thought it possible—

Her eyes opened wide with surprise. She almost laughed. But as he leaned her back on to the broken table, moving deeper, his face became serious.

She couldn't be doing this, she thought, as books, coffee cups and inventory forms were roughly swept to the floor. It had to be a dream, she told herself as he moved more urgently, the table creaking and groaning in the silent, dusty air. It wasn't happening, she breathed, holding on tightly as her body began to respond in a heated rush, which turned all her thoughts to Will.

'Enough,' she whispered.

But the slow smile returned, and the creaking and groaning continued, so that she cried out, moving against him with a violence of her own, aware that by doing so she was breaking something, something she told herself Will had already broken, so that things would never be the same again.

'Oh Mrs M. Armstrong,' he said, nuzzling her neck, and looking at her with such a stupid grin that she had to laugh.

The hospital letter was dog-eared and creased. It had lain in May's handbag for days, burning a hole in the lining, and in her consciousness, with its presence. She ought to throw it away. It merely confirmed what the consultant had said. That they thought it best to operate. Her lump, apparently, did not wish her well.

The consultant had answered all of her questions and said a good deal more besides, so that whereas last year May had managed to make light of her illness to herself, she found she had not now that option.

She was struggling with its reality. It felt like an unwelcome presence, an unasked for companion, persistently dominating her thoughts through the day so that the rest of the world became cloudy and dim; at night weighing heavily at the front of her mind, so that everything else seemed lightweight and distorted.

And in the mornings, half-conscious, aware of the discomfort at the back of her mind, trying not to know it, trying to keep it back, it would nevertheless move inexorably forward and resume its place of priority.

Never before had she felt so alone, or afraid. Face to face with her own mortality, yet without the courage to look.

She thought perhaps that if she confided in someone it might help. That if someone else knew, and someone else cared, maybe she would feel less alone. If someone else understood how frightened she felt, maybe she could then feel less so.

But she knew who it was that she wanted to tell, who only it was who could comfort her. And that was no longer possible, or appropriate. Which meant there was no one.

To tell Rose or the girls at the class would be to broadcast. Emily was back in London but seemed to have retreated more than ever into a world of her own. And it was not something you could tell your lover, not when he was as rakish and irresponsible, albeit as sweet, as hers was. Which left Alice, perhaps. Alice was and always would be her little sister. But perhaps there was Alice.

Alice sounded surprised when she answered the phone.

'But it's not our usual day to get together,' she laughed hesitantly, making May feel confused, and guilty, because it was weeks since they'd spent any real time together.

'If you're busy it doesn't matter,' May said, feeling obscurely hurt. Alice usually leapt at the chance to see her, was always grumbling that they saw too little of each other. Or used to be—

'No, no,' Alice protested. 'It's just that— on Wednesdays— Maybe you could come tomorrow?'

'Yes, of course,' May answered brightly. She put down the phone, wondering, and not for the first time, how guilty she was of taking Alice for granted.

*   *   *

135

Alice moved around her spotless kitchen, carefully made up and smartly dressed, even though her day consisted of nothing more that May could see than doing the washing and collecting her daughter from school. She'd tried repeatedly to persuade Alice to consider a part-time job. But she preferred it at home, Alice always insisted unconvincingly.

After the telephone conversation of the day before, May had been prepared to look carefully for signs that Alice was offended in some way. Ever since they were children, Alice had had the capacity to develop and sustain huffs, sometimes so mysterious in origin that May often only understood how she had offended when they were over. But Alice greeted her as enthusiastically, and as affectionately, as ever.

May watched her sister making the coffee. Alice was looking well. Her face looked different somehow, rounder, healthier, as it had been when she was pregnant, its angles and lines smoothed out, even her eyes were brighter.

May wondered whether Patrick was treating her more kindly. She doubted it, but it had been a while since there'd been any trouble. Alice certainly seemed less diffident, and happier. In fact she was almost glowing.

A thought suddenly crossed May's mind, but she dismissed it instantly. She knew Alice better than that.

They exchanged news and then lapsed into silence. May fiddled with her cup as her heart began to beat more rapidly.

'Alice. There's something I need to talk to you about—'

She stopped. The words sounded stagy, melodramatic.

Alice turned from gazing out of the window.

'Mmm?'

May paused, searching for the language that would fit.

'Alice—'

But Alice's attention had slid back to the window.

May shook her head, half-laughed. 'Alice?' This was not how she'd thought the conversation would go. Alice didn't even seem to be listening. She'd only once seen her like this before, dreamy and preoccupied, when she was expecting Jane.

'Please. I need you to listen.'

'Has Will finally agreed to go?' Alice asked, head on one side, trying to adopt a sympathetic attitude, although May knew she was totally against the separation.

'No, not yet. It's not that.'

May sat in silence, choked with unsaid words. How did you tell someone you'd always taken for granted that now you needed their support?

May looked at her anxiously. How did she tell her sister about this?

'I— I don't know how to—'

'What is it, May?' Alice asked, some sixth sense suddenly alerted. 'May?' She focused intently on her face.

May looked at her sister's anxious expression, the sister who had been there for her all her life, the sister she perhaps hadn't cared enough about recently, and the words wouldn't come. She looked down. Maybe now was the time to care more about Alice. Alice had enough pain in her life, married to a man like Patrick. She couldn't tell her.

She laughed shortly. 'It's nothing so terrible. Don't look so worried. It's a new man, that's all.'

Relief and surprise spread across Alice's face. Eyebrows raised, a half-smile on her lips, she waited for May to continue.

'He's a bit of a Jack the Lad, but sweet for all that,' May went on breezily. She couldn't tell her. Not yet. Once they confirmed it had to be the more drastic surgery, maybe then.

'I met him at the library, would you believe. A classic of the species – hunky, handsome, and doesn't he know it. A real Bella D'Arcy special. Except that he's only called Ted. Well, Edward on Sundays.'

Alice's smile seemed to waver a little.

'Yes?'

'Edward Hepple. He wants me to get engaged, of all things, once Will and I are finally divorced— Alice?'

The cup crashed, the coffee swirled around the new formica table, trickling steadily down on to Alice's immaculately pressed dress, but Alice didn't move. May rushed for a cloth, watching her sister anxiously. Alice's colour had drained away. She was sitting wide-eyed, holding on to the edge of the table.

'What is it? Are you ill? Alice?'

'Really, I'm fine. Don't fuss, May,' Alice said, moving like a sleepwalker up to her room. May arranged the covers over her and sat by her side, hesitating over what to do. Alice lay calmly staring at a crack in the ceiling.

'You're sure you're all right? You don't want me to fetch the doctor?' May asked a third time.

Alice closed her eyes and shook her head.

'I'm fine. You just go. *Please.*'

May quietly let herself out of the house. She'd bet a pound to a penny that Alice was pregnant again. But she wouldn't press. Alice would tell her in her own time. But she was sure that must be it. Which made her all the more relieved that she hadn't spoken.

Maybe you just had to cope with some things on your own, she told herself brightly, but feeling more alone and afraid than ever.

II

The Class
1968

Once a month my mother gets 'done'. This involves a trip to Fenwick's in Newcastle, to the beauty salon. The recipe is always the same.

1   Take one mother. Yank out bits of her eyebrows while she sits red-faced with the effort not to scream.
2   Next, tear hairs on her legs out by the roots with the aid of molten wax.
3   Then take hair on head, twist around metal spiky rollers, douse with a liquid that smells like a baby's nappy after a particularly productive night, and finally, roast said mother under a nice hot drier.

And apart from the pain lines that appear on her forehead, and that line where the hairnet's been that makes her look as if a completely new top has been added to her head – sausagy curls and all – she never looks any different.

She says that now I'm growing into a young lady (yu-uck) I should go with her. She wants me to have a perm. (My grandmother made her watch Shirley Temple films at a formative age.) When this fails she tries to tempt me with the promise of finery, ho-ho.

'But fine feathers make fine birds,' she says, giving my old jeans and shirt the once over.

'All cats are grey in the dark,' say I.

Her mistake was to give me a proverb book for Christmas.

'But clothes maketh the man,' she insists.

'And handsome is as handsome does,' I counter gleefully.

I'm as good as my aunts at it now.

All the same I agree to go to Fenwick's. I've discovered a corner of the book department where you can sit on the floor unnoticed. Last month I managed to read four chapters of Harold Robbins. Today I'm hoping to get to the 'good' bits.

But when we're half-way to town my mother says, 'You know, our Megan, when I'm in the salon you could go down to the lingerie department and see about getting that bra we talked about.'

I stare out of the car window. *She* talked about. I only listened.

'You're growing into a young lady,' she says cheerfully. 'You'll have to get one some day.'

I swallow hard. The corsetiere is a huge conically pointed woman who looks like a poster I once saw at the Theatre Royal for Wagner, no sense of shame or modesty, and there's no way I'm going to subject myself to the pushing and pulling she inflicts on my mother. I don't need a bra anyway. If you wear a really tight vest, and then a sloppy joe, no one can tell.

'What about Gran's?' I ask. 'Couldn't I go there instead?'

I know my grandmother has a class today, and I haven't been to the class for ages – I peaked at cards at an early age – but needs must, etc.

'I thought you hated cards,' she says, bobbing for my face in the driving mirror.

'Oh that was ages ago,' I say, refusing to feel guilty. This is survival. Necessity being the mother of invention, and all that.

'Megan!' the girls all coo. I turn my head away as each tries to kiss me, although I don't mind kissing Alice, but I have to hug her carefully because she's so thin. She's going to be the next Twiggy, she tells me. About eight of them have arrived. I flinch under a continued onslaught of Revlon's 'Crimson Kiss', 4711 Cologne and Coty's L'Aimant.

'Just her age,' my grandmother says, raising her eyes to heaven as I escape to the garden.

'Being mean, moody and magnificent, Megan?' May says as I pass. As if she's a one to talk. 'More flounces than on a frilly blouse, eh?'

'Megan? Come and make up the numbers, there's a girl,' my

grandmother yells. I've amassed a huge caterpillar collection and I'm now unsure about what to do with it.

'Megan!' she shouts, and it's an order, so I put all the caterpillars into a cabbage right at the back of the row and go into the house.

Uncle Will, my grandfather, and Alice's Pat have arrived. I kiss my grandfather, for a moment feeling guilty about his cabbage, but he pulls out a chair and tells me to sit next to him. Uncle Will and Pat aren't going to play cards.

Then Aunt Emily arrives. I haven't seen her for a while. I stare at her while she's taking off her coat, trying to understand why she always looks different from everyone.

'What suit are we in?' someone asks.

'Crimplene,' I say and giggle. It's true. Bobbly-patterned in pastel blues, lemons and pinks, as if they were all huge babies. But not Aunt Emily. Her dress is silk.

I watch her sorting her hand. Age is a funny thing, I've discovered. Once I thought anyone over thirty-five was old, but now I see there are varying degrees. But I don't understand where Aunt Emily fits. She's much younger than my grandmother, of course, and she's older than Alice, who, confusingly, is nearer my mother's age, but Emily seems younger than all of them. In fact, she's the same age as May, and look at her. May's the size of a house at the moment. She's so fat Gran has to put a cushion behind her back to make her more comfortable.

The room grows hot, because the sun is streaming in through the window and the fire's been lit. Everyone takes off their cardigans, and I see that even Aunt Emily's skin is different. The girls' arms are all white and a bit crêpey at the top, but Aunt Emily's are golden, with a sheen, although no one's that colour in Newcastle in April. I decide to ask about the brown arms later. I also decide to do a poll amongst the girls after tea so I can ponder this age thing further.

We play rummy. It's a doddle, and after four hands I've got the second lowest score. If I'm off next time, I'll have won, and it's not just because my grandfather is looking out for me.

'How are your mother and father?' Aunt Emily asks with a polite smile adults don't usually give kids. She doesn't know this, however, because she's never married and has no kids. My mother says it's because she's a hot shot at the Ministry in Newcastle and has to work too hard.

I tell them one or two uninteresting things as quickly as possible, because I want them to get on to *me*. I want to tell them about winning the competition and it's not the same if I have to bring it up.

'What's wrong with her?' Aunt Emily asks, when I say my mother's been to the doctor. Everyone is suddenly interested. They like things to do with health. All year they've been discussing Gran's operations. She was in Newcastle General for four weeks in February. They kept taking bits out of her. If she hadn't left when she did, I reckon she would have died.

'Just women's problems,' I say dismissively. 'You know what *they're* like.'

They laugh at me but I don't mind.

'Have *you* finished at the hospital yet, Alice?' Gran's neighbour asks, and I raise my eyes to heaven. They're off. No one will ask about *me* for ages now. Being 'bad with your nerves' is one of their favourites. Alice has been seeing a specialist to talk about her nerves, but Gran told me that was a secret.

'Last visit next week,' Alice says, with a bit of a laugh, though I can't see that it's funny. 'Then I'm through.'

Everyone goes quiet and Alice begins to sip repeatedly at her tea, which I suspect is something else.

'Ee, lass, what a to-do,' says May, changing the subject back to my gran's operations as she deals out the cards.

As we play, I imagine rows of jars, clear, sweet-shop jars, each containing a bit of my gran, strangely shaped, grey-yellow and waterlogged, like the appendix in the biology lab at school. And I'm so busy imagining this, I lose the hand. May has won the game. May bloody would.

She turns to me sharpish. 'And what about you then, Megan?' she asks. 'What have you been up to?'

She narrows her eyes against the cigarette she's had to stick in the corner of her mouth, because she needs two hands to scoop up all the pennies she's won. *My* pennies. 'What have you been doing?'

'Well—' I say.

This is my opportunity, but I wish someone else had asked. They're not even all listening. Alice and May begin arguing about the score. I wait until they've finished, pretending to fasten my sandal under the table.

'You can't bloody count,' May mutters finally.

'Says who?' Alice counters.

Then they laugh. But I can remember a time, years ago, when they had really nasty rows. Although May always seemed a bit bewildered by it all. They don't ever fight nowadays. Maybe as you get older you lose your fighting spirit, along with gall bladder, spleen, womb, etc.

'Well,' I say, appearing from under the tablecloth. 'Not much. But I suppose I did win a competition.'

'Did you, pet?' Alice asks, turning to me, and I know she's only done this because she can pointedly turn her back on May, but attention is attention.

'It was for writing a story,' I tell them.

'What did you win?' Pat suddenly asks from over on the sofa. Pat is always interested in *things*. He does competitions to win *things* and he likes to know how much people's furniture costs.

He makes Alice keep the house *immaculate*. She's always working at it, polishing and washing his things. Earlier I overheard him tell May that too much housework was the cause of Alice's 'nerves'.

'Well, why do you make her do it then?' I asked, although I still can't see the connection.

They both ignored me.

'Is *that* what you reckon?' May snorted back at him, in a tone that stopped everyone else's conversations dead.

I decide I'd better be a lousy housewife when I grow up, just to be on the safe side. Hate to be whisked off to the funny farm because I'd been caught ironing the sheets.

'What did you win?' Patrick asks me again.

'Well, I didn't win anything,' I admit reluctantly, wishing like mad I could tell him ten shillings. 'But it'll get published in the next school magazine.'

'And what was it about, dear?' Aunt Emily asks, gathering up the cards and shuffling them with a ripping sound like some maverick card sharp, which is funny when you look like Aunt Emily.

'It was about a fox,' I begin. Everyone's looking at me expectantly, apart from Pat who begins chatting to Uncle Will again, and suddenly I feel quite cheerful.

'You had to make up a story that showed all the things a city fox might be. You know, crafty, territorial and things?'

143

Alice nods and laughs as if I've told some huge joke. It's definitely sherry in that cup.

'Well, this fox is very crafty. On the outside he's quite beautiful, with a chestnut glossy coat and a thick brush which is going a bit white because he's quite old, and he has very blue eyes.'

'I don't think they have blue eyes, dear,' Aunt Emily says, dealing out cards with her beautiful hands. I watch and make my three hundredth resolution to stop biting my nails.

'But on the inside, he's really horrible,' I say.

Alice laughs again.

'He only *pretends* to be good to his family. But he's not. Not one bit—'

My voice trails off. I suddenly look over to Pat.

'Go on, pet,' May says.

I swallow. 'Well, after he's hurt one of the cubs,' I say more quietly, 'the other foxes find out, and they chase the man away, and he never comes back again.'

'Fox,' May says.

'What?'

'Fox, not man. You said man.'

'No I didn't.'

I look over to Pat again. He looks up, sees me and gives me a pantomime wink. I look down and pick up my cards. My hands are shaking.

'Fox,' I say, quietly. 'My story was about a fox. They live in communities, you see. They drive out bad foxes.'

I glance up. He's talking to Will again, and when I turn back May is still watching me. She looks at me hard, then looks across to Pat. I suddenly flush.

'Here,' she says roughly, reaching out for my cards. 'I'll sort these for you.'

'A dance?' I repeat, staring at Gran's over-bright smile, sure that I cannot have heard correctly.

The tea is over, the men have gone to the pub, and the sherry bottle is out. In fact, while I've been reading upstairs, I suspect several sherry bottles have been out. *All* the girls look flushed and there's a lot of cackly laughter going on.

'Here, Megan,' says my grandmother, sticking her cigarette in the corner of her mouth and getting hold of the table. 'Help me move this over to the window. And May, no, better not May, Emily, you can move those chairs to the side— yes, there— that should be enough room.'

'But here?' I say incredulously. 'You can't dance in here!'

But my grandmother is already stacking a pile of records on the Dansette which has appeared on the sideboard.

'Loads of room,' Alice says, standing and beginning to sway to some imaginary, and irregular, beat. 'You can partner me if you like, Megan,' she invites, beaming at me with her turquoise-lined eyes slightly out of focus.

Good grief, I think, thoroughly alarmed. My friends would kill themselves laughing if they ever got wind of this.

'I just need to freshen up,' I say, making for the door, hoping no one will notice, intending to go back to my books.

'I'll be with you in apple blossom time,' the Andrews Sisters chime out. The girls begin to pair off, Crimplene bust meeting Crimplene bust.

'I'll be waiting to change your name to mine,' Alice croons, a good two beats ahead of the music.

I'm slipping out of the door when May appears behind me.

'Good idea, Megan. Could do with a freshen up myself,' she says, following me up the stairs. My heart sinks.

She stands behind me at the dressing-table.

'I used to have long hair, you know,' she says, picking up one of the silver brushes and brushing my hair. She begins to plait small sections of it.

'Really?' I'm trying not to cringe too visibly. I'm going to look really stupid. I knew I shouldn't have come. Brunhilde and her bras at Fenwick's would have been better than this.

'Oh, it was a long time ago,' she smiles, looking a bit dreamy. I stare at her. May! Dreamy! She's *definitely* been on the sherry.

'Megan.' She lifts her head from the plaiting and looks directly at me in the mirror. 'I liked your story.'

There's a pause. Another plait appears. Oh my God, I think.

'Has Pat ever bothered you?' she suddenly asks.

This is so unexpected I don't know what to say. I flush.

'No,' I say quietly. 'I don't know what you mean.'

But I know that somehow she knows. Even though I'm not sure exactly what it is she knows.

145

She smooths the hair back from my face, affectionately, like my mother does, which makes me feel even more bewildered.

'Well, you just tell me if he does,' she says quietly. And then she becomes brisk. 'There you are. What do you think of that now?'

I look at my reflection with surprise. I like it. In fact I love it. I look like a hippy, vaguely romantic, straight out of San Francisco.

'Bet you thought you were going to get something stuffy like a French pleat, didn't you?' she says with a wink. 'Back to the dance now?' And she goes to the door, even though she's not freshened herself up yet. 'Ready?'

I turn to thank her for my hippy hair and suddenly stop. She's standing in profile, one hand to the small of her back in a gesture I've seen in other women when— I stare. Her stomach is big, but her arms and legs aren't fat at all. And then I'm blushing at the craziness of the thought, while she waits, eyebrows raised, an expectant smile on her lips.

'Yes—?'

I clear my throat. 'Ready as I'll ever be,' I say, feeling suddenly confused about a whole mass of things.

'Snowball, pet?' Alice asks, pouring from the bottle of Advocaat I usually see only at Christmas. She adds lemonade, stirring it to a froth, and plops in a sticky glacé cherry which immediately sinks to the bottom. I beam at her. I've already had a glass of sherry. My face feels very warm and it's permanently smiling. I take the glass and lick the froth from the top and then stick in my tongue, but I can't reach the cherry.

The girls are still dancing. I've danced with everyone except May, who said that if she took the floor there'd be no room for anyone else.

'Let's put on something modern for the bairn. Some of the stuff that *she* likes, says Gran, and I smile happily at them all. I had no idea that my grandmother had the Rolling Stones and the Incredible String Band.

'*Got myself a crying, talking, sleeping, walking, living do-oll,*' the Dansette blares out. '*Got to do my best to please her just cause she's a living do-oll.*'

I giggle.

146

'Ee, that nice Cliff Richards is such a canny lad,' Gran says, and they all take to the floor again.

The table and chairs are back in the centre of the room, the ash tray and glasses are in place, and everyone is chatting. I've never seen the girls like this. They're so funny! Nearly everything they say is making me laugh. Especially the rude bits. I didn't know old ladies knew jokes like that.

'And what do you call that, she says to him. A Swan Vestas?' May beams, triumphant with her punch line.

Everyone roars. I do too, although I haven't a clue what they're talking about. I decide to store it away for when I'm older, however, and then suddenly I remember my plan to do 'The Age Poll'.

'What's it like being old?' I ask everyone, with a grin.

They all look at me surprised, and then a few of them laugh.

'Easy on that snowball, our Megan,' Gran says, but it doesn't sound at all like a warning. I sit beaming at them happily, waiting for their answers.

They're all looking at each other with sort of wry smiles on their faces, and for a moment I wonder if I've maybe been tactless, but then everyone starts talking at once.

'Well, it's a funny thing,' says my grandmother, when the noise has died down. She's the eldest, and so it's right that she should start. 'You don't so much slip into old age as it creeps up on you. Or so I've been told,' she says, with a wink to the girls.

Everyone laughs.

May pours herself another sherry. 'It's strange,' she says, putting her elbows on the table and her face on her hands. 'You imagine you're young and lovely, and then you look in the mirror and it's such a surprise. All these wrinkles appearing, and inside you feel like you're thirteen.'

I can't imagine this at all. I'm thirteen now.

'When I was leaving the library the other day,' Alice begins softly, and everyone listens. 'I met this group of girls – I knew a couple of them – they must have been on their way to some do. They were all about nineteen or twenty. You know. Girls of that age so pretty they don't even have to be pretty.'

I laugh at this, but no one else does.

'And I was laughing and talking away to them, not aware of being in any way different, and when I got in the car and looked in the driving mirror, there was this old woman looking back at me. I got such a shock—'

I wait for her to finish, but she doesn't.

'Well, who was it?' I ask.

May reaches out and takes her hand. 'It's just because you've been poorly, Alice,' she says quietly. 'Soon you'll be right as rain. Then the weight will pile on, you'll see. You'll be blooming again before you know what's hit you.'

Everyone goes silent. I glance at May. I've never heard her talk to Alice like that before.

'So nice to have a dance,' Gran suddenly says, changing the subject. 'What's the best dance you've ever been to?' she asks, turning to Aunt Emily.

Aunt Emily looks at her, surprised, as if she's never danced in her life.

'She only ever went to dances to listen to the bands,' Alice says. 'She just used to stand there dreaming through the warm-up numbers, and then left before the action started.'

Aunt Emily frowns at her, but in a joking way. She puts an arm round Alice's back. I watch them, thinking, they're sisters, and wonder what they must have been like when they were girls.

'Well, as a matter of fact the best time was— August 1945!' Aunt Emily suddenly says with a laugh. 'I was in London, walking home when the streets began filling up with people, cheering, laughing. It was the end of the war, you see, Megan,' she says turning to me. 'And people were dancing. I got caught up in it. I was trying to cross Piccadilly Circus, and then next thing I knew I was dancing the Conga! With everyone. Soldiers with soldiers, Americans, Polish, Dutch, Czech— all together! An international Hokey Cokey it was.'

Everyone laughs, but softly, not the cackly sort.

'That was special— But maybe the best time—'

She stops and stares into space. This is an Aunt Emily I've never seen before.

'I used to dance in Cyprus, under the stars,' she laughs, then sounds far away. 'But that was privately. Not at a dance—'

Cyprus, I think. Good grief. And I've always assumed the girls have never got further than Newcastle.

'And who was that with, Em?' May asks, with a wink to Gran and Alice.

'Oh, someone special—'

'Always the enigma, eh, our Emily?' Alice smiles.

'Is that where you've got your brown arms from?' I ask.

Everyone laughs. But Aunt Emily turns to me, surprised.

'Well, as a matter of fact it is,' she says, looking at everyone as if they didn't already know. 'I go there each spring.'

And from the way they're looking back at her I can tell they didn't know this. My Aunt Emily must be a real dark horse.

'Why?' I ask.

'Megan,' my grandmother warns, but everyone's looking interested, and so I can tell they all want to know.

'Because of this special person,' she says with a slow smile.

'A foreigner?' I ask incredulously.

'No, not a foreigner.'

'And does he ever come to see you here?' I ask.

'No, I'm afraid he can't do that,' she says, examining her beautiful nails.

'But why?'

My grandmother gives me a look I can't fail to understand. I shrug. I was only interested.

'Because—' Aunt Emily suddenly seems far away again. 'Because we got caught up in something— and now he's not here any more.'

I shake my head. I don't understand at all. Why on earth does she go to visit someone who's not there any more? But then she looks up at me, and her eyes are so sad, and then I understand.

'I remember my special moment,' May says, after a long pause.

But I'm not going to ask any more questions, I'll wait for someone else to ask, and so instead I just smile over at May, as if we've got a special secret between us. Which we haven't of course. It's strange because in some ways May seems the same as ever, but I really like her, so how can that be?

'I was at the cinema,' she says, dreamy again. 'We used to go as often as we could during the war. It kept your spirits up. Will was in the RAF. One of the Brylcreem Boys, they called them then. We'd lost touch with each other— Anyway, he'd got through it all, but then he was sent to Australia. The war against the Japanese lasted longer than the war in Europe, you see, Megan.

'We'd lost touch, but I was in constant contact with his family, but then they lost touch with him too. And everybody began to fear the worst—

'Well, there I was watching the film, thinking about him – months it was without a word, not a word from him – and suddenly the screen goes blank, and a handwritten message comes on it. *Will May Charlton please return home immediately*, it says.'

May's voice goes very quiet.

'And I think, oh no, God. Please no, God. And I just sit looking at this message, unable to move, thinking, please not, when he'd got so far— not to be taken now, not before I'd ever had a chance to tell him—'

'Tell him what?' I ask, but she doesn't answer.

'So I stand up, heart hammering, make my way out, past all those people looking at my message, all knowing what it must mean— And when I get outside— there he is. Just standing there. Brown as a berry. Smiling. Waiting for *me*.'

I laugh. It's a great story. I look around expecting everyone else to laugh. But they're all looking misty-eyed. God, they're soppy, I think.

'An excess of sentimentality, girls,' I tell them in my headmistress's voice.

'Megan, in wartime everything sounded like an excess of every-thing,' Aunt Emily says to me with a smile, but I don't understand.

And then suddenly *everyone's* got a story to tell, and I sit there listening to their *Ee, o-ho! Ee o-hos!* – I swear if a foreigner landed in a group of Geordies he'd think we'd all been taken over by donkeys – and I feel really warm and happy and it's not just the sherry. I want to get up and hug each one of them. I feel a bit choked in fact. And as I look at them all with my smile that won't stop smiling, I think I'm never going to miss an opportunity to come to the class again. Not ever. And as for that Pat—

Well, I think, the hell with him. If he ever comes near me again, I'll— I'll—

I look to each of my aunts in turn, and then I smile. I'll set the girls on him, that's what I'll do.

And I continue smiling at no one in particular, until I realise they're all looking at me, and laughing.

'Bedtime, our Megan,' says my grandmother, ruffling my hair.

12

Emily
1965

'Watch the edges of that piece,' the foreman instructed as two tattooed youths swung out of the room carrying Emily's inlaid walnut bureau. 'It's a valuable piece of furniture, you great dolts, not a bleedin' sack of spuds.'

'Sorry about that, Miss,' he said, aware of the colour in his face, again. He'd never had a customer like her before. He'd thought she must be in the films when he first saw her, a right stunner. But no, the lady had laughed, she was just an office worker.

'Watch it!' He wasn't going to let any of *this* customer's possessions be damaged. He'd carry them all himself if need be.

He stared at her, trying to think of something else to say to keep her attention, but she turned back to the window. He scanned the floor, wishing there was more. All the room contained now was a small cardboard box of papers.

'That seems to be the lot in here then,' he said, hearing his voice come out loud and jolly, as if he were delivering the punch line of some joke.

'Mmm—' She continued to stare down into the cobbled mews where two young men were hoisting her bureau on to a removal van. Dobson's Haulage. Distance no object.

The foreman hesitated then strode purposively through the other rooms of the flat.

'Yes, that's the lot,' he repeated, returning and examining the room once more as if a piece of furniture that had been eluding him might suddenly give itself away.

'There's always more than you reckon, eh?'

She turned from the window. 'Sorry?'

'I said there's always more than you reckon,' he repeated lamely, the heat rising up his neck again. 'Not *us* of course, not more than *we* reckon, after all that's our job, to reckon, no, but you, well no, not *you* exactly, but you know, the customer reckons—'

'Yes, there's always more than you think,' she said.

He stood, unable to look away, unable to get a word out. There was a noise behind him. Gratefully he turned and saw that one of the hired kids had dropped the box of papers.

'No, not those.' Emily moved swiftly forward. 'I'll be taking those with me.'

He bent with her, catching her perfume, and his mouth dried. His hands moved mechanically. A notepad, a bundle of old airmail letters with USA stamps, beige file, a faded photograph of what looked like a coloured baby, another of four young girls – one red-haired, another small and dark, an older girl, all laughing, except for the tall, skinny blonde kid at the end who looked as if she'd been excluded from the joke. He paused at a third photograph. It showed a slight, dark-haired man smiling against a hard, blue Mediterranean sky. He had his arm tightly around the lady, while she laughed at the camera, her face all lit up. The foreman felt an unaccountable pang of jealousy.

Quickly he placed it in the box and reached across for a bunch of newspaper clippings held together by a bulldog clip.

Cyprus violence escalates, read the cutting on top. Her arm accidentally brushed his. He stared at the newsprint unseeing.

Security forces fail to root out EOKA terrorists— How did you get to know a woman like this?

Another bomb exploded this afternoon in Nicosia— He would love to ask her out—

The extent of the damage is not known— She would say no, of course, but—

A search of the nearby buildings revealed a further three bombs— He might never have the chance to meet such a woman again.

—while further threats of violence— She was putting the last papers in the box. He'd have to be quick.

'Thanks. I'll take these with me,' Emily said, standing just as the foreman reached a hand out to her. She looked down in surprise as he overbalanced. 'So I'll see you at my new address tomorrow afternoon. About three? —You said?'

Down below in the mews the lorry hooted. He stumbled to his feet.

'Well, have a good journey on the train,' he said, his voice coming out higher than he had intended. He nodded.

'Three o'clock, Fenham, Newcastle,' he said, still nodding, eyes fixed on his customer's face, deciding that green eyes had to be the most beautiful, especially accompanied by that complexion, and hair the colour of—

Emily raised a hand in warning as he bumped back into the door frame. Flushed and miserable, he turned and left.

Emily watched the tattooed boys grind out their cigarettes and jump into the cab of the lorry, followed by the rather odd foreman with his red face and strange voice. Perhaps he was drunk. She hoped her possessions would be safe enough.

She waited until the van had pulled out of the mews, then transferred the contents of the cardboard box to a leather grip and slowly looked around.

'End of an era,' she murmured to the empty room, and then left without a backward glance.

The seat Emily had reserved on the Flying Scotsman was occupied by a heavy, middle-aged woman in tweeds who was staring fixedly out of the window, perhaps through genuine interest, at the bustle on King's Cross platforms, but Emily suspected more to avoid eye contact with the person who had actually reserved the seat the woman was occupying. Emily cleared her throat and waited, but the woman simply leaned forward so that she could better watch the altercation that was breaking out between two couples trying to commandeer the same porter.

Emily frowned, then deliberately shrugged off her annoyance and walked on. The last thing she wanted was an altercation herself. In fact, if it were possible, she hoped to spend the next six hours without so much as a word to anyone.

So it was unfortunate that after several minutes of searching, the only carriage in which she could find a spare seat was occupied by a woman with a struggling infant on her lap, and four other excited children of varying ages.

'Going to Edinburgh?' she asked before Emily had time to sit down. 'Susan, move that bucket and spade so the lady can get to her seat.'

A girl of about ten grinned up as Emily placed her grip in the overhead rack. Emily looked down to see a trickle of sand run into her shoes.

'And Robert, get your feet off the seats.' The woman reached over and gave a small boy an unconvincing cuff to his ear, which nevertheless set up a wail that seemed out of all proportion to the child's size.

Emily shrank inwardly and toyed with the idea of going back and confronting the tweed-armoured lady. The journey was to take six hours.

'Edinburgh?' the woman repeated.

'Just as far as Newcastle.'

'Far enough. Although I love a journey. We've just come up from Bournemouth, been up since the crack of dawn this lot, staying with my sister and her brood which meant there were nine of us and honestly—'

Emily sat back and fixed the smile on to her face. Six hours—

The woman talked without pause until they reached the first station, and then suddenly, as if by common agreement or at some secret sign, the children settled down quietly. Books and comics were produced and two of the smaller ones closed their eyes. Finally the talker herself came to a stop with a contented sigh, as if she had got something out of her system. She sat back and gazed out of the window, stroking the head of the sleeping child on her lap as if it might have been a cat.

'And do you like travelling?' she enquired after several minutes' peace. 'Do you travel much?'

'No, not really. The last trip I made was returning home from Cyprus.' Emily smiled weakly. She preferred to keep details of her life strictly to herself.

'Cyprus?' Her companion waited.

'I was working out there,' Emily added reluctantly. 'I was there for quite some time.'

'A bit different from grey England, I'd imagine,' the woman laughed and moved the infant to a more comfortable position so that she could take up her knitting. It was obvious that she now considered it Emily's turn to talk.

'Very different.'

Emily hesitated, and after a few moments she began, surprising herself by the ease with which she could talk to this stranger.

'Diddleydee, diddleydah,' the little boy murmured next to her, in time to the click of the train on the rails. He moved closer and leaned warm against her, settling himself for sleep.

'Diddleydah diddleydee,' he whispered as the train changed track.

It was spring when she arrived. She was to be based in the city of Nicosia, but she'd been booked into a hotel on the north coast for the first two days. The old taxi bumped along the road, hazy and warm with early morning sunshine, and turned up a pass leading towards the Kyrenia mountains. In the back seat Emily sat braced against the vehicle's lack of suspension, trying to meet the driver's desultory conversation with a few words of recently learned coffee-shop Greek. At these poor attempts at his language the driver's attitude changed and his diffidence was replaced by an eager account of his family, which amounted to what seemed like hordes of relatives living scattered among a hundred villages.

Emily struggled to understand his broken English, but eventually the old man appeared to get caught up with his own momentum, and it was enough that she smiled and nodded at the weathered face that occasionally fixed her in the driving mirror.

The view either side was open, a clear, blue sky above the vast, flat plain of the Mesaoria. It was a bright, spring-green now, but soon would take on the scorched tones of the summer. Wild flowers lined the sides of the road and smells of thyme and orange blossom wafted in on the breeze along with diesel fumes from the old car. Behind them Emily could see misty outlines of the spinnerets of the cathedral in Nicosia, the fountain points of the Grand Mosque.

The old car began to struggle and spit as they climbed more steeply and the driver hunched himself forward over the wheel, as if by doing so he might impel the vehicle upwards.

'You stay at the Dome?' he asked, when they finally reached the top of the pass.

She nodded.

'Then you must look up my sister,' he said, taking a bottle from the front seat and offering it to her over his shoulder. 'I will give you her address. She and her husband make this – one of the best wines in Cyprus. Try!'

Emily hesitated. It was only ten thirty.

She shrugged. She wasn't in England. '*Endaxi*—' She raised it to her lips.

They passed through a small whitewashed village, brilliant with sunshine, groves of almond and peach blossom, silvery olive trees.

ENOSIS AND ONLY ENOSIS was daubed in black paint on the side of a run-down house. On another, the letters *EOKA* and *DEATH TO ARMITRAGE*. Further on, *LIBERTY OR DEATH*, and *THE BRITISH MUST GO*.

'But of course we like the British,' he said, half-apologetic, half-embarrassed, catching the direction of her gaze in his mirror. 'We don't want them to go. We want them to stay. But as friends, not masters.'

Emily could glimpse sea through the carobs and olives. A shepherd herding a flock of goats waved as they passed.

'My cousin Spiros,' the driver shouted, relieved to change the subject, and was off once more on the litany of his extended family.

Of whom, by the time she'd been dropped off at the hotel facing the ragged Turkish coast, Emily had the addresses of no fewer than five.

'It sounds wonderful,' the woman opposite beamed, moving a sleeping child further along so that she could place the baby on the seat too. 'Now me, I've never been out of England. Couldn't go far with this lot, could you really, but one day—'

The baby seemed to be on the point of waking. She took a teat from her bag, sucked it a moment and pressed it between the sleeping infant's lips.

'And you worked there, you said?'

Emily nodded. 'Five days a week. At the Public Information department in Nicosia. A beautiful old building full of mirrors on the edge of the Turkish quarter—'

'There's a new chap out from London,' her boss told Emily as she finished typing the last report of the day. She doubted anyone would pay it more than passing interest. Nowadays the news from her office was not what the government wanted to hear.

'They want you to go out to Government House and brief him. He's staying a couple of days at the lodge before moving to Nicosia. From the Foreign Office. He's coming as a diplomat of course, but obviously with intelligence links. I can't see why he can't get all the info he needs when he arrives here in Nicosia,' he grumbled. 'But you've been specially requested to go out and brief him on his arrival, although why it should be so bloody urgent—'

She'd packed and gone before anyone had a chance to change their minds. It was high summer, hot and dusty in the city, and the only breeze Nicosia felt was for an hour each evening just before the sunset. Government House was in the Troodos mountains. There it would be cool.

And she hadn't suspected at all. Why should she?

'Hot and dusty,' the woman repeated, pushing her knitting, long and multi-coloured, and without bearing any resemblance to any garment Emily had ever seen before, along its needles. 'We almost went to the Med. one year—'

'But it was cooler in the mountains,' Emily murmured, as if talking to herself. 'Occasionally I would attend a meeting with the Colonial Secretary – the HQ was in the Troodos. The air was cooler there—'

'Come in.'

Emily adjusted her glasses and straightened her skirt. She was to brief the whole board, but she was prepared. She turned the handle and walked in.

Her eyes went to him immediately. He was sitting at the middle of the large oak table, flanked on either side by government officials.

Behind her someone said her name.

She couldn't see his face clearly. Sunlight was streaming in through the huge stained-glass window directly behind him, making a bright halo of his dark hair, darkening his features, creating a negative of him. But she knew him, would have sensed his presence, even if it were pitch dark.

'Miss Charlton?'

The Governor was to her right, pouring coffee into small cups laid out on a heavily carved sideboard.

She took the offered cup, hardly aware that she did so.

When she looked back, the sun had passed behind a cloud. Now she could see his face clearly.

James.

'And did you enjoy your time there, dear?' the woman asked, producing a Thermos and pouring two cups from it. All five children were now out for the count. The boy next to Emily had snuggled closer, laid his head on her lap.

'I did. Very much,' Emily nodded. She paused. 'I spent most of it with someone dear to me.' She smiled, surprised at the ease with which she could make this admission, she who told no one anything.

The woman settled back to listen.

James.

She had left London without seeing him again. There had seemed little point. She had told him that morning at her apartment that their relationship had to be over. And so it had.

Maybe she should have contacted him before she left, told him how she felt, admitted that she wanted to stay with him. But they had given her no other choice. She'd told herself it would be better to write to James instead, not realising how difficult, how impossible that task would prove. Even though his face had filled her nights for months, occupied every spare moment of her days, she hadn't been able to write, to find the right words. She'd decided instead she must take the first leave home, face to face she would be able to explain. The first opportunity—

But now here he was. Looking back at her with unsmiling eyes.

'This is James Goldman,' the Governor said, motioning her to take the chair opposite. 'From the Foreign Office. Maybe you came across each other in London?'

Standing and shaking her hand with a cool politeness that had never been there before.

'Yes, we have. Only briefly unfortunately,' he added and laughed, unperturbed. 'You know what they say about it being a small world.'

And then turning to her easily, still the courteous stranger, 'So Miss Charlton, I believe you're going to get us up to date on the situation as your office sees it in Nicosia?'

Such a cool smile. But there was perspiration on his upper lip— patches forming beneath the arms of his khaki shirt—

How had she got through that afternoon? Had she delivered the briefing well? She couldn't remember what she said. They wouldn't have listened anyway. The government persisted in seeing Cyprus as a minor colonial problem that had to be dealt with, or as an unsinkable aircraft carrier, a strategic link in a chain of telecommunications. They refused to take the worsening situation seriously.

She told them that the protest on the streets was becoming less juvenile, more informed, and James listened intently. Then a final firm, cool handshake, while her own palms were damp.

She'd waited on the terrace after the meeting, hoping he would come to her, hoping there would be some explanation of his coolness, other than that which the formality of the meeting dictated.

She'd waited, watching the sun sinking fast, while swifts and swallows were replaced by bats darting round her head, and moths fluttering against blossom grown luminous in the twilight. But still he hadn't come.

She'd returned to Nicosia the same evening, declining the Governor's invitation to stay. And so she hadn't received James's note, and didn't know then the effort that meeting had cost him.

'And who was it? Was it a man, the person that was dear to you?' the woman asked, curious, years of child-rearing obviously undoing any awareness of social restraint.

'A foreigner, maybe?' she asked, without giving Emily time to answer. 'How romantic. When I was younger, before all this lot—'

Emily shook her head. 'No. He wasn't a foreigner.'

She'd spent the next few days in turmoil, trying to lose herself in work, barely leaving the office, immersing herself in any activity, as long as it was continuous, anything to obliterate the memory of James's coolness and the unsettling fact that he was there, on the island, and maybe only a few miles away.

159

It was obvious that he didn't want to know her. He had barely acknowledged their friendship.

But what else could she have expected? She had rejected him, callously it must have seemed, without a backward glance. Letters never sent, the leave home to explain never taken— And now it was too late. He had made that clear.

She thought she would have preferred hostility, even bitterness. At least that was personal. But such cool politeness— that was what you reserved for strangers.

On the Friday evening she walked back to her quarters via the market, lingering in the bustle, reluctant to go back to an empty room, reluctant to begin a weekend without the prospect of work to distract her. She stopped at one of the stalls and bought fruit, figs, cherries, a bag of oranges full of foliage off the tree from which they'd been picked. The market rang with voices and bustle. She stood eating cherries, watching. She ought to be careful. An Englishwoman, the wife of a soldier, had been killed here the week before. A recent EOKA pamphlet had promised 'to shed the blood of English and Americans'. She looked obviously foreign. She should go, not linger here. She scanned the crowd for faces that might give cause for concern.

It was no longer a case of mosquito raids by well-mannered sixth-form boys and girls, whipped up by local clergy rhetoric. In place of home-made grenades and Molotov cocktails there were now professionally made time-bombs. And they were placed more ruthlessly. When the bomb had gone off in Nicosia police station the street had been crowded with market visitors. And the week before Ledra Street had been rocked by a series of explosions.

She should go. Reluctantly she moved, but then paused, staring again into the crowd. She turned away feeling foolish. Now she was seeing him in daydreams too. She walked on a moment, but then turned again. Her heart began to beat faster. A flash of part of a face, eyes that she knew well—

Slowly she began walking back, as more of the face became visible, then a shoulder, a raised arm, brown eyes fixed intently on hers. Faster and faster, until she was struggling against the crowd, pushing and apologising in equal measure, never leaving the eyes, bobbing her head this way and that as they were obscured— But always they came back to meet hers.

And then rushing, pushing towards the figure that had finally appeared, that was running towards her, calling, shouting out her name.

James—

Tactfully the woman on the train looked away and busied herself with one of her sleeping children as Emily closed her eyes. Emily breathed steadily, unaware that she was smiling. She'd recollected the scene so many times, stored it up to be produced at all the bad moments, the good moments, the lonely moments, until it was engraved on her mind with the precision of a photograph. The market in the background, stalls closing, crowd thinning, and the two figures in the foreground, holding each other so tightly, as if their lives depended on it. She with her hair fallen loose, laughing, or was it crying, and James, his smile warm.

'I told you I wouldn't let you go as easily as that,' he'd whispered, holding her face in his hands. 'I warned you I'd be back.'

Emily opened her eyes. The woman had produced a book. She turned to the window. It was getting dark. Her own reflection stared back at her. She looked through it to the darkening landscape. They must be nearly there. They had already passed through York. Almost home. Just another hour.

Home. She smiled wryly at the word. She'd never thought of the North-East in that way before, would never have believed the day would come. She'd changed. And it was her time with James that had changed her.

She watched the dark-blue countryside rushing past the window, punctuated by occasional farms and the longer glare of a sudden town.

Diddleydee, diddleydah—

They'd had three years of happiness, years she didn't remember in the way she did other periods of her life. Her time with James was like a mosaic, made up of a thousand bright images— Turkish domes, deep blue Greek skies, herbs in old petrol tins, lemons heavy on a bough— And so many precious moments. Sitting at a café in the port, sweet Turkish coffee swinging towards them on pendulum trays, watching his profile, struggling with the effort not to touch—— while all around the world continued, fishermen repaired their nets, soldiers wandered in the cool air, children laughed and played under the battlements, while the sun set behind the castle walls and dipped into the sea. And later, lying exhausted in each other's arms, the twilight of a darkened room—

They'd driven out into the mountains one evening, escaping telephone calls and bomb alerts, the now nightly gauntlet of grenades and raids. The Kyrenia range lay in soft blue folds, stretching away into the dusk. He'd said they should stop to watch the changing colours, had made her sit on a hillside and try to guess where the sea ended and the sky began. And as it grew dark, his voice became serious. She listened, fixing her eyes on a star overhead, imagining the light in the sky condensing to this one point, everything in her life condensing to this one moment.

Turning to him, pushing back his hair, seeing his eyes soft and serious with love as he waited for her answer, she'd laughed.

'Yes,' she whispered, to the question he'd asked once before. 'Of course I will.'

'And did he return to England with you, dear?' the woman asked, glancing at Emily's ringless hand.

Emily shook her head. 'No. No, he didn't.' That was as far as she wanted to remember. She seldom went further than this in her mind.

'He didn't? But why? Sounds to me like you were made for each other.'

Emily hesitated. 'He died. He was killed out there.'

She swallowed, as if the words had bruised her mouth. It was the first time she'd said them aloud, the first time she'd told anyone. She closed her eyes, waiting for the pain to grip her, waiting for its familiar fierceness to overwhelm.

But it didn't come.

Moments passed. Emily opened her eyes.

'He was killed by a bomb,' she said quietly.

Then the words began coming quickly, fluently.

'He had a meeting at the Turkish Press Office. June 1958. We had arranged to meet for lunch in Nicosia. We were to plan a special weekend. We had something to celebrate.

'I was sitting at the café on the far side of the square when I heard the explosion.'

A deafening noise, cleaving the air, felt with her body as much as heard. Hot air rushing her face. A sudden silence— Then trying to stand, dust and masonry falling, everything slow-motion, half-stumbling, half-running, shouting out his name—

'EOKA terrorists. They'd bombed the building on the other side of the square.'

Pushing against unyielding bodies running in the opposite direction from hers, shrugging off a hand, wrenching herself free from an arm that was trying to detain her—

'The bomb took out the press office completely.'

Standing in front of where the building had been, eyes unbelieving, as the dust settled around her like a shroud. She'd whispered his name, knowing he would never hear it again, and then heard the scream, without realising it was her own.

'He would have felt nothing, they told me. The bomb was sited under the room where he was.'

'I'm so sorry, dear.' An arm moved across. Emily looked up. The woman was stroking her hand as if she were one of her children. 'How awful. How dreadfully painful for you.'

Emily nodded slowly. 'Yes. It was. For quite a long while.'

But now it was over.

The children all clambered on to the seat trying to get a look at the photograph Emily had produced. Faced with nothing more exciting than a picture of four girls standing in a row, the younger ones went back to their sweets and comics.

'My sisters,' Emily explained, amused with herself, that she who never gave anything away, was rocketing through her life history with a woman she'd never met before and five sticky-faced children. 'And that miserable-looking kid's me.'

'Her daughter is your age,' she told the eldest child, pointing to Alice. 'She is called Jane.

'And her *granddaughter* is your age,' she said turning to the ten-year-old. 'She's called Megan. Scottish, like you. Well, her name is, at least. Her grandfather's a Scot.'

The woman took the photograph from her. 'You're not very alike, any of you, are you?'

Emily reached over. 'I grew up with those two,' she said pointing to Alice and May. 'This one, my eldest sister Rose, was up and off as fast as she could. Our mother was a bit of a harridan.' She laughed, hearing herself say the words, marvelling that she could.

The woman talked about her own family for a while, then asked more questions. So Emily told her about May, and how she suspected that May wasn't as happy as she made out, which didn't make sense because she was married to a good man whom she loved.

But Alice was a different matter altogether, she told the woman. She too wasn't as happy as she would have the world believe. And this was much more worrying.

Emily thought back to the telephone conversation she'd had with May the week before. Alice had been caught taking something from a shop without paying. She hadn't been thinking, she'd explained to May, but the police had been called and it had taken a lot of talking to persuade the shopkeeper to drop the charges.

May had been half-ill with worry, but the strange thing was that Alice had merely laughed it off. It was as if she'd *wanted* to be caught, May said.

'They're lucky having a sister that cares,' said the woman, beginning to gather up the children's possessions scattered about the carriage. 'So that's why you're going home?'

Emily was about to mention her new job at the Ministry in Newcastle, the transfer she had applied for and got, but then she stopped.

'No,' she said. 'It's not because they need me. We've never been as close as we should have been. My fault, I'm afraid.'

She looked out of the window. The train was slowing down. They were crossing the river.

'I think it's maybe more that I need them,' she murmured.

'Roots,' nodded the woman approvingly. 'We all need roots.'

Emily looked down at the tar-like depths of the Tyne. Roots? Did she need this place? All her life she'd fought against the idea, tried to escape it, and now, here she was. Going back to the North-East, and calling it home.

'Maybe,' she smiled at the woman.

Whatever the reason, she no longer felt the need to fight, to struggle to be free. She had learned to let go with James; that had been freedom. It wasn't an escape to a different place, it was something she'd found in herself.

Emily picked up the photograph of her sisters, and her eyes rested again on Alice. She must have been about fifteen when it was taken, tiny, dark-haired, her outline blurred because, knowing Alice, she'd probably been unable to keep still. She was smiling, radiant, looking as if she would never have a care in the world.

The most recent photograph Alice had sent Emily showed the same pretty girl, a little older, but with the same hair, same figure, even the same smile. But Alice's eyes had been blank.

13

Alice
1968

Alice picked up a hammer.

She positioned a nail over a small pencilled cross she had just made and hammered it in with a few even strokes. She then reached down and picked up the picture lying against the bedroom wall. It showed a woman with long, dark hair, swept up but dishevelled, as if she'd just got out of bed. Except that she couldn't have, because she was leaning against a tree, was draped around the tree in fact, her face an uneasy mixture of innocence and knowing.

'Just the thing for the bedroom,' Patrick had said.

The woman had hung there for years, unageing, the tops of ever-firm breasts exposed, staring out of the frame through half-lowered lids, full lips parted. A red-haired woman and a blonde usually hung either side of her; Patrick had varied taste. But Alice disliked them all equally, these women with their open mouths and knowing eyes which seemed to say *we can do what you can't. We are what you can never be.*

The sort of women Edward Hepple would like.

Except that Edward Hepple had wanted May, and May wasn't like that at all.

'*They* were the sort of women who would know how to please a man,' Patrick had said with a laugh, as he'd hung up each one in turn, opposite their bed.

'And just like a woman to know nothing about art,' he'd added, when she'd asked if they couldn't perhaps hang elsewhere. But sometimes she wasn't sure that they were art. Although, of course, she had to admit that Patrick knew best.

She stepped back, looked at the line of the frame quizzically a moment, and then with a skill honed over years of living with the smug faces of these intimate strangers, adjusted it without seeing the image it contained.

Back on the landing she flicked through the large stack of pictures that needed rehanging: cheap prints, amateur water-colours and family photographs. Only one photograph from her own family, however, her great-grandfather, whose small snub nose Jane had inherited. A kind and gentle-looking man leaning on a gate, dignified in his clean but rough clothes, fob watch gleaming, sheep-dog at his feet. There were no other photographs of her family. Patrick had said they were too common.

She picked up the print of the red-haired woman. It had to hang on the left of the brunette. Or was it the right? She would have to be careful to make sure that they all went back in the right places. Patrick could be a stickler for detail.

'*Neat and tidy; tidy and neat. Won't you ever learn where things go, woman?*' he'd say, affectionately of course, when she got things wrong.

It would take her the best part of the day to put all the pictures back on the walls. But that was a minor chore compared to the work Patrick had put in over the last few days. Fancy painting the whole of the house, from top to bottom, in just four days! She should feel proud to have such a husband. Rose and May's husbands hardly ever lifted a paintbrush!

'Off you go to one of your sisters for a few days and let me get on with the work,' Patrick had said. 'Can't abide a woman under my feet when I'm trying to paint.'

'The girl can stay here and keep me company,' he'd added, surprising both her and Jane. But of course she'd taken Jane with her. Why would he want Jane under his feet?

Alice sorted through a small cardboard box full of screws and oddments and found another picture hook. Such a good man to want to make the house nice for them all. They'd discussed the decorating together, at a rare family conference, with smiles, all three of them around the tea-table. Like a normal family. Which was just what they were, of course!

Alice hesitated before making another pencil cross on the newly painted wall, then she brought the hammer down heavily on the

168

pin. Except something had gone wrong. Because instead of the pale-yellow she'd expected in the kitchen, it was purple, which clashed with the flowered curtains she'd made specially.

Bang, went the hammer.

And the front room was grey, even though they had agreed that as it faced north it needed a warm shade. Grey— like a cold death.

Bang.

And Janey's room was pink, not the usual pastel of her girlhood, but a vulgar, shocking, bordello pink, even though Jane had clearly asked for blue. Pink was for little kids, she'd said.

'Growing mature on us, are we?' he'd joked at that unusual, smiling, family conference. So he *had* heard. 'You and I can start on your room together while your mother's away,' he'd added, surprising them again, because he never usually paid Jane much attention.

But of course she couldn't have left Jane.

Bang.

Alice went back to the pile of pictures on the landing, which was now green, instead of cream. He must have misheard, or simply forgotten. And what did it matter, anyway?

Jane hadn't minded, although at first she'd seemed to turn pale, but that must have been a trick of the light, because she quickly took Alice's arm and squeezed it, even laughed a little. 'Don't worry, Mum,' she said. 'It's just a bit of paint. And at least it's clean.'

But in the larger room, the room in which Alice spent most of her day, their tight smiles had faded. The room was to have been white. It had always been white. The colour of peace and calm. The colour that soothed. But he must have forgotten.

'Everything depresses you nowadays,' he'd laughed, teasing her when she first admitted her dislike of dark colours, in a rare moment's confidence, emboldened and encouraged at that unusual, smiling, family conference. Although the smiles had gone when she'd insisted on taking Jane.

And there really was no reason why he should have remembered it was this colour that depressed her most of all, this dark and dusty red, which reminded her of ridiculous things, like old blood on new wounds—

Alice closed her eyes. The doctor had told her to try not to dwell on such thoughts. In fact last week he had insisted on it. She laughed out loud, the feeble sound echoing in the empty house. Fancy going on about all that, when she'd only gone to talk about a bit of a tickle in her throat! And then not being able to speak at all, just sitting there with the tears running down her face! Poor man must have thought she was mad!

He'd said such thoughts were simply the result of stress and not to be dwelt upon.

'I know you houseproud women, always working, I'll be bound,' he'd said and turned away to prepare himself for the next patient; the waiting-room was full, after all. At the door he'd handed her another prescription for Valium. He'd said that she would have to rest more, and do less. But by that time she was in the corridor, so there wasn't really time to tell him about the hours already spent lying on her bed, staring at the ceiling.

Where would she lie now? Where could she rest? Not in this dark and bloody room.

Alice opened her eyes and briskly hung up the print, carefully avoiding the red-haired woman's gaze. Patrick was a busy man. She couldn't expect him to remember everything. Jane was too young to understand.

'The bastard,' Jane had whispered the night before, and with such vehemence, for one so young.

Alice had tried to explain, but then, watching rays of evening sunlight disappearing into the dark walls, she had suddenly imagined herself disappearing after them, and for a moment it felt as if the room had shrunk, was shrinking further as she stood, and suddenly she found she couldn't breathe.

Alice walked back to the landing and searched for the next print. Patrick didn't mean any harm. He did his best. She would talk to Jane. There had been no need for her to eat supper in silence and then go straight to her room, locking the door like that. She never used to lock the door.

Alice picked up another nail and positioned the hammer. She paused and blinked. Her vision was clouding. She watched as the hammer moved forward as if in slow motion, its edges blurring. She shook her head and tried to focus on the mark on the wall. But her mind was already filling with images, at first crowded and distorted, like the new TV before it warmed up, a jumble of light and dark finally settling into recognisable shapes.

And there was the faceless woman again.

The faceless woman picks up the hammer.

The pills crunch under its impact. One hundred and twenty in all. All she has left from last month and the whole of her new prescription. It's always best to be on the safe side.

She brings the hammer down again. And again. And opens the tea towel. But there are still some lumps, a few pills surviving miraculously unscathed. She needs to crush them all to a fine powder. That's the way to do it.

She refolds the cloth and hammers in short, quick bursts. Bang, thud, bang, thud, then looks around the neat kitchen, takes down a pretty blue-flowered saucer from the wooden plate rack and carefully shakes the white powder into it. She assesses it critically. There isn't as much as she expected. But it's bound to be enough. Sure to be.

She hums as she moves around the kitchen. So what should she cook? He likes her meat pies. He likes them thick with gravy. He would never say as much, of course, but she knows they're a favourite because of the speed with which he wolfs them down, by the amount he manages to consume. The child and she always get small portions on the nights she makes meat pie.

Tonight she'll tell him that the child and she will be eating yesterday's left-overs. He'll approve of that. He likes a thrifty housewife. Especially when it means all the more for him.

'Knows how to stretch a bob or two, my wife,' he'd boast to those friends at the pub.

First to make sure the knife is sharp enough, scraping and pulling back and forth on the stone step by the back door, make it razor sharp so that it will slice through the flesh with ease, the well-hung meat, dark and dusty red—

Carefully cutting it into cubes, slowly and laboriously, thirty-six in all; it pays to be methodical and meticulous when one cooks, she has heard on the new TV.

Putting the meat on to boil, turning down the heat when a scummy froth whips up the pan and angrily spits out on to the cooker.

'Simmer gently, now,' she says, as if kindly instructing a boisterous child.

Kneading the pastry, rolling it, stretching it out as smooth and as white as a corpse, more flour for its winding sheet, putting it to one side.

Taking the hot chunks of flesh from the pan, adding flour to the grey-specked, scum-topped water that remains, whisk it up, whisk it up, a drop of sweat from her brow falling, hubble bubble, mix it in. Gravy browning, stirring smoothly, a little white powder, just a little more, emptying the saucer completely, why not?

Cooking is an art, the TV cook says. Three dinner party meals for ten and six, and proceeds to show the country how, her culinary lore beaming into households that never host dinner parties. But still, everyone watches, while her husband assists, respectful, deferential.

'Not like that!' Smiling at the audience. 'He does his best,' she says with a wink.

Finally more gravy browning, letting it bubble up rich and thick and dark. And the white powder is all gone.

'More pie?' the woman with no face asks the man with indistinct features.

He wipes his mouth on his sleeve, belches, thrusts the plate in front of her. She winces but spoons out another portion, positioning the food carefully on his plate, wiping a splash of gravy from the side. Presentation is all, echoes the TV cook.

Sits back, waiting, watching, eagerly looking for the first signs. And what will they be? Stares at his every move, intent, ignoring his suspicious glare, his angry fidgeting.

Laughing unafraid when he growls, 'What are you looking at, woman? Never seen a man eat before?'

Too late for him to do anything more to her now. Too late for him to do anything to her ever!

Biting her lip, suppressing the surge of giggles rising up inside, ten years old and up-to-no-good at the back of the class—

But then her smile fades. What if there wasn't enough white powder? Her eyes open wider. He's pushing back his chair, rising to his feet, glowering over her, reaching out for her shoulders, bellowing,

'I said don't stare, woman! You're enough to put anyone off his food!'

Shrinking back as hard fingers grip her shoulders, setting her teeth in readiness, for the shaking, for the fist—

But the grip suddenly relaxes, and the fingers fall from her arms as he blinks into her face, eyes glazing, unfocused.

She watches him sink to the floor, clutching at his stomach, twitching convulsively, moaning.

And as he gasps his last breath, she bends down and whispers gently in his ear. 'You bastard—'

Alice gradually focused again on the picture hook.

Bang. And another smug woman graced her bedroom wall.

Only one to go. The girl with the green face and the flower behind her ear. Who, although not like the others, was still dislikeable. People shouldn't be green. And she would clash terribly with the wall. But no time to think about that. She would have to get a move on if she was to finish before Jane and Patrick returned.

'Alice? Alice!'

Alice jumped guiltily. She put down the hammer and hooks and peered over the banisters. She could see the top of Patrick's sandy hair below; taking off his coat; turning to go into the kitchen. She shrank back. She hadn't been expecting him for lunch. Had he said? Had she forgotten? She stood wringing her hands at the top of the stairs.

'Alice!!'

'Coming, pet—'

Wiping her hands on her housecoat, quickly glancing in the mirror, adjusting her hair.

'What's there to eat,' he asked without looking at her. He picked up the newspaper.

Alice looked frantically around.

'Meals like you wouldn't believe, my wife—'

The TV cook would have something rustled up in seconds. Tin of corned beef, couple of tomatoes, and it would appear like magic. 'Fit for the Ritz for only one and six—'

'There's some meat pie in the fridge from last night.'

He looked up disdainfully. 'You know what I think about your left-overs.'

*　　*　　*

173

She watched him wipe the plate with a piece of bread. He had eaten in silence. Finally he pushed the plate away from him and leaned back in his chair. He looked at her quizzically.

'You didn't mention anything about the decorating,' he began, watching her face carefully. 'A man spends days making a home nice for his family and the two of you hardly say a word about it.'

Alice swallowed.

'Well?' He sat watching her, chin out, a half-amused look on his face.

'It— it looks nice and clean,' Alice answered and turned to the sink.

He snorted.

'You bastard—'

'Eh? What was that? What was that you said?'

Alice turned, surprised. She hadn't said anything.

'Nothing.'

He shrugged.

He read in silence while she washed up. The clock ticked, the refrigerator hummed. Outside the wind brought a squall of rain which clattered on the window pane. She looked up and stared at the neat garden, with its regulation lawn, the tidy flower beds, the orderly rows of marigolds and dahlias. Only her roses had any feeling about them. They were the only bit of the garden she was allowed to touch. Fed and nurtured them like children. Her hands stopped on the dishes. She stared at the flower bed to the right. Her roses were gone. The earth had been newly turned over. Tiny plants stood in rows, vegetables, marked by plastic tags. Her roses—!

For a moment the wind and rain stopped, the refrigerator turned itself off and there was silence. She held her breath.

'Eh? Did you speak?'

She shook her head. Her face felt hot. She turned back to the dishes. Ah well. Patrick had said they should go. Spoiled the symmetry of the garden, he said, and he knew about such things.

'I like the wife to have a nice garden,' he'd say to those friends at the pub. 'Somewhere nice for the little lady to sit in her leisure moments.'

'Bastard— bloody bastard—'

'What was that, woman?'

'Mmm?' Alice turned around, lost in thought.

'Nothing,' she repeated, surprised. She hadn't spoken.

174

*   *   *

Alice picked up the hammer.

Bang. The pin slipped. She winced. A dark red patch appeared under her thumb-nail.

'Can't do a bloody thing right, woman,' she heard a voice echo in her head.

She held the pin steady. Bang. A little plaster crumbled to the floor. But the photograph would cover it. The photograph of his father in full military uniform had to go there, on the landing outside their bedroom. Patrick liked to see it as he came up the stairs. A stickler for detail.

She smiled. *'The wife keeps the house looking like a new—'*

Her smile faded. *'Can't do a bloody thing right— thick as two short planks—'*

Bang.

More plaster fell to the floor. There was a definite hole now. The pin wouldn't hold. She would have to try another spot. But she paused and stared at the hole she had just made, imagining it growing bigger, a peep-hole into their bedroom, imagined herself putting her eye to it, spying on the pale-faced woman and the tall, belligerent man. Imagined them lying together on the bed, the man laughing in that particular way, before doing those things to her, things that were getting worse, as if he was putting some creative thought into it, seeing how many ways he could degrade her—

Bang. The hole grew larger.

The faceless woman picks up the hammer.

The hole in the wall will have to be about two inches in diameter to take the hose.

Bang.

She puts her fingers into the hole and pushes the plaster out the other side, picks up the dustpan and brush, sweeps away all traces.

'Neat and tidy, tidy and neat—'

Downstairs she uncoils a length of rubber hose. She's bought thirty metres. It's always best to be on the safe side. She carries one end upstairs and tries to poke it through the hole into the bedroom, then unhurriedly, fetches a penknife and cuts until the hose fits snugly.

Back downstairs, she takes the other end out of the back door and pushes it through the garage window.

All so easy!

She positions the end just below the oil slick on the garage floor. And it's exactly the right length. Not stretched, but neither so long that it will lie in folds and thereby impede the flow.

She laughs out loud at her own cleverness. Her only regret is that he will never know. Will never know just how clever she is, she, the 'bloody useless woman'!

He'll never see her slip into the garage after he's fallen asleep, drunk as usual, and attach the hose to the car's exhaust. He'll not see her turn on the ignition and slip back quietly upstairs, position it next to his sleeping face—

Which is a pity. Because she would like him to see.

But she will see his eyes open and bulging, his choking face going blue— will hear him begging for help— will laugh— will have the last laugh—

Alice picked up the hammer.

She had three more paintings to go and then she would be finished. Just in time. Jane was already back, doing her homework in her shocking-pink room. Patrick would be home at any moment. He liked the house to be orderly, everything in place.

'*Like the house to be nice for my lovely wi—*'

'*Can't do a bloody thing right, thick as two short—*'

She closed her eyes tightly, but the echoes kept coming, discordant and jangling, other pictures crowding in, other voices, more and more! Putting her hands over her ears, *Bastard— bastard— neat and tidy, tidy and— Bastard!*

'Pull yourself together, Alice,' she whispered, holding on to her arms. 'Time to make tea.'

'*Meals like you wouldn't believe, my lovely wi—*'

'No!!'

Alice put down the hammer. Her hands were shaking. She felt as if she'd been whirling round, arms outstretched, spinning like a top, so that colours, images, thoughts, even sounds had merged. She sat down heavily at the top of the stairs. She must be going down with something.

* * *

176

The book lay in her lap, open at the same page as it had been all evening. In the armchair opposite sat Patrick, long legs stretched out in front of him, hands clasped on his chest, eyes closed, chin back, mouth open. From time to time he gave a loud snore and spasmodic splutter. Then he would rearrange his hands on his chest and go silent again.

'Mum?'

Alice stared ahead at the fire. She could see pictures in the orange and red flames that leaped from the coals. Occasionally a small blue flame would spurt with a hiss. Her legs were hot and scorched; they would be red and mottled, but she couldn't be bothered to move back. Not while the pictures flickered and moved.

'Mum? I'm off to bed now.'

Flickering and moving, pictures of a sleeping man and a pale-faced woman, a petrol can, a lighted match, all playing in the grate as if it were the screen on a Friday night down at the Odeon.

A hand touched her shoulder. She looked up surprised.

'Janey.' She smiled, lifted her cheek to the child, put her arms out in response. 'Sleep tight, my lamb.'

Back to the flickering, entranced, hypnotised. A lump of coal emitted a thin stream of smoke, and the pictures changed. A station, a waiting train, the smell of soot, a crowded platform, the train moving off, everyone crushing forward to wave, the woman's eyes on the tall man's back, the hiss of the engine as it approached, the woman's hands carefully positioned in place, her feet braced, ready for the moment, ready for the push— And then the sudden scream!

Alice opened her eyes with a start. She must have been dreaming. She sat for a moment with her heart pounding. The room was hot, terribly hot, so that she felt drowsy, half-drugged, just as she did when she took an extra Valium, on those days when she really didn't want to think any more. But she hadn't taken any Valium. Her eyes moved to the cup of coffee Patrick had unusually made for her. A few dregs remained. She put the cup tentatively to her lips. Did it taste bitter? But the room had been hot, that's all. She usually woke when the fire died down. Patrick must have banked it up.

Where was he?

She took a few deep breaths and looked uneasily at the door. Her heart was still pounding, the vestiges of the dream hung around her, the scream was still in the air, echoing in the room, as if it had happened in reality, and not in her unconscious mind. There had been a scream once before, long ago, a terrible scream, May, on a farm—

She tried to stand, but she felt dizzy. She *must* be going down with something.

'Get out!!'

Alice froze, and knew instantly that she had not dreamed the scream. It was Jane.

The hall was cold, mercifully cold, shocking her awake, helping to clear her head. She could hear raised voices. Patrick's with a familiar tone, a mixture of mockery and bullying. She tried to hurry, but her legs felt heavy and slow.

'I said get out! Don't you dare touch me!'

Sounds of a scuffle as she approached Jane's room. The door seemed jammed; she had to half lean, half throw herself on it to make it open.

She stood staring. Jane was sitting, legs drawn up at the back of the bed, flushed and angry, clothes dishevelled, buttons on her school blouse torn. Patrick standing over her, fists clenched. Neither noticed Alice.

'I said get out!' Jane spat, as Alice watched her pulling her blouse more tightly round her. Her hair was coming undone from its pony tail— Alice swallowed. *Jane.*

Suddenly Patrick swung round.

'What do you want, woman?'

'It's all right, Mum,' Jane said in a hard, low voice she'd never heard before.

'What are you doing, Patrick?' Alice asked dully. Pray that she could believe him. Pray that she could.

'I'm only making sure that the girl is doing her homework, idle little bugger that she is, and all I get is a load of lip for my concern.'

Silently Alice turned and walked out of the room.

'I need to talk with you, Patrick,' she said slowly, without turning round, formulating the words carefully because her tongue felt too big for her mouth. Drugged. She felt drugged.

'Janey, go on with your homework, there's a love.'

There was silence behind her. Then, '*You* want a word with *me*!' He laughed humourlessly. 'Well, there's a turn up.'

178

His tone was sarcastic, but she could hear him following her, all the same.

Alice picked up the hammer.

The blow caught him on the side of the head. Blood immediately appeared from his ear, but she had missed, it was only from the fleshy part. She raised the hammer again as he stood, too stunned to move, just staring at her. But the hammer was suddenly too heavy, her arms too weak. She blinked, trying to focus on his head, peering at him as if through a fog, a fog that was permeating her senses, dulling her strength. Her legs were beginning to weaken. She would have to be quick. She brought the hammer down as hard as she could, this time aiming at his temple.

But Patrick's expression suddenly changed. He caught her arm and jerked the hammer out of her hand.

'You little bitch!'

He twisted her arm, and then, after a moment's pause, and with an expression she was never to forget, he jerked her arm once more. Alice heard the sickening crack, almost before she felt the pain, and as she sank to the floor, mercifully all went black.

It was clear and light and bright in the hospital. Her room was quiet and calm and white, and there were no cracks in the ceiling. Sometimes she liked to lie staring at it all the same, but only occasionally; now she preferred reading, or talking with the other women.

The doctors have said she could go home quite soon.

Her arm healed long ago, but that was not why she'd been brought there.

'Why do *you* think you've been here, Mrs Sullivan?' the doctors all asked her. And now she knew what to answer, which words would gain her freedom. It was important to co-operate. To get it right. Otherwise she wouldn't get home to Jane.

'Why do *you* think you're here, Mrs Sullivan?' they asked.

She told them she realised now that Patrick had brought her there for her own good. That now she could see that he had her committed so she would get better. That her wild accusations were simply part of her being 'unwell', as they liked to call it.

Because she needs to see Jane.

So she told them that she was looking forward to going home, to being part of a happy family.

'Got my family together again,' he'll say to those friends at the pub. 'My two lovely girls.'

And she stopped talking to the nurse on the night shift, the girl who always seemed to have a black eye, always walking into doors she said, who chatted in the small hours when Alice couldn't sleep, which used to be often. She stopped listening to her words.

'Leave the bugger,' the clumsy girl exhorted, through a split lip the last time. 'Don't go back.'

Now she pretended to be asleep instead, so she could assure the doctors next morning that she could see things in their true perspective, and acknowledge quite frankly how 'unwell' she must have been to tell such stories, because no one behaved like that.

And as a result they nodded and smiled and scribbled in her file, and said *now* she could go home.

At the gates of the hospital, Alice paused, suitcase in hand. The sky was high and blue, the air crisp and clear, a fresh north-easterly wind sprinkling cherry blossom from the trees like confetti. She breathed deeply, drinking in the air, as if it was entirely different to the air in the garden of the hospital. And it was. It was the air of freedom.

She looked down the road. Patrick would be waiting. She was looking forward to going home.

So she turned in the opposite direction. Because home is where the heart is. And that was where May lived, and Emily, with whom Jane was staying, had been staying for the past six months.

With head held high and a smile on her face at the promise of the day, Alice began briskly walking. For the first time in many years, she was looking forward to going home.

14
May
1968

May put down the romance she was reading. She held on to the edge of the counter, feeling light-headed. She had stood up too quickly, she told herself, that was all. She began to stamp the books of a queue of people that seemed suddenly to have appeared out of nowhere. Had they all been waiting there a while? She took a deep breath. She wasn't feeling good at all.

At the end of the queue stood Edward Hepple. She could just see him, glancing repeatedly over his shoulder, no doubt in the direction of some woman he had his eye on. Edward never changed. She hadn't seen him for a few months. His comings and goings had tended to follow a pattern over the years. He would work for a year or so, in which she saw little of him, and then he would take a few months off.

Sabbaticals, he called these periods of unemployment, during which he liked to spend a fair amount of time at the library, pursuing his alternative career of chasing women. Here he followed them through geography, social science and natural history shelves, and with nice irony finally cornering them in the biology section, which was set back and relatively private.

He reached the front of the queue and pushed his book towards her. There were a few more grey hairs to streak the black at his temples, a few more lines crinkling around the handsome eyes.

'Out of work again, Edward?' she asked sympathetically.

He gave her a quick grin and shrugged. 'You know how it is. Quarter of the work force laid off this time.'

He glanced over his shoulder as she stamped his book. She looked at its title. *Motorcycles in Action.*

'I'll bet you're a design engineer now,' she said archly, remembering the old game they used to play.

He looked at her blankly.

'No,' he said slowly. 'Still a welder. I'm fixing me bike.'

And giving her a doubtful look, he walked off to where a young woman stood flicking unconvincingly and nervously through some cookery books. May saw the young woman's colour heighten as he approached her. Edward Hepple never changed.

May sat down with her book, still feeling light-headed and nauseous. She must have picked up a bug. She watched the young woman drop her book, Edward bend close to pick it up, and she smiled. With Edward it was a continual case of off with the old and on with the new. He probably hardly remembered their own affair; certainly he didn't remember their communicating with obscure book titles and pretending to a matching range of odd professions. He'd looked at her as if she were mad when she'd suggested he was an engineer.

Mad— Looking back over the years, she herself thought of the weeks of their affair as her 'mad' phase. Weeks in which she'd been sure that she was going to die, so crazy with fear that she'd run from Will, accusing him of all sorts of ridiculous things. And ran to Edward Hepple of all people. Even Alice, who hardly said a bad word about anyone, told her she must have been crazy to turn to such an incorrigible flirt.

Edward suddenly left the cookery section and went instead to lean nonchalantly against the fiction shelves opposite. He was still glancing around, obviously waiting for someone. He caught May's eye and smiled his toothpaste advert grin. She smiled back. She couldn't help liking Edward. It was impossible to take the man seriously enough to dislike him.

She was also unable to feel ashamed of the affair they'd had. There were too many mitigating circumstances; you had to learn to be kinder to yourself, Will had said when she finally told him about Edward.

Edward was an opportunist, admittedly. He'd known she was in a crisis when he'd made his move with her, some predatory instinct telling him just when he could leap in. But he'd also been funny, with a warmth that had helped in those weeks when she'd feared the worst, believing she could confide in no one. She'd refused to tell Edward the details, but he had nevertheless sensed the extent of her fears. And he'd told her that she must confide in Will, perhaps also sensing her true feelings.

She watched Edward casually examining his fingernails. Maybe he wasn't that sensitive. Maybe he'd merely thought he had bitten off more than he could chew, and wanted to offload the responsibility back to her husband. But she would always choose to believe that Edward Hepple had a kind heart.

She saw his face light up as he looked to the door. She stood so she could see better. Whoever it was had obviously arrived because he was smoothing back his hair, adjusting his leather jacket. It must be someone special, she knew those gestures, that familiar body language. Edward was firing on all cylinders. Pity the poor woman—

A young man joined him. May watched in surprise. She had been wrong. But her book slipped from her hand as she watched Edward lean back in the familiarly provocative way, then whisper something in the young man's ear, put an arm around his shoulder, and guide him towards the biology section.

May put her hand to her mouth, for a moment wanting to laugh. Edward *was* ringing the changes. On with the new indeed. God, Alice wouldn't believe it—

Slowly she sat down. But she would let Edward keep his secret. Just as he hadn't pried into hers, all those years ago. But you must at least tell your husband, he had exhorted. She would always have a soft spot for Edward Hepple, if only for that.

She hadn't told Will, however. Because Will had guessed.

She'd been standing in the bathroom, had forgotten to lock the door. Will had come in and found her half-naked, staring at herself in the steamed up mirror, lost in fearful imaginings, with God knows what in her eyes.

'Excuse me,' he muttered quickly, turning away. 'I didn't realise—' They hadn't been close for some time, hadn't been intimate for even longer.

In the mirror her eyes followed him as he went to the door, and inwardly she screamed his name. As if he heard, he swung back and caught her expression.

'What is it, May? What's the matter?'

Staring at him, at her own reflection, back to him, unable to speak, so fearful—

'May? What the hell is it!'

He'd taken her shoulders, made her face him, and seen the fear that was swamping her thought, blocking all words of explanation.

And so he'd ignored her resistance and held her, until at last she could weep, and at last the words would come.

If it hadn't been for Will, she would never have gone for the second opinion. It was he who did the talking at the consultant's meeting, he who found out as much as he could, he who said they should delay the proposed surgery until they'd had a second opinion.

They moved automatically through the following few days, together, his arm always around her shoulders. There were no more accusations of infidelity, Will's own doubts left unspoken. There was a truce. None of that was important now.

He'd steered her through one appointment to the next, until finally, in a green-painted cubicle at the back of an old Victorian hospital, after a very minor operation, they were told that there was in fact nothing to worry about. There was no need for major surgery. Nothing indicated anything sinister, the second consultant said. She should stay vigilant, he advised, but the condition appeared to be caused by hormonal changes, was not so uncommon, and was harmless.

The relief when it was over! It washed over them both, breaking down barriers, opening up channels, so that at last they could talk, at last she could see. Her crazy accusations were simply born out of fear, she told him, fear that she might have lost him if she were to be disfigured, fear that she would have *had* to lose him, if she were to die. The uncertainty of the whole situation had been so unbearable, she had deliberately created a worse situation.

'But there's only ever been you,' he said. And she realised she had always known this.

Over the next few months they continued to talk, through long evenings, and nights in which they no longer turned from each other, back through time, to their early years together, their youth, the war, and schooldays— where they finally reached Joe.

184

It was Will who brought up his name.

'And Joseph Graham?' he asked simply. 'Can you talk about Joe yet, May?'

The familiar silence encircled her like a gag, stifling, stopping her words.

'Don't you think it's time?'

May stared at him. What did he mean? How could he know?

'I know you took Joe's death badly. I know that it changed you. And somehow it came between *us*.'

Still she kept silent.

'You've never mentioned him, not once, over all these years, even though I know he was like a brother to you. Why? It *is* time, May,' he insisted gently.

And so after years of silence, May took a breath, and finally spoke of the friend she had loved, and lost. Of the day Joe told her he was leaving, how he believed he might never see her again. Then speaking faster, in case she should falter, she spoke of the night Joe had asked her to stay with him. Will looked shocked as she told of the illness that followed, and of the doctor's bleak diagnosis. But he held her closer.

And finally she spoke of Joe's death, how it had frozen any anger and resentment she might have felt, made such emotions seem inappropriate. Which meant she had never been able to come to terms with what happened.

'I couldn't tell you. I told no one. I thought I'd lose you. I'd betrayed you. I thought you wouldn't forgive me.'

He shook his head, holding on to her so tightly she could hardly breathe.

'May, May— Forgive? There was nothing *to* forgive. It was the war— It was just the bloody war.'

May put down her book. She breathed deeply and sipped at the glass of water on her desk. She needed to get home. If she could just lie down for a while she would feel better, she was sure. She and Will were supposed to be going to the class at Emily's, once Will returned from work— but she would feel fine once she was in the fresh air.

It was nothing to worry about. A virus could hang on and on, like this. Three weeks now— but no need to worry. No need to panic. She'd probably been working too hard, visiting Alice in the hospital over the last few months, helping Emily look after Jane, and all on top of her work at the library. It was enough to make anyone feel light-headed. She was forty-two, not twenty-two. It was just her body slowing down a bit. Nothing sinister.

Will had told her she should start thinking of working less. Maybe they both should. Maybe they could then get out of the city a bit more, spend more time in the countryside.

'One day,' was Will's frequent promise. 'When we've saved enough, it'll be to hell with the city and we'll live where there's not a factory or sooty street in sight.'

May packed up, ushered the last people out of the library, including Edward and his new friend, and then locked up. She would walk home. The exercise would help. There was no need to worry. She would tell Will and he would laugh, joke her out of it. Just because she'd had cause for concern once, he'd tease, didn't mean she had to worry about every sniffle.

All the same she would tell him as soon as he returned from his shift.

Will was already at home when May arrived, looking drawn and anxious, so that all thoughts of viruses went from her head. He had already lit the fire and she could smell the chicken roasting in the kitchen.

'Playing hookey?' she joked uneasily. Will had never come home early in his life, had hardly had a day off work for any reason.

He patted the seat next to him. 'Come and sit down. A bit of bad news, I'm afraid,' he said, struggling to look bright.

He took her hand. 'Pipe dreams— Just pipe dreams,' he muttered to himself.

'What is it?' she asked, feeling suddenly sick and light-headed again. 'Emily? Rose? One of the children?' But she'd seen them all earlier. Alice—

'Is it Alice? Is she worse?' she asked quickly, her face growing more pale.

He shook his head. 'No, no. Everyone's fine. Nothing like that.' There was a silence. 'I've been laid off, I'm afraid.' He laughed bitterly. 'After thirty years. As of Friday, not even a decent period of notice— I'm sorry, May.'

May breathed deeply, with both relief and despair.

Two other mines were to close within the month, he told her, so there was little chance of his being employed again. He was too old, the colliery manager had said.

'A double blow,' he laughed, trying to make light of it. 'Unemployed and old in one fell swoop.'

'But that's ridiculous, Will. You're only forty-six. You'll find something!'

But she knew the situation as well as he. He couldn't go back down the pits again after all these years, and the closures would mean there were few places for his management skills.

'At least we have some savings, which is more than many have. The cottage in the country can wait a while yet, Will.'

He put an arm round her shoulders.

'And we have our health, so I suppose that's the most important thing, eh?'

May nodded, and was silent.

They drove out to the farm in Stamfordham at the weekend. Since her uncle died May made a point of regularly visiting her aunt, which was no hardship. She loved the old woman. There'd been times when Lizzie Bolton had seemed like a second mother to her.

And she loved the farm and the surrounding countryside almost as much. As they drove further from the city, the view opened up with a patchwork of browns and greens and old gold, under a sky that grew wider and higher, until they were meandering along familiar lanes hemmed in by thick hedgerows. Around a last corner, and a huge winter-red sun hung over the cornfield that marked the beginning of the Boltons' farm.

'Alice and I used to take that short cut,' May nodded. 'Especially at bramble time. We'd arrive purple-fingered, almost too full for Aunt Lizzie's Sunday tea. She used to have a fit.'

'Wouldn't like to be on the receiving end of an Aunt Lizzie fit,' Will mumbled. 'A veritable harridan of a woman,' he shuddered, and she laughed, because she knew he loved her aunt as much as she did.

They drove alongside the copse whose every tree she knew from childhood, rooks and crows circling and perching in the high branches, their nests like footballs in skeleton arms. And finally the car turned into the muddy track that led to the farm.

The visit would do them both good, May told herself. She was still feeling weak, and frequently light-headed, although she had not mentioned it. Will had enough on his mind. He was not a man who would take to unemployment easily, despite his assurances.

Half-way along the track Will stopped the car and got out to clear away fallen branches blocking the path.

'The manager ought to be seeing about these things,' he muttered under his breath. 'The man doesn't know when he's well off, neglecting his job like this—'

It was painfully clear how he really felt about being unemployed.

The farm was quiet when they arrived, no dogs to greet them, no geese to hiss at them. They could hear a drone of machinery from the back yard, starting up suspiciously the moment they arrived. In May's uncle's day, the farm had been relatively prosperous, had employed a half a dozen local people. Will had warned her aunt more than once that parts seemed to be getting run down unnecessarily. He used to enjoy helping Harry Bolton at weekends. It grieved him, as much as May, that the old man's hard work was being neglected, that it looked as if the farm might well die with May's aunt.

And as the old lady was now in her eighties, at each visit May wondered how many more there would be. The farm had played an important part in her life, the best weekends of her childhood, the years as a land-girl, a thousand Sunday teas since. But everything had to change. She walked slowly across the cobbled yard, her mind full of echoes.

The plants around the doorway and window were overgrown or dying through neglect. She'd tried to persuade her aunt to make a proper garden here. Now that the old lady spent most of her days at the window overlooking the yard, May wished she'd tried harder.

She saw the lace curtain at the window twitch and knew her aunt would be popping her teeth back in, the sixth set in as many years (all the wrong fit, she insisted), and would now be scurrying off to the kitchen to make tea. May smiled at Will, knowing he was thinking the same thing. She watched him pause at the doorstep and gaze around, breathing deeply, and he suddenly looked more relaxed than he had all week.

They both stared at the old lady, who was grinning mischievously, sucking her dentures loudly in the silence.

'So, what do you think?' Lizzie Bolton demanded, as impetuous as a child. 'At least say something!'

Will and May looked at each other.

'It was going to be yours anyway. I've left you the place in my will. If Harry and I had been blessed with children, well— but as it is— *If* there's anything to leave by the time that bugger's done!' She tossed her head contemptuously in the direction of the back yard, from which came the intermittent sound of machinery. 'That manager's getting worse,' she muttered. 'I may be old but I still know what's necessary. He can't fool me.'

She grinned toothily again. 'Seems to me that the change would do you both a power of good, as well as solve all your problems. And you don't need problems at this particular stage of your lives,' she winked at May.

She waited impatiently, barely able to keep still. 'So, why the silence?'

'But Aunt,' May began. She felt stunned, thrilled, yet maybe Will wouldn't—

'You'd have to give up the job at the library, of course,' her aunt went on. 'But you were already leaving anyway.'

May shook her head. She wasn't following. Had she missed something? Was her aunt really asking them to come and live on the farm, that she and Will should manage the place together?

'You would have had to leave soon enough, you know,' her aunt repeated, nodding towards her.

'No, no— not me. It's a wonderful offer! But I don't know, I mean it's up to Will, and it's *Will* who's being laid off, aunt, not me. He's already finished, in fact.'

'I know that, I know that,' snapped her aunt. 'All the more reason. So why the hesitation?'

The old lady looked frustrated. She wanted this all settled. It was time for her nap and she was itching to take out her teeth.

'Look,' she said with good-natured impatience, turning to Will. 'I need the help, my lad. You can see that. In fact if I don't get decent help soon there'll be no farm left to run. And it was all going to be yours. I'll be gone shortly anyway.'

Will suddenly found his voice. 'Not that shortly,' he laughed. 'You're going to be around for a while yet, I fear.'

The old woman cackled as if she'd been paid a compliment and settled back to watch the faces of her favourite niece and her husband. They were going to accept, of course. She knew they were. She'd hardly been able to contain herself all week waiting for this moment, for this look on their faces. They looked like a couple of kids for whom Christmas had come early. She rubbed her hands together.

'So? What's your answer?' She laughed gleefully. Look at them! Staring at each other like a couple of love-sick teenagers. At their time of life. Although she and Harry— Well, she supposed they'd had their moments too. It would be good to have someone else at the farm. Things had been quiet around the place since Harry had gone. Too many silences. Too many empty spaces. She hadn't planned on being long before she joined him, in fact. But now, and especially looking at May, well, maybe she'd wait just a little longer.

May was still staring at Will. Like her, he appeared stunned, his face was flushed. Farmers! She wanted to laugh out loud. Her aunt was offering them the farm!

'Well, only if it's what Will wants too,' she said, trying to sound neutral, trying to keep the hope out of her voice. She didn't want him to agree just for her sake. She wanted *him* to want—

'Want?' He leapt to his feet. 'Good grief, May. I would jump at half the chance!'

He strode over to the window and stood looking out over the view. When he turned back, his eyes were wet.

Everything's going to be all right now, May chanted in her head. Everything will be fine.

Will took the old woman's hand, and one of May's, and crouched down beside them both.

'And what more could I possibly want, if I have you two as well.'

'Seems to me you're going to get more, whether you like it or not,' her aunt cackled.

May turned questioningly, but the old lady just nodded happily, so she leaned forward and kissed her cheek.

'And I can't think of anything I would like better too,' she whispered.

'Aye, well,' her aunt said, pretending to shrug off this display of affection, but the pleasure showed in her face.

'It'll work all ways, believe me. You'll both do me and the farm a power of good. And it's just in time for you both, I can see that. Things have a way of working themselves out in this world, I've always said.' She nodded again at May. 'How long is it?'

May shook her head, again with the feeling that she was missing something.

'It was just last week. Will was laid off last week,' she repeated patiently.

'Not that, you silly goose,' her aunt said. 'I'm talking about *your* condition. How much longer have you got?'

May frowned and opened her mouth to correct her aunt again.

But a thought was beginning to take shape at the back of her mind, an idea whose parts must have been there for some time, because it grew rapidly, astonishingly.

She stared at her aunt, suddenly knowing not just what the old lady was talking about, but with the startling conviction that she was right.

Will sat looking from one to the other, bemused, waiting for someone to enlighten him.

May put a hand to her mouth. It wasn't possible— Couldn't be— She did some rapid mental calculations— She'd assumed it was the menopause beginning— It couldn't—

Dear God, could it be?

Her aunt was sitting forward expectantly, small eyes shining in her brown walnut of a face.

'You can't fool me, May Charlton. I've known you all your life.'

'May?' Will asked, puzzled.

May stared back at him, wanting to laugh. The way she'd been feeling, the weakness, the light-headedness, the nausea—

'Good lord, girl, if you can't tell your favourite aunt,' her aunt said exasperated. She suddenly fixed May with a shrewd look. 'You can't tell me you didn't know, child?' There was a pause. 'My God, you young girls!'

May's laughter rang around the room. 'But I'm forty-two— forty-two!'

'That's as may be,' said her aunt, patting her hand. As much as she loved her, this girl had always been a funny one. The sooner May started living on a farm, closer to nature, the better. Maybe it was just as well she'd decided to hang around for a while longer. Harry would wait, after all.

'That's as may be,' she repeated. 'But I was a midwife for long enough, and a farmer's wife for long enough after that, and I know when someone's expecting. Now, my dear,' she said more gently. 'Now, isn't that right?'

May looked from one face to the other, at Will's jaw appearing set to reach the floor, at her aunt managing to look both smug and conspiratorial at the same time, and the laughter surged up inside her.

She nodded slowly. 'I think you might just be right, Aunt Lizzie.'

'Stuff and nonsense,' the old woman muttered, taking out her teeth because it was time for her nap, now that the business of the day was done. 'There's no "might" about it.'

15

Emily
1969

Emily leaned forward on her shovel and pushed a few stray strands of hair from her face, unaware that as she did so she streaked mud across her cheek. It was a Saturday morning in October, and despite a cold wind that brought the tang of the sea a few miles east, Emily was perspiring. The flower beds contained tall, bronze chrysanthemums and thick, purple Michaelmas daisies, but her attempts not to disturb these plants had been abandoned, and small clumps were being broken off and buried as she strenuously dug and turned over the heavy clay soil.

She would talk to May. May would know what to plant here. She continued digging, panting slightly, ignoring the ache that was beginning to make itself felt in her lower back. Tomorrow, no doubt, she would know all about aches, but for now she would dig, because then she wouldn't think, and then the time would pass.

Dig— Mud pies for adults, May called gardening. Herself, she knew little about it, but she found it freed her mind, like playing the piano. Which she had also done with equal vigour that morning, alarming the neighbour at the other side of the party wall with a spirited rendition of Beethoven, before breakfast.

Keep busy. That was the way. Then the time would pass. She wasn't going to look at her watch. She had promised herself she would wait until she was sure that at least an hour had passed, and then she would look. She glanced at her watch and was stunned to discover she had only been digging for a little over fifteen minutes. She hacked at the earth more earnestly, cutting into the soil with renewed energy. And another clump of daisies disappeared under the earth.

He'd said about one. He would be coming at one. She dug on as a cold rain began to fall steadily, soaking her hair, running into her eyes, colouring her cheeks pink behind the streaks of mud. One o'clock. She wondered whether he liked gardening.

Mechanically she moved around the room, straightening and tidying. The room was pale and sparely but elegantly furnished. All her homes had looked like this, whether it was a mews in Bloomsbury, an apartment in Nicosia or a house in Newcastle. Pale walls, little but well-chosen furniture, a bubble of peace and calm. She wondered what his home was like, and whether he would like hers.

In the kitchen she took down plates and then opened the refrigerator. She hadn't been sure what to prepare and so had opted for salad, cold salmon. There was a bottle of wine chilling. With care she laid the food on the table. Fresh raspberries she had paid a fortune for because they were out of season, Cornish cream to go with them— She took a step back, hesitated, then moved all the things off the table and into the dining-room. Of course she didn't know whether he drank wine or even ate fish. She knew nothing about him.

Upstairs in front of the mirror she looked at herself critically. Too pale. She applied make-up. Too much jewellery. It might give the wrong impression. She took off the gold chain and pendant. But some jewellery perhaps. With trembling fingers she placed pearls at her ears, and examined herself again. Maybe she should have worn something bolder, more colourful, something that would make her look younger. She didn't know what he would be expecting. She took off her cream silk dress and hurriedly swapped it for a colourful sweater and jeans. She didn't even know what he looked like now.

She looked at the photographs dotted around the living-room, of her sisters and her mother, her early life. What would he think of them all? There were none of James. Those she kept hidden away; she needed to keep James to herself a little longer. One day she might speak of him again, as she had to the woman on the train the day she moved north. Or maybe not. Maybe she no longer needed to.

194

Would she tell him? Would she ever be able to speak easily to him of the important things in her life? Would they be able to talk, to share things about their lives? She laughed nervously, reprimanding herself. They might not even get past the weather.

At five to one Emily chose a record and put it on the hi-fi, Gershwin, 'Rhapsody in Blue', maybe he would like that— took it off immediately to replace it with Chopin— took that off, and then sat in silence. Maybe he wouldn't like her style of music.

One o'clock, he said. She sat holding her hands in her lap. Would he be able to find her? What if he couldn't? Of course he could. If he could succeed in tracking her down after all these years, then he could surely find his way through Newcastle. But maybe he would change his mind. Maybe he'd decide it was a mistake to think you could go back. Maybe he wouldn't come—

At two minutes past one Emily suddenly leaped to her feet. It was obvious that he wasn't coming. She hurried to the kitchen and began putting away the food. It was a crazy idea to think they could meet after all these years. Absolutely crazy. *He might not even have liked her as she was now. And then the embarrassment of that!* After all, what could they have said to each other? They would probably have been transfixed with embarrassment. It was all a mistake. He must have realised. She had known deep down all along that he wouldn't turn up. A foolish mistake—

At three minutes past one the doorbell rang and Emily froze. She stood for a few seconds, her heart pounding. Behind her, it rang again. She turned and stared at the sunlight streaming through the stained-glass front door, at the dark silhouette behind it. There had been another moment like this, another man, another time— It rang a third time. She walked down the hall and opened the door.

Standing on the doorstep was a tall young man she had never seen before. But she knew him, would have known him anywhere. Even if it weren't for the deep familiarity of his eyes, the turn of his mouth, the slight hesitation of the smile that was so like Alice's, and therefore presumably also like her own. The hands lifted nervously to push back wild, dark hair were the hands of his father, the hands of a musician, but the gesture was her own, and at that moment her own hands were mirroring his action. Yes, she knew him.

Smiling, tears forming in her eyes as she did so, smiling more widely, unable to stop, hands fluttering out towards him wanting to touch, pulling back as she told herself to stay calm, that this meeting must be more difficult for him, being so young. But he was smiling back easily, and it was she who felt out of control, wanting to take this young man she had never seen in her arms and hug him and hold on to him.

She held her hands tightly in front of her, smiles and tears spilling from her, opening her mouth to speak, not trusting the steadiness of her voice.

'Matthew?' she breathed, in hardly more than a whisper.

He nodded, his eyes wide, face expectant, waiting for her to say more. And then the tension was suddenly broken with his laughter, dark and rich, so that Emily had a recollection of a voice from long ago.

'Matthew,' he nodded, his accent distinctly American. 'And you must be my mother.'

He'd thought she'd be so 'cool', he admitted as they sat close, hands still touching. She sounded so 'together' during their telephone conversations, and from what she'd said in her letters. He had hopes— but he'd been unprepared for the emotion from this trembling, beautiful woman. He admitted all this, simply, as a child might, and Emily was grateful.

Because it meant that in time they would laugh and talk and admit to a great deal more. It meant that she and her son were going to be close.

16

The Class
1973

I hop off the bus and walk through the red-brick council estate and along the Two-ball Lonnen. Two clay balls on squat pillars give the adjacent few yards of green a pretension of incongruous dignity.

I haven't been to Gran's for a while. The shop where I used to buy ham for tea and sherbet lemons if there was any change is boarded up.

Some of the houses I pass are boarded up also. The area is going through a bad patch. My grandmother says it's because many of the people who moved in when it was built – and such luxury it was in those days, she tells me – many of the oldies, as she likes to call them, are dying off. And in their place my naïve gran tells me the council is housing problem tenants. As a first year sociology student I can assure her this is unlikely. But she insists that the house next to hers is now inhabited by a burglar, because his dog barks all day, his curtains are permanently drawn, and he only goes out at night. Bill Sykes would never have survived these curtain twitchers.

He's harmless, I assure her, his biggest crime is that his garden at the back is overgrown, and if my grandfather were still alive, he'd have a fit at all the weed seed that blows in to run amok through his lovely garden.

I'll do some gardening while I'm here, while Gran and my aunts are playing cards. I peer over squat brick walls to the concrete patches that now front most of the houses. At one time every house in this road displayed a patch of green and a bed of flowers. I'll dig over Grandad's vegetable patch and tie up the rose arch. There's only so much rummy and second-hand cigarette smoke you can take, after all. (I didn't think this the night before, however, when the pot was circulating freely. Although I don't enjoy it as much as I ought – unless everyone's pretending, Emperor's new clothes and all that.)

I can't say the same for Gran's 'girls', however, who take to their fags with gusto and relish, waggling them in the corners of lipsticked mouths as they chat, inhaling hugely only to exhale through a surprising number of orifices.

I pause at the house with the monkey puzzle tree. Gran says the old man is dead and his wife has moved away, but their tree is growing a new shoot regardless. Life goes on, as my mother says, always a one for the proverbs.

She wants Gran to move in with us, now that my grandfather is dead. Chance would be a fine thing, however. I know my gran. You'll only get her out of that house with a crowbar.

The road bends and the red pillar-box outside her house comes into view. My mouth suddenly dries. I've hardly been here at all over the last year. I'm only back during the holidays and I see quite a bit of Gran at home anyway, I told my mother, when she asked why I didn't want to go.

She gave me one of her eloquent looks which said 'Bullshit, Megan'.

But the first time I went to the house after my grandfather's death it seemed so empty, so empty I hardly knew what to say, rattling on to my aunts about nothing at all. Then I behaved even more badly, although Alice and May put their arms round me and Aunt Emily told me to let it all out. Blubbering like a baby at my age, right in the middle of blind horse. Honestly.

The funny thing is, my grandmother seems fine about his death. Grief is your friend, she says, it lets you mourn and remember, it lets you cry. But I don't understand. She and my grandfather were so close they were like a TV couple. *The Love Boat* comes to Fenham. I miss him.

She joked last week that when *she* goes, she's going to be cremated so that when I do anything bad, she'll blow into my eye in the form of a speck of dust, to tell me off. At least I think she was joking. You can't always tell with Gran.

I open the gate and walk up the path. The small tree at the edge of the tiny lawn is stiff with white lilac candles, fragrant and luminous against the grey air. It's the end of April, but it's as cold and bleak as November. I hesitate at the front door, for a split second tempted to turn and walk away. I'm not ready yet. Even though it's not the whole class, but just my three aunts, I know it'll be all 'ee o-hos', shrieky laughter and God knows what. Which doesn't seem right yet.

I pause, hand on the knocker. A first few tiny rosebuds are splitting dark crimson on the wall below the window. I wonder if anyone else has noticed. My grandfather would have. There were things I should have said to him, wish I had said to him. But in the last few months he didn't resemble my grandfather at all, but a poor, thin rambling form, occasionally making my heart lurch with a lucid 'twopence!' only for the recognition to fade after a second or two. So I couldn't tell him then how I felt, how important he was to me. Instead it was a relief when this stranger finally died. It was months before I realised I had lost my grandfather.

I fix a smile in place and knock loudly and for too long. All the old biddies will be going deaf I tell myself grimly, giving the knocker a last loud bang. I stand listening to the echo bounce around the still air of the estate, and then I breathe deeply. Because I know I'm not being fair. I know no one is going deaf. My grandmother could still hear the munching of forbidden jam tarts at a hundred paces, and as for my aunts, they're barely in their fifties. May is a young mother and Emily recently turned my *boyfriend*'s head, for goodness sake. So no, hardly old biddies.

I try to change my mood, aware of unfocused aggression, of the need to kick. *If they're not old, he shouldn't have died. I wasn't ready.*

'Megan! Megan!'

There's an excited high shriek from behind Gran's legs as she opens the door.

'God, what a racket, Megan! I thought it was the fire brigade,' she says, face lit up all the same, struggling to keep her balance as something pushes from behind.

'Beth, for God's sake,' she scolds as a mop of golden-red hair appears over a small pink face, beaming delightedly in my direction. May's daughter looks like a pixie.

The child immediately latches herself on to my legs so that I walk, with exaggerated clowning, into the living-room, groaning with mock pain as I drag her along with me. Then I laugh and quickly pick her up before saying hello to anyone, using her as a shield, but against what I'm not sure.

Coty's L'Aimant from Alice, bending to get a whiff of Max Factor pancake from May, something spicily and expensively undefinable from Aunt Em— I should have been a chemist. My grandfather used to say I had the nose for it. I could recognise the flowers he picked with my eyes closed, right down to the colour of the roses: pale pink from the arch, lemon from the kitchen wall. And I'm suddenly filled with the memory of him as I stand there smiling fixedly at them all. Not just the memory of his voice or face, or his smell, but everything, his essence, and in that instant the busy room is empty. Echoes of *'Dance fer Grandaddy'* die in the air.

'Let me look at you!' I say heartily, putting the child down and standing back.

May's daughter is a peach. The colour of a peach, she smells like a peach, and I'm sure if I nibbled her neck she'd taste like one.

'How are you, Aunt Em?' I ask when we're all sat down. Unusually my aunt has circles under her eyes and for the first time actually looks her age. Beautiful as ever, of course, but her age.

She tells me she is 'champion', lingering over the word with a wink – it was my grandfather's word and one of my favourites. She gives my hand a squeeze.

'God, I'm sorry about that bairn, Megan,' May says, attempting to take Beth, who has clambered up on to my knee again, determined not to be physically separated, but it just makes her squeeze my neck all the more tightly. 'She's been looking out of the window waiting for you coming for the last hour.'

She disentangles arms and takes the child from me.

'Well, that's more than I ever used to do for you, when *I* was that age,' I say with a grin. 'Or at least if I did keep a look-out, it was only so I could keep *out* of your way.'

She laughs. 'Get away with you,' she says with a dismissive wave of her hand. 'I was the perfect aunt.'

I pull a face, challenging.

'You were a right little madam, anyway,' she snorts.

Beth is regarding us with wide-eyed seriousness. I suddenly remember listening to my aunts' arguments at her age and I stop. But Beth just waits expectantly a moment, then bursts into laughter.

'You are funny, Mummy,' she says, giving my once-ferocious aunt a hug and settling back in her lap.

'Alice?' I say. She's been uncharacteristically silent through all this. She turns to me. I know that look on her face. I wish they wouldn't worry. I'm not a kid any longer.

'You look great,' I say brightly, to take the worry lines from her forehead. And it's true. She looks better every time I see her.

I stand examining her critically. 'What is it? What have you done with yourself now?'

Since she stopped living with Patrick she's abandoned the old-fashioned perm and now wears her hair loose so that she looks much younger. Last time I saw her she'd replaced her specs with contact lenses, and now—

'It's the clothes!' I announce triumphantly.

She's obviously been talking to my Aunt Em. The rather prim, stiff outfits she used to wear, 'costumes' she called them, are gone. Her pale-blue wool dress is soft and casual and fashionable. She isn't as thin as she used to be and she looks great.

'C & A's perhaps? Or is it Fenwick's French—?' I enquire, all guile and innocence, looking her up and down. *Haute couture* if ever I saw it. Five years away from Patrick have given her a new lease of life.

'And that's not all,' says Aunt Em drily.

'Go on, tell the bairn,' urges May.

Bairn. I'm eighteen and I'm still the bairn.

But Alice just grins. I swear *she* can look nearer sixteen than I do, since she got rid of Patrick.

Although the rumour round here is *still* that he got rid of her. Which is so unfair. She lives in a poky flat, and he has the house, although it was bought in joint names. In fact it was she who put down most of the money after her mother died. She loved that house. Women get all the really lousy deals.

'Go on, Alice,' May urges. 'Tell her.'

Women of my aunts' age still haven't a clue. It's all little lives attached to the kitchen up here. Betty Friedan *et al.* haven't reached this far yet.

Alice shrugs. 'I'm sure Megan won't think it's any big deal.'

I give a smile as if to say of course I'll think it's a big deal. She's probably done up her flat.

'I've been doing a business degree,' Alice says.

My mouth opens but nothing comes out.

'A degree?' I eventually repeat, not understanding.

'See,' Alice turns to May. 'I told you it was no big deal. People get degrees all the time in the circles in which Megan mixes.'

'Get on with you,' May insists. 'Blow your trumpet. Go on. It's about time you did.'

Alice just shrugs and laughs so Emily interrupts. 'She's got an honours degree and has just been offered a job at the Ministry.'

I sit gawping.

'Not at our Emily's level,' Alice explains, almost apologetically. 'But it's a start.'

I shake my head, then laugh out loud. Alice. My Aunt Alice! My poor downtrodden Aunt Alice! I want to pick her up and twirl her round the room like she used to do to me when I was little.

'Jesus! You sneaky old aunt!'

'Less of the old,' she says drily.

'Where? I mean how?'

'That new Open University. Over the last four years,' she says.

I do some mental calculations. She must have started soon after she came out of hospital.

'It was to keep me sane initially,' she nods as if reading my mind. 'Emily suggested it and kept me at it. In fact she was a bloody slave-driver a lot of the time,' she adds pointedly, but Aunt Emily is staring out of the window.

'What?' Emily turns to us, preoccupied. 'Oh, it had nothing to do with me,' she says, raising her hands. 'You always had it in you. You just let that idiot persuade you otherwise for too long.'

Alice shrugs again, and to my surprise changes the subject. This is disappointing, because there's nothing my great-aunts are better at than a spot of 'Patrick bashing'. They love it. It can get quite hilarious, outrageously wicked, but always funny, as if there's some unwritten rule that the man must not, on any account, be taken seriously. But sometimes I'd like to talk seriously, to know if Alice ever sees him, if Jane is ever in touch.

I try to ask Alice if she's seen him recently, but again she changes the subject, which makes me feel annoyed. For all the scathing jibes at his expense, it doesn't change the fact that he's won. He has the house and public sympathy for having a wife who was not only loopy (although not as loopy as he made out when he had her committed), but also left him, and everyone still keeps out of his way while he strides around unconcerned. Moreover, despite their bluster, I know there are places my aunts actually won't go in case they bump into him.

We begin to play cards. Little Beth flits off to the garden on a caterpillar hunt, not remotely interested in the game. She must take after Uncle Will in that respect; he can't tell clubs from spades.

We play a few hands and I begin to relax. They're obviously not going to talk about my grandfather, as they did when I was last here. I bombard questions at Alice. I want to know how she accomplished her amazing, secretive feat. But although she chats back easily, she changes the subject if I ask about her future plans. I feel she is being too modest.

Uncle Will arrives, fit and well-looking; he never looked like that when he worked for the mines. Farm life obviously suits him. It suits them all, I think, watching him put his arm around his wife. They smile at each other. My heart warms to them both, and to the precious red-haired bundle in the garden raiding my grandfather's cabbages. Maybe all does come to them what waits, as May puts it, succinctly if not grammatically.

The serious business of cards over, tea is served and I sit back, waiting for the easy chat to flow. But it doesn't. I can't quite put my finger on it. The conversation is too staccato, there are too many non-sequiturs, not like the girls at all. These sisters can conduct conversations at top speed using only half-sentences. Alice is repeatedly steering the conversation away from herself and Aunt Emily seems preoccupied.

Uneasily I begin to wonder if it's because of my outburst at the last class, and whether they're all treading carefully on my account, avoiding mention of my grandfather in case I get upset again.

But as the sherry comes out, and the chat loosens a little, my grandfather becomes part of the conversation. In fact he moves to the heart of the conversation. It's all 'John said this', 'John always liked that'. And in the whist post-mortem, 'Now if John were here he wouldn't have partnered a hand like that, I ask you—' And with regard to Beth, 'Poor John would have had a fit if he could see what she's done to his vegetable plot.'

I sit in silence. I don't know how they can, as if he wasn't dead, as if he'd just gone to the shops— *He's dead.* I feel my colour rising.

'Can you remember when your grandad found *you* digging up the cabbages?' Gran asks me directly.

I look at her, startled. My aunts are all laughing in anticipation. The story is part of family folklore, they know it well. They look to me, smiling, waiting. My mouth dries. *But he's dead—*

'Of course you do,' May says, as the pause lengthens. 'You found an old seaside bucket and spade, and thought you'd solve the caterpillar problem—'

'By getting rid of the cabbages!' Alice finishes, laughing. 'Covered in mud you were, clarts from one end—'

'It wasn't a spade. It was an old trowel,' I say, my face hot, my heart beating faster.

They wait patiently, deliberately letting the silence lengthen, as if they're determined to make me talk.

'And was your grandad cross?' Beth eventually nudges me, still giggling at the picture Alice has conjured up.

I'm about to turn away, but her five-year-old face is beaming at me. And suddenly I'm telling her the story, about my grandfather and how he was never angry with me, not really, and all at once it feels easy, and I talk more and more, and it's not painful at all. While Beth laughs like a hyena at the end of my tale, embellished and adorned with years of telling, my aunts smile at each other and clear the table.

I sit watching them. I'm not daft. 'That's right,' those smiles say. 'That's the way,' their satisfied nods say. They leave me on my own at the table.

Well, maybe they are right, I think, watching them whispering and half-falling over each other in the tiny scullery. Maybe they're right. If we talk, and let ourselves remember, then maybe those we love can stay with us. Gran looks at me over her shoulder and winks.

I sit peaceful and silent, contributing little to the conversation, concentrating instead on the sherry. I have to increase my capacity for alcohol if I'm to have any credibility as a student. It's a while before I realise that Emily and Alice are silent also.

'Something wrong with you two?' May asks after a while, looking at them both. 'Have you two been up to something together?'

Emily and Alice both look up, surprised, confusion mirrored in each other's faces.

'No!'

'Of course not,' Emily laughs.

But another silence follows.

We look from one to the other.

'Well, I do suppose I have something to tell you,' Aunt Emily finally begins. 'In fact I've spent nights wondering how to say this—'

We all wait. The clock ticks, it feels as if minutes pass.

Aunt Emily takes a breath. 'I'm going away,' she announces.

'Away?' chorus my gran and two aunts.

I look in dismay as Emily nods, her face serious.

'I'm taking early retirement— I'm emigrating.'

We all stare at her. All her life Emily has hankered after living abroad, somewhere with space, with the sun on her face, as she says. But to go *now*? At the age of fifty, alone, now that she's finally content and near her family? It doesn't make sense. It's taken years for her to feel close to people, she told me recently. And now that she has, she says she's leaving them!

'But why?' Alice tries to laugh, as if refusing to take it seriously.

'Where?' May asks quietly. 'Where are you going, Em?'

'To California.'

'But you'll be on your own again,' I wail.

'No, no I won't, Megan,' she says gently. Then she looks at each of us in turn, and takes another deep breath.

'It's a man!' Alice accuses suddenly. 'So that's it. You crafty old—'

Emily nods. 'Yes. It's my son.'

For several minutes you could have heard a pin drop. I stare at her, wanting to laugh. It's all obviously a joke. My Aunt Em always did have a dry sense of humour. It's a great joke.

'You had us all going there,' I say, giving her a nudge.

But she's still watching her sisters, waiting, anxious for their response. And Gran and my aunts are looking back at her in a different way now. It isn't a joke.

'He's been in touch then,' May murmurs.

'After all these years?' Alice shakes her head in disbelief.

It's only when photographs are produced that I can take in this extraordinary fact. 'Little lives,' I thought. I don't know the first thing.

'He's gorgeous,' I mutter, handing back the photograph to her. And he is. Tall, nice face, brilliant affro, and he has my Aunt Em's smile. And he's my cousin! Of sorts.

In the silence that follows Aunt Emily begins to talk, about a love affair in Liverpool, years before I was born, about a black American trumpeter. About a baby she had, and had to part with. And as I listen, I realise with a shock that she must have been about my age then. All that pain, to love and lose so much—

Little lives? They were huge, compared with mine. I've done little more than go to school. I look at them all, and get a sudden glimpse of another time, which is all I can get; but it's enough to make me feel sheepish and stupid and vow I'll never judge again, knowing of course that I will. But I'll try not to, at least not until I know my arse from my elbow a little better.

The sherry bottle does the rounds again. There's much to say. I call home to say I'm sleeping here after all and my mother sounds both pleased and unsurprised. 'The first step is the hardest, Megan,' says my proverbial mother. And then we talk, as the twilight deepens and the shadows lengthen in the tiny room. She's going to live near him in California, Emily tells us. At least for a while.

'And if I don't like it, I can always come home,' she finishes, raising her palms upwards.

It's late and dark but the conversation is still flowing. Gran switches on the lamp, and lights the gas fire that has recently replaced the coal fire I loved. We've talked about much, love stories coming from nowhere, not just about the trumpeter, but also about a man named James who died in Cyprus, whom Emily loved.

And after Will has taken little Beth away, May talks of her youth, of misunderstandings and crossed wires, of an Italian who died, about her feeling that *she* had died, because for a while she lost Will. Things that must have caused such pain, now talked of easily and quietly.

It's an odd evening. Even my gran, who despite the love she heaps on others prefers to keep her own emotions secret, even she tells

206

of a love story, between a gardener and a young girl. And I'm so wrapped up in it, for a while I don't realise it's her life with my grandfather she's describing.

I look at the photographs on the wall, going back through all the years, and then at my gran and aunts, and I think, *and now* I'm *part of it all*. I nod, impressed with this thought, in the way one is, when a little drunk, and convinced you've stumbled across a great truth. Gran looks, tuts, and moves my sherry glass away.

The gas fire hisses and pops in the pauses of the conversation. The room becomes warm, the overhead bulb flickers in power occasionally, casting odd shadows. I've missed coming here, I realise. Maybe that's why I've been dreaming of it so much over the last months.

It's always the same dream. It begins at the top of Gran's estate and I'm walking through the network of streets, past oddly-shaped trees, until I reach a giant pillar-box outside a blue door. When I open it, Gran and my aunts are there, waiting for me.

I go in and everything is entirely as it is in real life, except for one difference. In this room I can move things without touching them. And I can float, if I choose to, although I don't. In fact there's nothing I can't do in this room.

In my dream no one thinks this is in the slightest way odd. Gran's and my aunts' smiles are accepting and unsurprised, as I will glass, pen and paper to move towards me to take down the scores of our card games. As I play I'm aware of this power as a richness within me; it's there should I choose to draw on it. And it comes, not from the room itself, but from Gran and my aunts. I've been made up of bits of all of them. Because of this, I can do *anything*.

I giggle as the dream moves from the profound to the ridiculous, and my grandmother claps her hand over mine.

'Enough sherry, our Megan,' she tuts. 'You're all pink, as usual.'

People stand and stretch, and coats and scarves are produced. It's only when Alice loudly clears her throat that we notice she's still sitting at the table.

'Now that our Emily has us all well and truly stunned with *her* news,' she begins, 'maybe it's a good time to tell you my own.' Her laughter sounds unconvincing.

I turn back from where I was heading to the kitchen, thinking, good grief, not another revelation. Is Alice now going to come up with some secret love-child, some man of her dreams hidden in her cellar? I smile to myself. I wish she would. Despite the laughter and jokes, we all know that behind the jibes at her husband, behind the fact of her hospitalisation, behind Jane's choice to live far away from home, lie a fair few horrors.

I look at her hoping that she's going to tell us of some man friend, and for a moment can almost believe that she is.

'I'm going back to Patrick,' she quietly announces.

For the second time that evening you could hear a pin drop. The clock on the mantelpiece loudly chimes the quarter hour.

'I decided a while ago. I wanted to finish the degree, get a job, generally get myself sorted out first,' she says, not meeting anyone in the eye. 'Then I promised myself I'd go back.'

No one speaks.

'I know you'll be surprised, and probably won't approve, but—'

And suddenly everyone is talking at once. Except for me.

'You can't mean it, Alice,' Emily's voice is finally heard above the others. 'You can't do this,' she states firmly, using the voice she must use at work, to pull the department she's in charge of in line. But the expression in her eyes doesn't match her tone.

'You can't!' she exclaims, as bewildered as the rest of us, when Alice looks down at her hands. 'Not when you've come so far!'

'But I have to.'

'For Christ's sake why?' demands May, jumping to her feet. 'The man's not worth the time of day. He treated you terribly, Alice, you can't delude yourself any more about that. Pretending to yourself he was a good husband, insisting your marriage was fine, it had you in the funny farm! He's *no good*!'

'I have to,' Alice repeats, trying to smile at the table-cloth. 'I miss my home. So I have to.'

'And it'll be different now,' she says. 'I've changed. He'll have to see that, and respect that.'

She pauses and looks at each one of us in turn.

'This time it will be all champagne and roses. You'll see. Champagne and roses—'

17

Emily, Alice and May
1973

Alice walked along the landing of her home, in the direction of her husband's room. The house was warm with sunshine. Shafts of light streamed through the skylight and bounced off the newly painted walls. The first thing she'd done when she'd moved back home was to hire a couple of decorators to paint the house from top to bottom. Now it felt clean and peaceful and light, like her home again.

At his insistence, Patrick's room had not been painted, and so it was still the rather darkly-violent pink it had been when her daughter last slept there. He'd said if Alice wanted to waste her money she could go ahead, but she wasn't going to inconvenience him by imposing the smell of paint on where *he* slept.

He'd looked startled when she said she'd prefer to sleep separately for the moment. But he quickly recovered, satisfied by the familiar apologising tone when she explained that she slept so restlessly nowadays it would disturb him.

'Just for a while then, mind you,' he said. He could afford to be a little generous after she had come back so cap-in-hand. 'A husband has rights, after all.'

She didn't answer, but he didn't notice.

Instead he'd told her how he knew she would come back sooner or later, adding that she was lucky to have a husband who would take her back after the trouble and fuss she had caused. He misread her expression, thought the colour which flooded her cheeks was embarrassment. And he said that for the time being she could also continue with her job, it would be useful pin money and he could use a bob or two extra at the moment. Again, so easily satisfied that Alice had seen no need to correct his impression that she was a filing clerk.

'It keeps you off the streets, I suppose,' he said airily, disappearing behind his newspaper. 'Although I imagine it was your sisters that put you up to it. You wouldn't have the initiative.'

Unseen, Alice stared back coldly, then muttered something about Emily's help, causing him to reappear for a moment with a smug smile that said, no, his wife hadn't changed at all.

He wasn't a one for bearing grudges, he told her magnanimously at the end of their first week together, during which time they had seen little of each other, she being out through the day, he out (where, he didn't say) each evening. He would let her settle down, he said. He was man enough of the world to know that changes took time, but then things would have to go back to normal. And no nonsense about it. Which meant that he was going to return to her bed.

At the door of his room Alice hesitated. The curtains were still drawn, the air was stale. It was the first time she'd entered this room in years. It was here that she'd read her daughter to sleep, comforted her after nightmares, helped with homework, listened to problems. Jane wouldn't set foot in the North-East any longer, let alone in this house. And so it was for Jane also that she had to do this.

She walked over and opened the window. A cold gust pulled at the curtains and she breathed deeply, letting it fill her lungs, replacing the stale air. Below her, the garden lay totally overgrown. The vegetable patch Patrick had made just before she left, digging up her beautiful roses, had obviously been short-lived. But of course, it hadn't been vegetables Patrick had been interested in. He'd been more concerned with hurting her. She turned away from the overgrown patch of earth and began the task in hand.

It took her only a few minutes to find what she was looking for. At first she wasn't sure if she would find anything, and thought that perhaps her suspicions after this morning's telephone call were the product of hopefulness. But there it was, hidden between the base and mattress of the bed. A pale-blue exercise book. And Alice suddenly knew, with absolute certainty, what it would contain.

She took it back to her own room, and sat, savouring the moment. The room was white and restful once more. Prints of old paintings she loved had replaced Patrick's half-naked, knowing women. Strange that he hadn't objected to their removal. Had he changed? Or was he merely treading carefully, for some unknown reason?

She opened the exercise book, flicked through its pages, read a few of the tiny cramped blue entries, and then she sat in the silence of the room, her eyes closed in an attitude of prayer. A prayer of thanksgiving.

After a while she went downstairs to telephone the anxious woman who had called earlier.

Then she called her sister Emily.

'Champagne and roses. Which do you want to do?' she asked, without even announcing who it was.

'Really? You're sure? You've checked?' The caution in Emily's voice was overridden by eagerness. 'I mean this morning you weren't sure. It was only speculation, you said.'

'Quite sure. And what's more, he's written it all down. Typical, pedantic Patrick.'

There was a silence followed by a long exhalation of breath from the other end of the line.

'Champagne it is,' Emily said with a sudden laugh. 'Much more my style. Leave the roses to May.'

Alice then dialled the farm at Stamfordham.

Emily put down the phone and rolled over in her bed. There was something delicious about being in bed late on a weekday morning. It was the same feeling of luxury she remembered in bed ill as a child, watching the clock hands move round to the magic time when she should have been in school – now they'd be queuing in the yard, now standing in assembly, sitting in class— She laughed at herself. The novelty would no doubt wear off soon enough. She'd only been retired for a week. In a few months she'd probably be up at six, pacing, desperate for something to do.

But deep down she doubted it. There were a million things she wanted to do with her time, with her life. She'd rediscovered her passion for music, she wanted to take up the painting she'd never had time for, to have enough time to read the list of books that had grown immense over the busy years. But most of all she wanted to travel. There was a brave new world out there.

She stretched, got out of bed, and walked over to the window to see what kind of a day it was. It was a glorious morning, crisp, clear and spring-like, the ghost of a moon still hanging in a pale-blue sky, trees unfurling fresh green foliage, undulled by the city's dust. But most of all it was a glorious morning because her sister Alice had finally found a way.

She'd been convinced Alice was wrong to risk her safety by moving back with Patrick Sullivan, and suspicious of the man's motives at having her back. But it looked as if Alice had been right. It was the only way, her sister had insisted. And she seemed to have played him like a fish on a line. When Emily visited the week before, she'd seen Patrick look puzzled once or twice at what Alice said, but then Alice would quietly defer, and the stupid man's frown would lift. His arrogance was keeping Alice safe.

Emily quickly dressed in track suit and trainers, pulled her hair back into a band and went out into the morning, looking light years away from a retired senior civil servant of fifty. She walked with a light step. If Alice had really cracked it, well now she could make her plans. She'd been delaying only until she knew her sister was safe. Maybe she could even write to Matthew today?

But first, Alice—

The wine merchant was helpful, dispensing recommendations quickly so that he could ask Emily about her plans. Everyone in the community seemed to know about her proposed move to the United States.

'Soon now, I think,' she answered him, examining the dustily expensive bottle he directed her to. 'This will be perfect. Just a few loose ends to tie up and that will be it.'

'We'll miss you,' said the shopkeeper with genuine regret, and Emily was touched. Over the last five years the area had come to feel like a community she was most definitely part of.

'I'll be coming back from time to time, I expect.' She smiled and added, 'You won't get rid of me as easily as that.'

Someone else had once said those words to her. And it was because of James she could say them now.

She carried the bottle carefully. The champagne would be old and golden and delicious. It wasn't chilled, but she had plenty of time; it wouldn't be needed until later in the afternoon.

*　　*　　*

'Roses? You're sure, Alice? Already?' May demanded.

Her smile broadened as, at the other end of the line, her sister talked.

'Jesus. You be careful. You know what the bugger's like,' she warned, but her smile was growing wider. Her sister seemed more than able to take care of herself nowadays.

By her side her daughter was pulling at her skirt, demanding to be able to speak to Aunt Alice. Not today, she was told. Today they had to get busy.

Holding the child's hand May walked quickly through the farm yard and out through the cowsheds to where Will was ploughing up the far field. They were moving the farm away from dairy and more towards arable. They had devised the five-year plan together, sitting up late, night after night, too excited at the prospect of their future to want to do anything as mundane as sleep. Neither had any doubt that it would work and the farm would be successful.

She and Beth walked briskly, the child breaking into a run every now and again to keep up. The day was bright. They passed through the orchard, where some of the apple trees were already showing blossom after the mild winter, yet late primroses were still tucked in cushions at the base of the trees. Even the weather was being kind to them. They'd fallen on their feet in every way. The farm looked set to do well, Beth was growing strong and happy, and both she and Will were in better health than they had been for years. Every day May felt like giving thanks that this was *her* life, every morning brought a consciousness of contentment, an excitement at the prospect of the day ahead.

Somewhere along the lines, she must have done something right to be rewarded with all this, she had said at the class the week before. Everyone had laughed, and said she deserved it, but they couldn't understand how good it was.

The only thing that blighted her happiness was Alice's situation. But roses, Alice had said. And she seemed sure.

Will was on the tractor at the far end of the field. The new green vehicle slowed and stopped as May and Beth picked their way through the ploughed earth, rooks and crows swooping around their heads for what the earth had turned up.

'Alice says she's ready,' May said simply, shouting above the noise of the engine.

He looked surprised. 'Already? But she's only been there a couple of weeks.'

May nodded. 'Long enough. She seems sure. I don't think she'd risk anything if she weren't. The bugger's too predictable. She's going to tell him this afternoon.'

'Do you want me to be there?' He frowned.

He knew Patrick Sullivan. In fact he knew a lot more than his wife realised. He'd made it his business to know; his wife cared about her family, and so he did too.

He knew Sullivan had few acquaintances and even fewer friends, but he had a large capacity for trouble. There were many stories circulating; last year there had even been a court case when he'd broken some poor kid's nose in a pub.

And, more recently, Will had learned of gambling debts, just from the dog tracks admittedly, but made with pretty dubious parties. He had tried to find out more, in case it would be of help to Alice. He'd been surprised that Sullivan had let her move back; Sullivan made no bones in the pub about what he thought of his wife. But the gambling made sense of it all. Sullivan was in trouble. He wanted Alice back, no longer as someone to bully, but for her money. Alice now had a wage-earning job, as well as her savings.

'I think I'd better go alone,' May said, but grateful for his concern. She told him everything, involved him in all aspects of her life, but Alice had insisted. They looked at each other thoughtfully, each knowing what the other was thinking.

'But you could deliver a bag or two for the roses if you want. And if you deliver this afternoon, say around four, you might just be in time for a glass or two?'

He nodded. 'I know my place.' He grinned, turned the tractor round, and headed in the direction of the stables.

May and the child made their way back to the farmhouse and out into the garden. Unlike in May's aunt and uncle's day, there was now a lawn, on which stood a swing, a well-used sand-pit, several ornamental trees, and at the back, just before the field sloped away, there was a rose garden.

Here, in a sunny spot, sheltered from the wind, May grew old-fashioned roses, Gallicas, Damask, Bourbon and China, seeking them out from nurseries all over the North-East, some that maybe only flowered once a summer but did so perfectly.

And here, among these tidy, well-tended plants, stood five special rose bushes in containers, awaiting delivery. These were a different kind of rose altogether. Flowers ranging from white to deep scarlet would pour from these plants, in a wild and free profusion. They were not May's taste at all. But Alice would love them.

Alice made her way through the red-brick estate, carrying the large brown envelope tightly in her hand, hoping Rose would be at home. Her eldest sister lived closest, so that was best. She didn't want to waste any time. Letting herself in, as was always the way between the sisters, Alice found Rose sitting with Megan, reading in a companionable silence in front of the fire.

She declined their invitation to stay for lunch, and stalled their anxious questions.

'But if you could look after this for me, Rose,' she said, handing over the envelope that contained Patrick's book. 'I'd be grateful. It's valuable.'

Rose and Megan exchanged a look, but asked no more questions.

'And I'll call you later,' Alice promised.

Alice sat in the living-room, waiting. She'd made a few more telephone calls, just to make sure. Most of the people she called were surprised to learn that she was back and helping Patrick once more. Years earlier she used to ring to make appointments with those who hadn't been at home when Patrick called to collect their premiums.

Only one woman sounded less than pleased to hear from her. Her tone, and its rising volume as she stated she would only conduct business with Patrick, suggested she perhaps did more than merely conduct business with her estranged husband.

But the others had been helpful and were more than happy to give Alice the information she needed. So that she now had verbal confirmation that there were several families from whom Patrick was collecting money, that did not appear in his official books. Their premiums were not being handed over to the insurance society. They were going into Patrick's pocket.

Alice sat calmly reflecting. She couldn't have expected help like this. Moving back with Patrick had not been without its risks, and despite what she said to her sisters, Alice knew she would need a lot of luck. But she'd felt she had no other choice, and that she was as ready as she ever would be. She had run from Patrick the last time, run away to her sisters when she left hospital, too frightened to face him. Well, now she wasn't prepared to run any longer. To be free, really free, she told herself, she would have to face him, and confront him.

Over the last two weeks she'd repeated this like a litany, a charm to give herself courage. She was no longer a victim, she'd whisper, as he mumbled disdain behind his newspaper. Between abuser and abused there was a complicity, she'd chant, as he smiled smugly, so sure of her compliance. She could no longer be bullied. He no longer frightened her. In fact at times she could hardly keep the scorn out of her face. And it was time Patrick saw that.

But there was another reason for moving back. It was time to reclaim her home, for herself, and for Jane, she hoped. At first in defeat she had been prepared to lose it. But not any longer. Alice wanted it back, and all her instincts told her that to achieve this she would have to move back. Patrick had always been susceptible to the temptation of money, but he could also be stubborn if he thought this would hurt; he could refuse to sell his share, purely out of spite.

But now she'd found a way to guarantee his co-operation. The anxious woman who had called earlier, saying she couldn't afford this week's premium, had given her a gift, handed her the solution on a plate. To think, if she hadn't tried to check up on the woman's account, and then been unable to trace it in Patrick's official book, she would never have known.

Alice had felt many things over the years about marrying Patrick, regret, disappointment, pain and even horror, but for the first time in her life she now felt shame. Her husband was not only defrauding the company he worked for, but he was also stealing from the people he lived with, people who hardly had anything anyway.

The front door slammed. She'd told him she'd be home today, that it was her day off. She waited, her heart beating at the same steady rate, her hands still cool in her lap. The truth was the man was no longer some monster to be feared, but a petty, contemptuous thief who would stoop to stealing from his own, a bully who would take money from the smaller kids in the playground.

'Alice? Alice!'

He looked surprised to find her sitting comfortably in the living-room, and not in the kitchen.

'What's all this then,' he muttered gruffly, going back into the hall to hang up his coat and hat. 'Sitting around the house like lady muck?'

His tone was ambivalent. He could have been joking. She saw him glance at her. Patrick still wasn't sure of her. He was definitely treading carefully. Maybe because of a realisation, conscious or otherwise, that she could no longer be bullied. But she suspected it was more because he wanted something from her. And it had to be money.

'So where's the dinner, then?' he asked a little more belligerently. His wife hadn't leapt to her feet as she would have done at one time.

'There's plenty for lunch in the fridge. You can help yourself,' Alice said evenly, managing a small smile.

He frowned, a little thrown.

'But it's a bloody cold day and when I get back I expect—'

'Patrick,' she interrupted. 'Sit down. We need to talk.'

He stared, surprised.

Alice nodded in the direction of the armchair opposite.

'Go on. What I have to say will take a while. You'll be glad of the seat.'

He laughed shortly. 'What the hell is going on with you, woman, ordering me to sit down in my own house, not getting the dinner, sitting here like you own—'

'But I do, Patrick,' Alice said quietly. 'I do own this house. I own the major share. Which is what I want to talk to you about.'

He stood stunned a moment, and then burst into explosive laughter.

'You! Own anything! Look, woman,' he said, smiling easily again. Now he felt he knew where he was. 'It wasn't so long ago that you were in the bloody loony bin. Then you deserted me, *and* this house.' Still smiling, but his colour had heightened. 'You walked out on me, madam, so don't go on about what you own. You forfeited everything. In fact the way I see it, you owe *me*. The maintenance of this house has cost me money. And I know you have savings.'

Alice shook her head. 'Patrick, listen—'

'Although I'd like to know where your savings book is,' he

continued, with less effort at control. 'You must have left most of your stuff with your sisters because I'm damned if I can find—'

He suddenly stopped. Alice was smiling at him, actually smiling.

'I knew you'd go through my things,' she said wryly. 'I knew that you'd take whatever was in my purse.'

'What the—? I would never—'

'You always did,' she interrupted. 'So let's not pretend. We both know exactly what our relationship was.'

He stared at her as if he had never seen her before.

'Sit down, Patrick.'

Wary, suspicious, he slowly sat down. 'You've changed,' he said, half-statement, half-accusation.

He sat watching her in silence, then with a smile that looked as if it caused him pain, he sat forward.

'Now, Alice,' he began carefully. 'I'm your husband. I know you've been ill, and that we've been living apart for a while, but things *were* beginning to get back to normal.'

He reached forward and self-consciously took her hand. 'So let's not spoil it. I'm an easy-going man, I don't even mind you working if you contribute your share. I know the clerk in our office gets a tidy little—'

'I'm not a clerk.' Alice looked down at the hand covering hers and withdrew her own. 'I'm an officer at the Ministry.'

He raised his eyebrows. 'Alice, Alice, where do you get it from?' He laughed, amused. 'You have to have an education for that. Still in fantasy land, I see.' His eyes narrowed slightly. 'You're not still seeing those doctors, are you?'

Alice sighed.

'Here.' She took her business card from her bag, handed it to him, and watched him reading it over and over.

'It was you who assumed I was a clerk. And as for the doctors, well I never really needed to see them in the first place. All I needed was to find the strength to get free of you.'

She leaned forward.

'Listen,' she said. 'Not that this has much to do with anything, other than the fact that I can afford to buy you out, but I'll tell you anyway. I have a degree, a staff, and a good salary—'

As she named the amount Patrick's colour faded further. She laughed. He looked like a wide-eyed child.

He cleared his throat and tried to collect himself, the salary she'd named still ringing in his ears.

'Well this is a turn-up,' he said trying to sound pleased. 'I never thought you had it in you!' trying to laugh.

'You never really thought about *me* at all,' said Alice, quietly. 'Let's face it. We were a disastrous couple.'

'But that's rubbish,' he said, alarm now showing in his face. 'We were happily married for—'

'You used to beat me up, to say nothing of the other forms of cruelty you managed to inflict—'

The words hung in the air.

He shook his head, as if he truly didn't understand what she was saying.

'Nonsense— A slap now and then when you deserved it, but—'

With an effort, Alice resisted putting her hands over her ears.

'Don't say that. Don't you dare say that.' Her voice was little more than a whisper. 'We both knew how it really was. I kidded myself for years. You'd better not start pretending now. Anyway,' her tone became brisk. 'I want my house. You never had any love for the place. And Jane needs somewhere to come back to. If she has a home here she might consider getting a teaching job in Newcastle. The flat was too small for both of us.'

She looked him directly in the eye.

'I want my home back, Patrick. And I want you to leave. I'll give you—'

His sudden laugh was loud and humourless.

'God, you're stupid,' he said, face suddenly serious. 'You might have your bloody degree but you still haven't a brain, have you. As thick as two short—'

Alice raised her eyes wearily. 'I was trying to say I'll pay you what it's worth.'

'And what makes you think I'd sell to you?'

'Because you don't really want this house. Because you only kept living in it because you knew it would hurt me. Because you get a thrill from hurting people, even if it is someone as weak as you perceive me to be.'

His face darkened again.

'And because you want the money. Badly, I suspect, or you wouldn't have had me back. And you wouldn't be still sitting opposite, looking like that, twitching your fists because you're dying to hit me, to shout at me, and generally make the fuss for which you are justly famous.'

There was a few moments silence in which neither could believe this was Alice who had spoken.

Slowly Patrick sat back in his chair and folded his arms.

'So maybe I *could* do with the money,' he nodded. He sat looking at her, thinking. 'But I've got other sources— And I'd rather get it from them, than give you any satisfaction.'

The clock struck three. Alice's palms were damp. She stood up and walked over to the window.

'I have a book,' she said quietly, looking out over the overgrown tangle of weeds at the back of the house. She turned her head to look at him. 'A book I found this morning.'

'Aye, well?' he said confidently, sure of his position once more. His wife was changing the subject. She always knew when she was beaten.

'It's your book I found,' Alice said, still gazing out of the window. 'It was under your mattress. It's similar to the one you hand in each Friday to the insurance office listing the premiums you've collected. Except it contains the names of those people you collect from— but keep the money for yourself.'

There wasn't a sound from behind her.

'And the amounts you take— And for how long you've been taking their money.'

Slowly she turned.

He looked as if he'd been slapped.

'That's theft, Patrick. And because of that, you *will* leave this house, or people will get to know. And I suggest you also make some sort of repara—'

Patrick jumped to his feet and began making for the door.

'The book is no longer here,' she said calmly. 'I'm really not stupid, you see. It's in a safe place.'

He moved a few paces towards her and stood, white with fury, his face working.

She made herself hold his gaze. 'There's no point looking like that. I have the book, you see.'

She turned back to the window. Behind her the silence lengthened. Her heart beat faster. She tried to steady her breathing. She mustn't let him see her fear. The back of her neck was pricking, his eyes were still on her. Maybe she should have told her sisters to come earlier, agreed that May could bring Will. The clock ticked. Still he hadn't moved. Now she hardly dared to breathe. From outside came the noise of a lorry stopping, followed by the sound of someone in the alley.

'I'll pay you your share,' she said to fill the tense silence. 'Emily has said she will lend me the money if I can't get a bank loan arranged, but now that I'm working—'

She could sense him moving closer, knew from years of experience what his expression would be.

She swung around quickly.

'Someone's out the back,' she said, although she had heard whoever it was leaving the alley. 'It's probably the dustbin men. I need to speak with them,' she lied, wishing it was, wishing she'd moved sooner.

She turned and moved past him as slowly as she could manage, seeing him out of the corner of her eye, his mouth set, fists clenched. She walked into the kitchen and out into the garden, fighting the urge to run. And as she knew he would, Patrick was suddenly following, rapidly.

'Why, you little bitch,' he shouted from behind. 'You'll bloody well pay for this—'

'It wasn't the dustbin men,' she said, her mouth drying, knowing what was to come, again, *God, again*, after she'd determined he would never harm her again. She'd got it wrong. She shouldn't have played it like this. She should have moved sooner. *She'd got it wrong.*

She stared at the pile of manure that Will had dumped at the side of the garden.

'It wasn't the binmen,' she whispered again, licking her lips.

And he was behind her, she could feel him at her back. She moved quickly, sure the first blow would come from behind, and turned to face him. Fist raised, cursing under his breath, Patrick darted forward. She sidestepped a sack of coal, no longer laboriously emptied into the coal shed, as he'd insisted she did in the past, and braced herself, closing her eyes. God, *again*. *It was going to happen again*—

The blow didn't come.

221

She opened her eyes as Patrick tripped against the sack, stumbled to regain his balance, his fist still outstretched, and for a moment time appeared to stop, frozen, as he leaned precariously, his body suspended in mid-air as if by strings. In slow motion, Alice saw her hand move out towards him, she stretched out her index finger, and pushed. Ever so lightly. That was all that was needed. And in equally slow motion, Patrick toppled into the steaming pile Will had kindly emptied from his stable, and delivered for Alice's roses.

'Champagne and roses,' Alice said, holding on to her arms to stop herself shaking, to stop herself laughing, to stop herself from jumping up and down like a six-year-old. She smiled at her sisters who had just arrived.

Emily was holding a large and expensively labelled bottle in one hand, while May had her arms around a tub containing a white rose bush, which was small but would grow, grow gloriously, Alice was sure. And both were staring down at Patrick Sullivan. Both also appeared to have lost the power of speech.

'Bloody hell, Will, would you come and look at this silly bugger,' May suddenly shouted over her shoulder down the alley.

'Are you all right?' Emily asked Alice, but still with her eyes on the prone, dung-covered form.

Alice nodded. She was trembling, but no longer with fear. The adrenalin coursing through her veins had nothing to do with fear.

'I'm fine. Absolutely fine.'

In fact she was more than fine. A great deal more. She'd done it. *She'd done it.* And by God, from the way she'd done it, someone up there must have been looking after her, she was to tell everyone later, as the story turned into family folklore, to be related with the 'Megan-and-the-cabbages' story, 'the-day-Beth-tried-to-milk-the-donkey' story.

She was never to add that if her sisters hadn't turned up when they did, she was under no illusions about what would have happened to her. He would have half-killed her. Of this she had no doubt.

But she was fine. Absolutely fine.

'Champagne and roses,' she repeated, her voice lifting as if in song, and smiled broadly at them both.

She stood, holding herself quietly. She had escaped his fists, and now would never be threatened by them again.

She looked up at a noise in the alley. Rose and Megan arrived with Will. There were several minutes' silence as everyone watched Patrick pick himself up and dust himself down as well as he could.

'You're just in time,' Alice said quietly to no one in particular. 'Patrick's just leaving.'

18

The Class
1990

Youth, large, lusty, loving – Youth, full of
grace, force, fascination,
Do you know that Old Age may come after you,
with equal grace, force, fascination?
                                    Walt Whitman

A thick sea fret has clung around my village all morning, shrouding the houses, muffling car engines, making eerie echoes of the footsteps and voices of those mad enough to brave its chill, but now I see it's lifting, and rolling out to sea.

I bend to the window to scan the sky for more scraps of pale-blue showing through the once-dense whiteness. Strands of mist are swirling, careering down towards the beach as if racing against time.

Good. I didn't like to think of my gran and great-aunts making their way in this. No old ladies they, they insist, but these sea mists can chill through to your very bones, June or no June. Half a mile away, of course, it will be clear as a bell. My road is the last in the village, although village isn't a very apt description for a place that can grow while your back is turned, creeping ever closer to Newcastle, stretching fingers just a little further up and down the Northumbrian coast.

But not eastward, because here we overlook the sea. And, as a result, have a micro-climate all our own.

Beyond the window my garden is springing into existence, hedges of fuschias suddenly appearing, a lawn grey with dew gradually extending down to a still looming, ghostly shrubbery. It will be bright and sunny by the time they arrive. Not that Gran and her sisters would mind if it wasn't. Put those women together and the chat flows so freely they wouldn't notice a hurricane. But I want things to be perfect today.

Everything is ready for them. I've stuffed the wrappings from the fondant fancies, jam tarts and chocolate cake to the bottom of the bin, not that this will fool anyone for a moment. They all know that despite my apprenticeship in Gran's kitchen I couldn't make a swiss roll even if I pushed it. I've produced a couple of doilies from my daughter's craft drawer to line the plates, which will no doubt raise eyebrows. *Our Megan pushing the boat out.* And the sherry, pale cream, nothing but the best. I want things to be special. After all, this *is* the class, and more importantly, it's the first class at my home.

At least that's what I've told Laura, my daughter, who is sitting with her nose pressed to the window in the living-room, anxiously waiting for signs of arrival. All week she's been full of the 'knitting class'.

'It all began when your Gran and aunts, and their friends, got together to knit clothes for soldiers during the war,' I told her, all set for a make-history-fun session.

But it was the subsequent card-playing that has fired her imagination. It must be in the genes. They're all coming to teach her to play rummy, she tells anyone and everyone who will listen. She has two packs set out ready on the coffee table and her face is pale with excitement.

'Who's coming apart from Gran MacIntyre?' she comes to ask for the third time.

'Your aunts Emily, Alice and May,' I tell her, buttering white bread for sandwiches. Her eyes grow enormous. *She*'s only allowed white bread at parties. But it is a party, I say. And May pulls my leg if I serve brown. Middle-class lunacy she calls it, pointing out we're happy to have white if it's fashionably long, and called French. You don't get away with anything with my aunts.

'Emily—' Laura repeats. She knows the others quite well but she's forgotten Emily, whom she only met once, when she was last over from the States.

'Aunt Emily,' I nod. 'Another of Gran MacIntyre's little sisters.'

She laughs, and tells me they're not little at all, but big and old, and goes off chanting their names, Emily, Alice and May— Then she sticks her head back round the door.

'You're humming "Popeye the Sailor Man",' she accuses.

'No, I wasn't,' I say, surprised, and then laugh, catching an echo.

Emily, Alice and May— To the tune of 'Popeye the Sailor Man'.

She nods with satisfied finality. 'And you say *I* watch too much TV,' and goes off, still nodding, six years old going on sixty.

Upstairs I hear the baby stirring. Undoing my blouse I hurry off. I want him to be sweet and happy and peaceful when he meets the clan. Crazy, because they'll love him anyway. How could they not? Admittedly he's at the end of a long line, but he'll figure as largely as any of us have in their affections. The spotlight moves on. And he'll provide yet another name to add to the growing list which precedes my own. Whenever Gran addresses me nowadays, it's first with my mother's name, then May's daughter's, then Laura's, before she finally gets to me.

'Betty-Beth-Laura-Megan come and thread this needle for me,' she'll say, rattling out the names with an enviable fluency and always in the same order. In time, no doubt, the baby's will be added, as he takes centre stage.

They arrive at the front door while I'm still feeding him and I come down to find Laura doing the honours to a Geordie gaggle of excited talk and laughter, unseasonal fur and wisps of chiffon. From the noise level, you'd think they were sixteen and arriving at their first dance. I smile and bend to kiss a powdered cheek or two, but my eyes go to Emily. I haven't seen her for three years. I put out my arms, catch her familiar perfume and the emotion surprises me. My emotions seem perilously close to the surface nowadays.

Emily whispers as she holds me tighter. 'I'm so sorry about your mother, Megan,' and I stiffen, caught off-balance. It's only three months since she died.

She draws back, holding my arms outstretched, beaming, looking me up and down.

'And another baby?' she nods, delighted.

I see with a small shock that one half of her face doesn't move as she speaks. Perhaps she notices, because she turns quickly to Laura.

'My God, she looks like you, Megan,' she exclaims with a laugh. 'A proper little clone!' And she bends stiffly, but still with grace, and introduces herself to Laura, with as much dignity as Laura is addressing her.

'Well, you don't sound like an American,' Laura announces, looking at Emily hard, as if she might prove to be a fake on closer inspection.

'Geordie-Americans are different, my sweet,' Emily says, taking her hand easily. Laura nods, and her frown lifts.

'*This* one's going to be an actress,' my grandmother proudly announces, as my daughter leads the way into her first knitting class.

We busy ourselves with our cards, tactfully pretending not to look as the fan May has made for Laura collapses yet again. I did try to tell Laura that she would only be able to manage seven cards, but she was determined to have eleven. A very determined young lady, May calls her.

Red-faced and frowning with concentration, Laura arranges them again. Only four are visible, I see, but she doesn't seem to mind. Assorted helpful hands, sparklingly bejewelled with pearls and paste, diamanté and diamond, lined and blotched with work and age, reach across to take or add to her fan.

'That five goes there, pet—'

'Pick up the Jack now, there's a girl—'

And, 'You *do* want that, you know.'

'The queen goes there,' May says in a stage whisper.

'But I want to keep *her*,' Laura whispers back equally loudly. 'She's pretty.'

May nods. 'Good idea. And here's another pretty one,' she says, handing Laura the Queen of Hearts. 'Better dress sense.' She gives the child a conspiratorial wink.

I look at them all in surprise as Alice proceeds to dig out a queen from her hand to give to Laura, then Emily produces the fourth. I laugh and put down my cards. Maybe next year. Laura's obviously not old enough yet. Although I was red-hot at cards at her age. Maybe cards isn't in your blood after all.

I apologise as Laura pretends the four queens are having a conversation, and I know we are seconds away from their removal to the doll's house. But Alice just laughs.

'Ee, she's just like you were at that age,' she says fondly. 'You weren't any different.'

Rubbish, I think, surprised. I was *ace* at cards. And I joined in their games as an equal, didn't I? Card games were serious business.

'It could be thirty years ago,' Emily agrees, and they begin helping Laura to create a house out of the two packs.

'Just like you, Megan,' May chimes in, forming a careful triangle for the roof.

I stare at their indulgent smiles, thinking, Rubbish! I can remember! It wasn't like this at all!

The cards collapse and whirl to the floor. I watch my aunts patiently begin again and think, could they really have been like this with me? Did they humour me too? Wasn't it all rummy and whist?

'But that's not how I remember it,' I tell them, confused, picking up the cards at my feet. 'We played cards for real, surely.'

'Later maybe, but we had many a silly game with you as a bairn,' May says.

And again, I feel caught off-balance.

I flush, and see them exchanging glances.

'Megan—?' says May.

I shake my head. 'It's just that I've been thinking back a lot recently,' I say, with a small laugh. 'At least I've been trying to— But it's difficult.'

The card castle is abandoned, and Laura gathered on to someone's lap.

They smile at me, waiting patiently as always.

'It's as if my mind won't co-operate, is denying me access—' I attempt to laugh again, but I can't. Because it frightens me that I can't remember, that since my mother's death I've been unable to hear her voice, that when I look back I can only see my childhood self without her. If you lose your memories, you lose part of yourself. If you lose it all, who are you?

'Give yourself time, it will come,' says Alice, gently.

They know, of course. They always know.

May reaches out for my hand. 'Grief takes a while.'

I nod, and take my daughter on my lap.

Aunt Emily reaches over and pats my hand.

'Time— give it time,' she says.

Then, 'Don't you remember how we used to make card castles with you?'

I nod, but I *don't* remember.

Maybe it's *their* collective memory at fault, I think, as Laura begins another castle. Maybe they weren't like this with me, at all. Maybe they've just mellowed with time.

Laura screams with delight as the cards fly everywhere again.

'More!' she yells, and they laugh. 'Again!'

Was I like this? Were they? How can we know that what we remember is what actually happened? That after a lifetime of sifting, evaluating and editing, those events we've stored away really happened?

Did I really dig up all my grandfather's cabbages? Unlikely, but they tell me I did, so I must have done. I think I remember the story, not the event.

And did five-foot-nothing Alice really push fourteen-stone Patrick Sullivan into a load of manure, or is that family folklore too?

And did he really come into my bedroom to abuse me, or was it that I disliked him so much my mind constructed words, to describe events, to fit that emotion?

How can I tell? Most conscious memories are just words, and the words I have now are not those of a child. So how valid does that make my memories?

But they are mine. And now, when I want them, now, when I need *them, they're not all there.*

'Time,' they repeat gently. 'You just need more time.'

My new son is produced, the real reason for this visit, and he's pronounced a bundle of the most wonderful, beautiful, edible, etc., just as they've pronounced every other baby that has appeared over the years. Instantly bored, Laura goes out to play and the talk changes. I used to think they talked with me as an equal. Did they wait until *I'd* gone out to play?

My son is passed from lap to lap like a precious parcel and there's much clucking and cooing.

'There's good stuff comes in little bundles,' my grandmother says and glances at me, because the proverb was one of my mother's.

'Come and have a dandle on your Great-Gran's knees,' she suddenly half-says, half-sings, and everyone laughs.

I'm quiet as they talk. Repeatedly my eyes flick to Emily. The right side of her face is stiff, which gives her a slightly lop-sided look when she speaks, but only slightly. She must be in her late sixties, I calculate, and she looks it, and she looks beautiful. But it's a different beauty to that of her youth, because now, in addition, there are grace and maturity and contentment in its lines.

She's been aware of my glances of course; she always could read my mind.

'It's nothing, Megan,' she assures me between bounces of my small son, worryingly energetic for a 'mature' lady, as they all call themselves. 'Not even worth writing home about. I had a small stroke, that's all.'

And she proceeds to talk about some place she's visited recently, and I think with irritation that she's changing the subject, but then I realise she's building up to telling us something.

'It's in Arizona,' she says, describing a town set on tall red bluffs, near a river, high in the Arizona plateau. 'Only an hour away from Matthew and his family by plane, and—'

'You're moving again!' Alice accuses, admiration and envy in her voice.

'*Enormous* skies,' Emily says. 'Somewhere with space, with the sun on your face—'

Her sisters and I smile at each other. We can't help smiling. We've heard these words many times before from Emily.

'So it sounds like you've finally found it, eh, Aunt Em,' I tease.

'If you could only see it, Megan!' she says, sounding so excited, not the cool Aunt Em of old at all.

I ask about the retired lawyer friend she's written to me about over the last year, already knowing somehow that she will not be going alone.

'We're thinking of getting married, if he can persuade me it's not too ridiculous at my age,' she laughs.

Space, the sun on her face and people to love. I'm more happy for her than I can say.

'And you must all come and visit!'

Gran and May laugh. As well they might. You'll not prise them out of the North-East, let alone get them out of the country.

But my indomitable Aunt Alice will be there like a shot, of course.

'You try and keep me away,' she nods.

As if we could. At sixty-two my Aunt Alice is formidable, one of the greatest gad-abouts in Newcastle. Since she retired it's as if there's not enough time in the day, or places in the world. Her energy puts me to shame.

She laughs as May pretends to take her to task about her latest jaunt.

'Grief Alice, such timing! Eastern Europe! Walls coming down, and six countries in ten days?'

'I'm simply behaving like the woman I was always meant to be,' she says, with a wink to me.

And it's true, of course. Jane never did move back as Alice had hoped, but still, she's made quite a life for herself, has my Aunt Alice.

'And better late than never,' May tells her gruffly, with a nod.

May too is happy, despite the perennial gruffness that fools no one nowadays. Her contentment shows in her face, still unlined after all these years, beneath a mane that grows more outrageously and improbably red as the years go by. Aunt Belisha, I'm threatening to call her. She and Will grow roses commercially on the farm now.

'Better late than never,' May repeats, giving Alice a nudge in the ribs. 'Though you left it late enough.'

They pretend to argue. I watch them, amused.

When I was very young, about Laura's age, I remember them arguing for real. I asked them recently what it was all about, and was it over a man, I suggested, some echo or other sounding in my mind.

Alice looked away, flushed, which said it all. But strangely, May, who is as upfront as they come, denied all knowledge.

'Edward Hepple,' Alice muttered under her breath after a while, and May looked astonished, her eyes suddenly the size of saucers.

'Never—! You as well? You daft bugger!'

And they both proceeded to roar with laughter for the best part of an hour. I couldn't understand a word of it. But I suppose I can't expect them to share *all* their secrets with me.

The card games start again and Laura returns to join us. We play blind horse and she suddenly catches on, becoming totally focused, to the point that she begins to clean up. Purses have to be sought from handbags as her pile of twopences grows. She beams at us and scoops up her winnings gleefully. Maybe it *is* in your blood.

She whispers to each old lady in turn, seducing them with her intimacy. I wonder how she sees them all. She huddles conspiratorially with May, who laughs and nods. Was I like this at her age? I vaguely remember being afraid of May, at one time. More tricks of the memory?

She disappears and comes back with a 'treasure' for her 'new' Aunt Emily, uncurling sticky little fingers to reveal a bewildered beetle, its legs in the air. Alice joins in with the appropriate exclamations, and rights the poor creature after admiring it for a suitable time. Satisfied, Laura returns it to its home, hopefully not in my bed, and comes back to whisper again with her great-gran and great-great-aunts. She loves them, how could she not?

I used to think of these women as having little lives, that they were deprived in some way by their class, their sex, by the area in which they lived, by their time. But love, hate, passion, pain, loss – it's all been there, along with endurance, in a way my generation has never had to know. They coped and cried and laughed and loved and *lived*. And even turned things round. And look at them! I laugh suddenly, startling them all. Maybe it doesn't have to be Dostoevsky. It can all happen in a council estate in Fenham.

'Ach, nearly forgot,' Alice exclaims, rummaging in her handbag. 'I dug out some photos of you at her age,' she says to me, and nods towards Laura who is just visible with my grandmother in the kitchen. 'And also a couple of your mother when she was that age. Peas in a pod, I tell you.'

She rummages deeper and a host of extraordinary objects are laid out on the table. 'Now where are they—'

I swallow. Not yet. I'm not ready yet.

'In a while,' I say, handing the baby to May.

I leave them to their cigarettes and sherry and go into the kitchen where Laura has dragged my grandmother. I find them making pastry, Laura balanced on a stool at the kitchen bench. I stand quietly in the doorway. My gran is almost eighty. One day I'll visit and she'll have turned into an old lady.

We're representatives from four generations. Except that a generation in the middle is missing. It's wrong, that. Middles aren't supposed to be missing. Is that why I can't remember?

I watch them cutting shapes out of the greying dough. As Laura works, my grandmother adjusts the tea towel around her waist and pulls up the child's tights, and instantly I remember how that feels.

'But that's got three legs!' she says feigning shock as Laura squashes raisins into her pastry creation.

'It's a monster,' my daughter answers unruffled, adding with the faultless logic of a six-year-old, 'Monsters don't have to have two legs.'

I stare at the scene in front of me, lost for a moment as echoes and ghosts and memories all merge; of caterpillars and coal sheds; of swinging round the kitchen, my face in a fur; shelling pea-pods on a back step in a warm pool of sunlight; lipstick lips on my forehead, reflecting back from a dark glass; my grandfather's Northumbrian burr as he sang——

And then, for the first time since her death, I can hear my mother's voice, loud and clear.

'*All that goes around comes around, Megan, eh?*' she says.

And I smile. Always a one for the proverbs, my mother.

After a while, I leave them undisturbed.

'We waited for you,' says Alice. They're all smiling up at me. 'We didn't want to show the photographs without you. Are you ready now?' she asks.

'I'm ready now.'

And I sit and join my great-aunts Emily, Alice and May in their memories, and my memories.